BY
ZACHARY
HILL

Published by White Feather Press. (www.whitefeatherpress.com)

ISBN 978-1-61808-057-8

Printed in the United States of America

Cover design created by Ron Bell of AdVision Design Group (www.advisiondesigngroup.com)

Image credit: <a href='http://www.123rf.com/photo_9607845_sky-colors-over-castel-sant-angelo-in-rome-italy.html'>jovannig / 123RF Stock Photo</a>

White Feather Press

Reaffirming Faith in God, Family, and Country!

Fifty Caliber Endorsements to Die For!

Zachary Hill is an author you want to keep an eye on. A professional historian, he is likely to weave lessons from actual history into his works. If you are not careful, you will find that you may learn a few things... little nuggets of knowledge... Like gold fillings amidst the gore of smashed zombie skulls and the chaos of the *Uprising* Saga. Zach's *Uprising* story takes us from the despair of a ruined America to the shambles of what became of Italy. There is action; there is violence; there is a machine gun wielding Nun, and there is a Centauro armored fighting vehicle rolling into the Vatican. And there are zombies. Lots of zombies!

– George Hill, Creator of *The Uprising* series
and author of *Uprising USA* and *Uprising UK* –

Uprising Italia is a wild ride through Old Europe with gunfighting nuns, demons, explosions, intrigue and high adventure. A welcome addition to the *Uprising* saga! Did I mention gunfighting nuns?

– Louis Quarleno –

This book is both fun and thought provoking. Serious questions about life are addressed with humor and fun is had by all courtesy of a pistol packin' mutha of a nun!

– Leslie Williams –

Zachary Hill has hit it out of the park with *Uprising Italia*. An awesome ZPoc tale involving exploring Italy with a corrupted Nun and an Assault Rifle, I couldn't put it down.

– Erik Stern –

Zachary Hill's Uprising Italia takes you through a frighteningly beautiful tale of the retaking of his beloved Italy after the Zombie Outbreak. While the world is bleak, he has a way of showing the beauty that can still be reclaimed. There is action, art and a nun...what doesn't sound great about that?

– Caryn Bever-Jones –

UPRISING ITALIA

Dedication

To my nephews and nieces.

ONE

Uprising Day 4, Salt Lake City, Utah

I stood on top of the requisitioned Humvee with my binoculars looking out over the desolated Salt Lake Valley. Below me was the sprawling urban mess that was several cities all blended into one.

"Messy like a soup sandwich," my old drill sergeant would say.

Normally the valley would be hazy from smog but now it was hazy from the fires that blazed unchecked. That's what happens when people died without turning off their appliances first. Without people the world just wasn't the same.

This use to be a crowded, hustling, busy place with roads and highways packed with the worst drivers I had ever seen. I-15 was a nightmare during rush hour. Now it was cluttered and impassable due to empty cars. I tried not to look in the cars too much. Each one told a story I wasn't sure I was ready to hear.

I tried not to think about how much had been lost and what would be irreplaceably lost. There would be some things that I would never see again. No more Mars rovers. No new movies. No more New York Times Bestsellers. The end of the world had a way of putting a stop to people's plans.

The end of the world was filled with stories and this is mine. Truthfully, I thought the world would end in war or the Yellowstone Super Volcano. I never actually thought it would be the zombie apocalypse. Guess I was wrong about that. I was wrong about a lot of things, but this was kind of a biggie.

Four days ago me and my brother George were just driving along in his truck when we heard reports of people getting sick and then going crazy.

"Sounds like zombies!" George had said.

He was right on the first guess.

Seriously though, zombies? WTF? But then when it was confirmed we slung our rifles, grabbed our ammo and went to save who we could. I can't say I was terribly broken up about the whole thing. I wasn't a big fan of the world as it stood, so maybe this was a fresh start? I hoped so, anyways.

I looked over to the down town area of Salt Lake City. The tall, glass buildings were all there but they now seemed hollow somehow, like great tombs or twenty stories tall head stones. They wouldn't do anyone any good now. Eventually, they would crumble and fill the valley with ruins that, hopefully, archeologists would one day get to sort out.

That was something I doubted anyone really saw; the big picture. I've studied history all my life and that helped me see the future. The future looked grim. I saw small farming communities, vast ruins of cities and hard times.

Unlike many others I held no illusions as to things getting back to normal in our lifetime. Normal wouldn't be the same and it wouldn't happen for a very long time. I'd be dead and the world would be unrecognizable to us.

The world was crawling with the dead. Normal was out of the question.

I looked over to where George was making plans with his men. As if we didn't have enough to worry about with cannibalistic corpses, we now had to contend with a truck full of murderous red necks. It seemed that some people just need the laws of society to slip a little for them to lose their humanity and turn into animals. I would not become like that.

Kilo stood up in the turret and looked around the vista through his sunglasses and long hair. No emotion registered, but I knew he was thinking something.

"You see anything?" I asked.

"Nothing."

That simple word held more meaning then what was obvious. I nodded and turned back to look at I-80 that led down into the valley. Like most roads that lead out of the city, it was packed. I tried not to think about the people desperately fleeing the city and getting caught in the traffic jam, all the while the dead were swarming up the highway and smashing windows and grabbing people out of their cars.

In the past four days, since the Uprising began, millions of people had died. Numbers that large were hard to really comprehend. I knew that each one of those numbers was a real person with hopes, dreams and loves. Maybe the zombie I shot an hour ago was a single mom that was just starting to make it. Maybe she was engaged to the only man she had ever loved. I didn't want to forget that each one of those mindless killers had been a real person once.

And somehow it had all started with someone getting sick on an airplane. I didn't buy that. There had to be more to it than a simple virus gone bad.

In the ruins of our civilization my brother George had somehow become the governor of Utah. The United States, and for what I could tell, the rest of the world, had fallen apart and was now crawling with homicidal dead bodies.

We used to talk and joke about a zombie apocalypse, but the reality was far more horrible than I had ever imagined. A real corpse was something that was so obviously devoid of life and to see that almost human thing rise up and come after you, well… it felt wrong on every level imaginable.

Somehow I found myself heading back into the valley to risk my life for books. If I were to die, dying for books wasn't a bad way to go. After all, I was now Utah's official historian. I checked the batteries in my camera and took a deep breath.

There were worse causes to die for.

Uprising Day 4 Zach (In Salt Lake with Governor Ogre.)

After splitting up with George and the rest of the convoy, I drove to a Barnes & Noble I knew would be less crowded than some others. While they were off hunting the psycho murderer punks, I had my own mission. Now that I was the official Historian of the State of Utah I needed to do my part to preserve what we had left. The fact is, the world was dead and would never go back to being how it was. Both the east and west coasts were gone and if Utah lost more than 80% of its population, other parts must have done far worse. There was no more central government and no more infrastructure to support the country the way it used to be.

I wondered how long it would take for that to really sink in. Probably once the food of the "old world" ran out.

My job, aside from taking photos of Vernal and a devastated Salt Lake, was to preserve what was and educate the future. If there was no future then there was no hope. People at least needed the illusion of hope.

Maybe that made me a snake oil salesman. I didn't know about giving people hope, I just wanted somewhere quiet to lay my head down while the world worried about getting back on its feet. Leave me out of it and call me when you're done.

George's older son, his code name was Kilo, but I modified it to Killa, came along with different motives. He heard I was going to Barnes & Noble and somehow talked his mother into letting him go. What he wanted was manga. He'd risk his life for Japanese comics. Granted, I'd do the same for some mountain dew.

Unlike our last little visit, there weren't nearly as many zeds around. I wondered if it was because they were off looking for greener pastures. We encountered a lot of resistance coming in, but the downtown area now seemed kind of quiet. I preferred quiet.

We drove past empty banks and apartment complexes that looked like a hurricane had torn through them. For being surrounded by death, there were very few actual dead bodies lying around. Also, the place was just quiet. Whenever I came to the city, it was always loud and obnoxious. Now it was painfully silent.

I pulled up in front of the Barnes & Noble with the back of the Humvee almost right up to the door. The pickup-like bed was full of plastic tubs I looted from a Walmart. I grabbed my silenced FS2000 and jumped out. There wasn't a single shambler in sight. I kept my AK "Elizabeta" and my PSL "Animala" in the truck for emergencies.

"Killa, stay there and keep an eye open with the… with my SAW. Be careful with it, it's my baby."

"I'll try not to break it."

"Don't shoot anything unless it looks like it wants to kill you."

"That can be interpreted loosely."

"Well, just don't waste ammo then."

The parking lot was empty and I didn't detect any movement. I made sure the Aim Point was on and tested the door. Locked. Thankful for a silencer, I shot the lock and went inside. The lights were off but the large, glass front of the store let enough light in.

Still, the shelves of books created dark shadows where anyone or anything could be hiding. Maybe it was a zombie or maybe it was an employee trapped there for days and partially insane from waiting out the apocalypse and having nothing to eat but expensive cafe cappuccinos.

"Hey! If you want something to eat, come get it! I'm right here!"

I didn't hear anything, not even a moan. For room clearing there were few things more ideal than a short Bullpup. Fighting from vehicles and clearing rooms was what we've been doing the past few days and that happened to be the FS's forte.

Nothing. No sounds, no groans, no movements.

The store was clear and pristine. It must have been locked down before it got too crazy. Not wanting to waste time, I grabbed the first tub and ran to the history section. I quickly filled it with American history books and took it back to the Humvee. Then I filled a tub with world history. I made sure to get plenty of Roman history and anything Byzantine they might have because those were my passions. I saw a book on the Napoleonic wars that looked interesting and it went into the tub.

Next up was literature. Classic literature told us where we came from and where we should be going almost as much as history. I paused long enough to pocket a small copy of "Heart of Darkness," one of my favorite books. The next tub was filled with sci-fi and fantasy. Not a necessity but entertainment had a place as well. Besides, I think that sci-fi has just as much literary worth as anything else. Also, it was going to get boring at times and it would be nice to have a book to read. I made sure to get the last copies of Monster Hunter International and the Grimnoir Chronicles.

The last tub was for Killa. I watched the outside while he filled his tub with manga. Knowing him, he wouldn't just grab anything. He would take his sweet time and choose only what he considered the best. He was a connoisseur of manga and anime and I've learned not to question his judgment.

I settled down in the turret with my SAW while he took Elizabeta with him. This was a familiar feeling. From two deployments in Iraq I knew the feeling of doing over-watch in a Humvee all too well. As I sat there my mind wandered back to my memories of the Iraqi desert.

I hated thinking of the war, but it happened often so I had to get used to it.

It was strange to see the sun shining on a nearly cloudless, beautiful day. Everything was quiet and peaceful and it didn't feel right considering we were in enemy territory and the world was falling apart. I took a picture of the scene so others could see a side of the Apocalypse that they wouldn't have known about otherwise. Just like in Iraq, there were moments that Hell opened up and spewed forth its furry, and sometimes, it was like this; peaceful, quiet and strangely beautiful.

When Killa finally came out, he had a manga in one hand and was dragging the tub behind him with the other hand.

"What you got there?" I asked.

"'Gunslinger Girls'. I thought it appropriate."

"You calling us girls?"

"No, the gunslinger part," he said, slightly flustered.

"Come on. We got to meet back up with the others. But first, I'm going to find some Mountain Dew Throwback."

"And frozen pizzas."

"Well played my friend. Hey, did you find any zombie mangas?"

"Nah, I don't like those."

"Not very realistic, huh?" I said looking around.

I climbed back in the driver's seat and began driving to a supermarket I knew about. I was hungry and if there was one thing I hated, it was being hungry.

We were in Sandy, near a mall that normally was bursting with traffic. There wasn't a moving car in sight and the roads were mostly clear. I saw a lot of zeds but they were considerably spread out. I noticed that many of them were slogging along much slower than before. It wasn't until I saw a woman with shorts that I realized why. All their blood was coagulating in their legs.

Gross. I hate zombies.

We pulled into the parking lot of the grocery store. Zeds were milling about and when they saw us they started their shuffling jog towards us. I ran a few over with speed bump sounds and jumped out with my FS and took care of the others. I told Killa to hold fire because the SAW went through too much ammo and this wasn't a big enough threat.

I had to keep my mind on the big picture. Ammo was now worth more than gold. I had to think 'long term.'

The drill was the same. We pulled the rear of the Humvee up to the door and I ran in to grab what I could. They had eight bottles of Throwback and many pizzas. I was happy. I took a shopping cart of canned food and hoofed it back to the truck.

"I think I hear something," Killa said as I came out.

"What?"

"Screaming."

I stopped and listened. A few moments later I heard it as well. It certainly sounded like a scream, but I wasn't about to jump to conclusions. From a distance many things could sound like a scream. One time in Mexico I thought I heard someone screaming bloody murder. It wasn't until later that I found the source of the sound. A freaking goat.

"Let's go take a look," I said.

We drove around the super market towards the direction of the scream. When we came around the corner we saw the source. In the middle of the parking lot was an RV surrounded by zombies. They were banging away like they were desperate to get in.

"There must be someone inside," I said. "Make sure not to hit the RV. Aim."

We pulled up a short distance away and Killa opened fire with the SAW. I jumped out and took careful aim at their heads, firing in a steady staccato beat. I had to angle away so as not to shoot the RV. If there were people alive in there, I didn't want to shoot them.

My military training kicked in and I knew to be aware of what was in front and behind my target. Geez, if there was a survivor I definitely didn't want to kill them. The world was kind of short on people as it was.

The small crowd began falling away as most were simply mowed down by our bullets. Some zeds began to charge us, but I placed my red dot on their faces and fired. The whole encounter lasted maybe four seconds.

My heart was pounding and adrenaline was pumping. I flipped the safety back on and scanned the area for more threats. Nothing. I took a moment to catch my breath.

Once they were dead I walked up to the carnage. One of the corpses looked very chewed on. One of the zombies was still alive. I had hit it in the head but apparently not enough to kill the brain. It was squirming on the ground, but it didn't look like it was able to do anything else: like a chicken with its head cut off.

I bent down and took a long look in the thing's eyes. The blank, gray eyes didn't see me. It was a man in a blue buttoned up shirt. I wondered who he had been. Did he have a family? Were there people that loved him? I wondered if he was lucky and went early or if he saw his loved ones die in front of him. Was he funny? What were his dreams? He was probably just a normal Joe trying to make it through life.

"Killa, keep your Mark I eyeballs open. Also, anything happens to me in there, hose this RV like you were watering the lawn."

Killa nodded and I went to the door. It was locked so I did "shave and a haircut."

"Hello?" A girl's voice said through the door.

She sounded scared and I couldn't blame her. Seeing as how she was locked in an RV, I guessed that she didn't have any weapons. That was the extent of my Sherlock skills. I couldn't even tell how old she sounded.

"I'm human and I won't hurt you," I said. "We killed the dead out here."

The door opened to reveal a young girl, about fourteen or so holding the hand of a kid that looked to be about nine. I'm terrible at judging ages. The girl had short blond hair, cut into a boy-cut and wearing a "Twilight" T-shirt. She was team Edward.

"Are they all gone?" The girl asked.

"Yes, we killed the ones around here, but there's still a whole valley full of them." Man, that sounded dumb. It needed to sound more official. "What are you doing here?"

"We were trapped."

"This your RV?"

"It was our dad's."

She didn't need to say anything more. I understood the story there.

"I'm Zach. What's your name?"

"Rebekah."

"What about him?"

"He's my brother, Dan."

"I'm glad to meet you."

I kept my voice calm and relaxed. He looked them over for any wounds. If they had injuries I could treat them. I was trained as a "combat lifesaver" in the army which meant I could treat basic injuries, but they looked alright. Of course, if they had bite marks that would be something I couldn't help and didn't want to think about.

"Listen Rebekah. We have to get out of here. There'll be more of these things coming. Do you have somewhere to go?"

"We were going to go our Aunt's house in St. George. We're from Seattle."

"I don't think St. George is a good idea right now."

"Why?"

I really didn't want to get into details right then.

"We live in Vernal. It's safe there; no infection."

"Are you sure? None of these monsters there?"

"Yeah, I'm sure. We're here taking care of business right now but we can take you there. We have shelter and food for you."

The girl looked about to cry so she just nodded.

"Okay, get whatever you need and let's go," I said. I was eager to get her away from this place and somewhere where she could feel safe. I was no psychologist, but I figured she didn't want to hang around a place she'd been trapped in for days.

As they quickly packed their backpacks I called up the Governor.

"Hey, Gov, I found two survivors. A girl and a boy. They were trapped in an RV."

I could hear the girl sobbing behind me.

"Status?" He asked.

"No bites. They're clean."

"Well, there's not much we can do. Just bring them with us for now. Too bad I already sent Willie away."

"Alright. Hey, I got a Dew Throwback for you."

"That's a beautiful thing."

TWO

Zach-Day 4 Salt Lake

I got Rebekah and Dan situated in the back seat of the Humvee with their backpacks in their laps. They were silent and wide eyed. I knew that look; desperation, confusion and fear. They were afraid of the world and of their future. Their whole world was in turmoil and they didn't know what was going to happen to them.

"I'm guessing you guys are hungry, right?" I asked the two kids.

Rebekah just nodded.

Poor kids. 'Traumatized for life' probably didn't cover it. They'd seen their whole world destroyed. Heck, it took me a while after my first deployment to Iraq to get my head on straight. As I watched them I knew that I'd never really understand what they were going through. Being young and having your world shattered really sucked.

We went to a grocery store and got them some fruit, canned chili and corn beef hash. As Killa and the kids were chewing I heard the Blue Force Tracker come to life.

"Whisky Six to Ogre, looks like the explosion was on State Street just north of I-80. The Salt Lake County Government Center just blew up... Hold on... we've got movement. Trying to get an ID," the radio said.

I sat up and listened closely. Zombies didn't cause explosions, despite what the movie "Planet Terror" said.

The Blue Force Tracker was a wonderful thing: probably the best invention designed for war in the past three decades. It marked all friendly and known unfriendly units on satellite maps showing everything in real time. It was point and click and made war just like a strategy game on the computer.

Then I heard the radio say, "Target located."

"Killa! We got eyes on the target! We're rolling!"

"Okay," he said with a shrug and put down his manga.

I cranked up the engine and we were off. The BFT kept us updated as to everyone's movement and the helicopter kept eyes on the target. I listened as they reported the targets switching vehicles. George marked on the BFT where he wanted us to set up for the ambush. I pushed down the gas and raced through the empty but cluttered streets of Salt Lake. Empty of people, cluttered with cars and trash.

As I followed the progress of the white truck on the BFT I saw that we were still far away from the target area. I pressed harder on the pedal and felt the acceleration push me back into the seat.

One wrong move and our Humvee would be smashing into the nearest parked car. It was foolish to drive this fast in the cluttered streets, but I had no choice. If I played it safe we wouldn't get there in time.

"Hold on, Killa!" I shouted up to the turret.

I narrowly missed a tipped over fire truck and heard the tires screeching. Okay, maybe that had been a little too close. I kept my eyes open for the clear paths in the road and said a quick, silent prayer.

When we safely got to the area I saw that it was a small business district with only one tallish building and it happened to be where I was supposed to set up. Perhaps it was where I was meant to be. It was some kind of unimaginative glass square which I couldn't guess the nature of the business. It didn't matter anymore.

I stopped the Humvee with a screech and scanned the area. I looked for a good ambush spot like I had been trained to do. Unfortunately, I had two non-combatants in the back seat and I couldn't risk them getting in the way of fire. So I pulled in behind the building out of sight.

"Killa, stay here and make sure they're safe. I'm going up into the building here."

I busted the glass door with the butt of my rifle and ran up the stairs of the office building up to the fourth floor. My boots were pounding on the metal emergency stairs.

The shooting was about to start any second so I had to go faster. Killa was down in the alleyway waiting for sign of the red necks, then he'd pull out, jump up into the turret and let loose with the SAW. I felt my legs turning into jelly.

I had my PSL, "Animala" and had to get into a good position. The ambush was a classic "L" shape to avoid friendly fire, but I was going to be on the opposite side George was going to be on. However, I'd be four floors above. That way I'd be out of danger and have a good vantage point. I wasn't an idiot and wasn't about to allow friendly fire on my watch.

On my thigh was my Beretta 9mm and on my back was my AK and an Indian "Gunstock Club." It was a working design by Cold Steel. I remembered that time in Farmington, outside the pharmacy where I had almost ran completely out of ammo. I don't care what some survival guide said, this thing was way better than any crowbar.

I hate stairs. I hate running. I really hate running up stairs. By the time I got to the top, I was out of breath. I rested by the top, leaning on the long barrel of the PSL.

Then I heard an explosion outside and the rattle of the windows. I had been expecting gunfire, not a howitzer going off. What was George doing?

I quickly went to the window and looked out. The target truck's entire front end was a ball of roaring flames and the killers were jumping out. Suddenly the entire street erupted in gunfire. Both sides began laying down a hail of bullets. I watched from above and it almost looked like the aerial footage from the news. I could see everyone as they ran for cover and took aim.

The window wouldn't open so I drew my pistol and shot it out. I quickly looked for a target. The only guy I could see was someone hiding behind a truck. I had learned with dramatic demonstrations that vehicles simply didn't make very good cover and only slightly better concealment. I found the range with my scope's built-in range finder and dialed my scope in. Then I took off my gold Elvis glasses and took aim at where I thought the man's center of mass was.

Yes, I know gold Elvis shades aren't the most tactical accessory a guy could have, but I wasn't going to lose my style just because the world had ended.

That was one thing that always pissed me off about Halo and other such craptastic video games. I was trained to shoot COM, yet those games were all about head shots. That and the pistol was better at long range than the rifle. Lame. Halo is lame.

I lined up the cross hairs on my guesstimate of the man's chest and slowly squeezed the trigger. It was only a second or two, but pulling that trigger made it feel like an hour before the gun finally fired. The gun kicked in my hands and my bullet went through both car doors and I saw the man jerk back.

I could smell whatever the weird powder and primer the Bulgarian ammo used. It was a familiar and very pleasant smell. I fired again and he jerked again, throwing his rifle into the air. Through my scope I could see blood splatter all over the broken glass of the truck he had assumed was cover.

Then I couldn't get a shot at anyone else. They knew I was up here now and they were staying out of sight of me and Killa's SAW. Well, it was my SAW, but he was using it. The murderous thugs dressed in hunting camo were focusing all their attention on George now.

I was about to run back down stairs when the helo came into view and tore apart the street and everything on it with a mini-gun. It was like the roar of a demonic dragon. I could hear the constant stream of bullets smacking into the pavement. Shreds of cars, asphalt and people flew into the air forming small, violent clouds.

I didn't stop gawking until the helicopter stopped firing. I had seldom seen such destruction and never in an American city. Smoke and dust filled the street now and through the gray clouds I could see a body lying on the ground. I really hoped it was one of the killers.

It was, because when George walked over, he gave the body's head a good, solid kick with his heavy boot.

Once I was satisfied that they were dead or at least not a threat, I put on my sunglasses and hurried back down stairs.

Out in the street George was standing over a survivor. The red neck murderer's Mini-14 was laying several feet from him. I kicked it further away. I didn't like those things. Crappy guns.

"Collect the weapons," George said.

"I'm not touching a mini," I said.

"What? Just get them in a pile and away from here."

"I ain't touching that Ruger piece of crap. I'll feel dirty and soap's in limited supply now."

So, I got Killa to do it.

As George interrogated the survivor I took all their ammo and supplies from their truck and loaded it into George's Humvee. One good thing about the Mini-14 was that it used the same ammo as my FS 2000. Bonus.

"Is everything alright?" Rebekah asked from the back seat of my Humvee.

"Yeah. We got the guys that have been murdering people."

Then I heard a now familiar moan.

"Killa! George! I think we attracted some unwanted attention!"

"Okay, we're going to have to boot scoot out of here fast," George said.

Killa ran to George and helped him with the prisoner. Down the street I saw a dozen zeds pouring out of a building and I heard moaning coming from other directions.

Then one Zed came from around the corner, running directly at me. It was only one and unlike some people, I knew that ammo was going to become more scarce than diamonds.

I quickly pulled out my gunstock club and swung when its head came into range. I heard and felt the bones of the skull crack and cave in. The Zed tumbled off to the side and twitched in the gutter. The putrid smell of the congealed blood on my club told me that I'd have to disinfect it later.

Not wanting to push my luck I jumped in the driver's seat and started it up.

On the way back to Vernal, after George put into practice his new penal code on the survivor, we grabbed some snacks from a convenient store. The canned food in the grocery stores would last a long time and when food started to get scarce in Vernal, there'd be more raids into the city. Every Mormon was supposed to have a year's supply of food, but that was the ideal and there were a lot of non-Mormons in Vernal. The food would not last. Raids would be necessary until the farms got up and going for full food production.

"We heard on the Radio, before it went out, that St. George had the sickness," Rebekah said from the passenger seat. She was staring out of the window with blank, dead eyes.

"We heard that as well," I said.

"Does that mean its like Salt Lake and Boise?"

"Probably."

I didn't want to take away all hope, but I didn't want to make any hopeful statements. It wasn't a position I liked to be in.

"It's okay. My brother's asleep. You can tell me."

"I don't think many people made it out of St. George."

"What's going to happen to us when we get to Vernal?"

"We've set up a temporary place in Lapoint's elementary school. You'll have food, blankets and anything else you need until we figure out something a bit more permanent. We even have electricity."

I was trying to be authoritarian and reassuring.

"Who were those men you fought?"

"People that thought they could act like animals and do whatever they want."

"And what do you think?"

"I think that we need to act civilized now more than ever."

"Are you Mormon?"

"Why? Just because I live in Utah?"

"Yes."

"I am."

"Me too. Is that man really the Governor?"

"As far as we can tell. I usually just call him bro."

"Oh, you're a family."

"Yeah."

"Got anyone else?"

"Yeah."

"Who?"

"Another older brother and a twin."

"Where's he at?"

"Last I heard he was grabbing a bunch of military trucks and heading out here from Virginia."

"I don't know, but I think…"

"I'm sorry."

"Zach?"

"Huh?"

"Will you take care of us?"

I hadn't expected anything like that and the question was like a sucker punch to the face. She was either a bold, gutsy thing or very desperate. What did she mean by that exactly and why would she trust me so easily?

"Take care of you?"

"Yeah. We're targets."

Crap. This wasn't exactly my usual thing. Substitute teaching is one thing, taking care of two kids I barely knew was way out of my league. Still, I had to do something.

Damn, I hate being put in these kinds of situations. I didn't want to be relied upon.

"I mean personal protection, as in, somebody messes with us, they have to face you," she said.

"I can do that. I promise."

I could. Watching out for them wasn't beyond my means. It might mean a huge pain in the butt. I had hoped to just have to care about "Number One". I had a hard enough time with that. What was I supposed to do with two others?

It would be so easy to slip into darkness and let go of my humanity. It would be so easy to enjoy the killing, the chaos and the end of the world, but if I did, I'd become like those militia freaks. I'd become a mindless animal. I wouldn't have to think about the people that died. I wouldn't have to think about every zombie I kill was once an average person with hopes, dreams and feelings. It would be so easy to forget all that and become a heartless 'thing'.

Helping people was much harder than killing them and right now it was very hard to help people.

"What did you do before all this?" Rebekah asked.

"I was a broke, starving artist and substitute teacher. A nobody."

"You never were a nobody."

"You didn't know me."

"I know you now."

I didn't like the topic at all. That was one introspective piece of humanity I could do without right now.

"What did you do before all this?" I asked.

"I was in a band."

"Oh, yeah? What kind of band?"

I was expecting Hannah Montana or Lady Gaga kind of crap.

"We had a heavy metal band. I was the lead guitarist."

I turned to look at her. Then I noticed the black wrist warmers and the heartagram necklace.

"I play bass," I said.

"Really? What kind you got?"

"An Ibanez four-string signed by Disturbed, Filter, Dommin and Birthday Massacre."

"You're kidding me! I love Birthday Massacre!"

"They seriously rock live."

We talked music the rest of the way back. Maybe protecting this girl wouldn't be such a pain in the butt after all. If all else failed we could start a post apocalyptic band.

We passed through the Duchesne road blocks and arrived at Lapoint late at night. Rebekah and her brother slept on a couch at Ogre Ranch because it was too late to go fixing up everything she needed at the school/shelter. That could wait until the morning.

It took two trips to bring all my guns and ammo back into the house. Killa took his tub of manga and disappeared down to his room. We wouldn't be seeing him for a while.

The next day Mrs. Ogre and Rosa helped get Rebekah situated in a tent with blankets and inflatable mattresses in one of the classrooms of the elementary. Rosa instantly took a liking to Rebekah and her brother. She thought they were the cutest things.

I didn't have much good to say about Rosa, but at least she treated the kids like they were royalty.

I sat back, put on a Godzilla movie, (the most escapist movies ever) and began to clean my guns and gear.

My cousin's kids came in to watch Godzilla. Their attention spans lasted a good fifteen minutes before they ran off to go do something crazy. Though, to the credit of Godzilla the two boys were pretending to breathe fire and roar.

Retaining my humanity wasn't easy and it had a cost. As I cleaned my guns I thought about the faces of the zombies I had killed and thought about each of their lives. They could have been like me, just average guys trying to make a living and find what little happiness they could. Some were little children like I taught at the schools.

I was wrong to have ever thought this whole thing was ever good. There was nothing good about this. Rebekah and many like her had lost their families, one of the worst things that could happen to a person.

"You okay?" Rosa asked from the door. I hadn't even noticed that she was there.

"Yeah, I'm fine."

She came in and sat down.

"Oh! I love these movies. My father watched them all the time." Her thick Mexican accent made every word come out like warm butter.

"Sounds like he had good taste."

"He liked bad movies."

"My kind of guy."

"There's something wrong. I can tell."

"Oh, nothing. Everything's fine, you know."

"I was psychology major at BYU. I'm not stupid."

"Why?"

"Why? That's a question everyone asks from beginning of the world. I think you need to get mind off things."

Then Rosa's hand came up and rubbed my head. She leaned in closer until I could feel her breath against my face. Her eyes closed and she waited.

Then I moved in closer.

Uprising Day 6 Zach. Salt Lake City.

After resting for a day, I went back out. As the newly appointed Official Historian of Utah, a title I made up and George approved, I had a duty to perform. I took a crew of two Humvees with three people per team. Kevin was in charge of one Humvee and I captained the other. One of the other guys drove while I chilled in the team chief's seat, or "Shotgun" in civilian parlance. I carried my FS2000, so I couldn't honestly call it "shotgun" anyways.

I took out a homemade burrito that Rosa had made me and a glass bottled Coke. Coke always went best with Mexican food. Handmade flour tortillas were one of the few things I fell in love with during my two years in Mexico.

George had told me of a clear route to the Salt Lake Airport so that was where I was heading. As the historian, I figured I should try to document how it all went down. The infection had come to Utah through the airport so I'd start there, then maybe hit up hospitals and police stations. I brought good cameras, digital and traditional and a camcorder.

I had always figured I'd be pouring through military reports from the Civil War, not documenting the downfall of Utah. Outside of Utah I knew only what my Blue Force Tracker told me. I could see military units and that's about it.

One thing that was interesting was what was happening in Iraq. I looked around and found a whole gaggle of military vehicles heading north. There were tanks, APC's, Strikers, LAV's, tons of Humvees and other trucks, all heading north into Turkey. It was a real life "March of the 10,000." They were hauling butt out of Iraq, probably trying to reach Germany where Ramstein Air Force base was. I'd be keeping an eye on them and wishing them luck. I didn't imagine that anyplace in Europe was doing well at all. Few guns: crowded population.

I thought of Italy. I loved Italy. It was where my heart was. I thought of Rome, Florence, Assisi, and Venice. I wondered if Venice was okay. The only land way into Venice was a small bridge and a railroad track. If they could defend it, block it or destroy it, I don't see how zombies could get to it. There were numerous small medieval towns that still had their stone walls. Perhaps those would fare well. Rome had the Vatican and the Castel Sant'Angelo. If people could hold up in there, maybe some would survive.

They were distant thoughts that wouldn't help me now. I had to focus on the here and now.

Still, I wondered about the rest of the world. Where was the US government? There had to be some of it left somewhere. I didn't want their "help" and at this point, all they'd do is interfere. We had a plan and a system going here.

"Okay, if you were a survivor, where would you hide?" I asked my driver. He was a Vernal local that George vouched for. He had his own AR and he had taken Crusader Weaponry's carbine course, so he couldn't be so bad.

"Apartment buildings? If I were trapped down town, maybe try to get to a top floor and block off the stairs?"

"You got the megaphone, right?"

"I do."

"Alright, we'll go through downtown and wherever else. We'll look for survivors still holding out on our way to the airport," I said.

We stopped in Heber long enough to syphon gas from a gas station. A small crowd of zombies were heading our way. Instead of wasting ammo, we hurried and peeled out as fast as we could. Then we went north and drove through the mountain passes into Salt Lake.

The view coming down from the mountain overlooked the whole valley. It was a beautiful gray and rainy day but I could still see the whole valley. It looked quiet except for the occasional pillar of smoke rising up from scattered fires. Growing up in Washington I had developed a love for gray, rainy days. Sunny days just bugged me.

Normally we could take a freeway straight to I-15 and straight to the airport, but this time we were taking a detour through the city. We had to push through a few cars on the freeway and run over a few zeds, but we made it into the very quiet downtown.

One thing I wanted to know was exactly the order of events. I wanted to know when the general chaos happened. When did people realize they should leave or not go to work?

I got up into the turret with the megaphone. It would attract a lot of attention, but we were staying on the move and Humvees could plow through zeds.

"Attention any survivors! We are here to help! We are what's left of the government in Vernal. We'll be back in three hours. If you want help, put up some kind of sign or signal to us that won't put you into danger. When we come back and we see your signal, we'll come to help you."

We drove all through the city doing that, careful not to double back to avoid zombies we may have stirred up. I didn't hold out much hope though.

When we finally made it to the airport, the place was completely torn up. Cars were crammed together as if people had parked in a hurry without any intention of coming back. Torn up, stinking bodies were scattered along the sidewalk in front of the terminal and baggage was everywhere.

We all got out of the Humvees with weapons at the ready and made our way into the terminal. Inside wasn't much better. There were a few zombies that charged at us, but we dropped them before they got near. We had seen them coming from across the terminal, but there were a lot of places a zed could pop out of. I didn't like surprises, not even surprise parties. That was why I wore black racer bike type leathers, with white stripes down the arms, from neck to toe. I had my old Army helmet on, but my face was still exposed. (I had my Elvis glasses, but they were zombie resistant.) Let's see the zeds try to bite through that!

Since acquiring the FS, I had to get a whole new set up for it. I only had one thigh rig and that was for the AK, so I used another chest rig I had lying around for this. AR mag pouches were easy to find and Get-Some had a few. All of it was black. I know that's tactical faux pas fashion now, but I didn't care what the zeds thought of me.

To top it all off, I had two shoulder holsters for my Skorpions. I was the height of fashion.

"Why two Skorpions?" Kevin asked.

"You telling me you want to go through the entire Apocalypse and not once go two fisted with badass pistols? Is that what you're telling me?"

"I'll make sure to get a photo of it then."

"As historians we have to document everything badass. That's our sacred duty."

Kevin was wearing his "Heavy Metal Shop" black hoodie with skulls and had the M4 we had given him when we rescued him. He wasn't as proficient with it as I would have liked. In fact, he was still a beginner, but if I didn't bring him, he probably would have kicked the crap out of me. Also, he was smart, knew the city better than I did and was quick thinking. Three things I wasn't.

"Kevin, Jason, you two come with me. The rest of you, go back and stay with the Humvees. Keep both eyes open. This isn't some Romero movie where everyone dies just because they don't pay attention. Jason, bring the thumper."

The three of us went further in while I began taking pictures. I tried to figure out what had happened, but I wasn't David Caruso and I couldn't know everything by simply looking at the crime scene. I took out my small note pad, wrote notes and took more pictures.

Then I saw the gift shop. There were sodas. No Mountain Dew, but I could use a Coke.

I walked over and saw that they had a lot of magazines, snacks and drinks. As I reached for a Vanilla Coke I heard several moans. I looked around and saw two zombies coming out of a back room of a McDonald's. One of them wore a McDonald's uniform. Poor guy. He never had a chance at life; killed before he ever amounted to anything. Still, he had been special to someone and he certainly deserved better than this. My FS was silenced so I quickly shot them both in the head before they could alert others. Even a silenced weapon made sounds and I immediately began to hear more moans coming from elsewhere.

I took a long drink of Coke and began looking around for the source of the sound.

"I think one's in the bathroom," Kevin said. He pointed his gun towards the men's bathroom.

I nodded and went to the open doorway. I could hear the echoes of the faint moans inside.

"Hey! Worm food! Come out!" I shouted and quickly stepped away. I could hear the patter of bare feet on tile as whatever was inside came running out.

It was a little girl with blood covering her face and the entire front of the pink summer dress she was wearing. The white, lifeless eyes found me and glared at me with what I could only describe as a look of hatred. She only looked about eight years old at most.

When I saw her I saw the faces of all my students I had taught. I saw the little elementary kids and their small, stupid problems they thought were so important. I saw their bright eyes and big heads and could hear the squealing laughter as they ran around on the playground.

I had to.

I shot her.

Then I looked back and saw Kevin's face. He had a little girl not much older than that. His eyes were wide and I could see pain written all over his face. I felt sick, but I couldn't think about it right now.

"Let's go out to the tarmac," I said and took another swig of Coke.

"What for?" Kevin whispered, still looking down at the dead little girl.

"To see what's out there of course."

We went outside. There was a slight drizzle coming down and the puddles along the tarmac reflected the dull gray of the sky, almost like the ground was flat as paper and had holes in it, showing the clouds that surrounded them.

There were baggage cars lying around, some with scattered baggage. Airliners and fuel trucks were also where people had left them.

I took a bunch of pictures and wondered which flight it was that had brought the first infected person. Was that flight even here or had it flown off before the chaos started?

We walked over to one of the fuel trucks. It was full. I turned a valve to let some of the fuel out.

"Alright, start the thumper," I said.

I had gotten an Idea while reading the book "Dune." Instead of a rhythmic pounding, I used a boom box with a megaphone. I had a tape of women screaming. Rosa and Rebekah had provided the screams. They liked the theatrics.

Once the thumper was set we ran off to hide.

We didn't wait long. Soon zombies from all over the tarmac were converging on that one spot. One or two came out of parked planes. A few came from the baggage rooms and the others just wandered in.

We waited for them to gather together and I set my camera rolling. Maybe I'd post it on what was left of the internet.

"Now" I said.

We all fired at the same time. We weren't aiming for heads, however. We hit the fuel along the ground and set the whole thing off into a giant ball of fire. It almost looked like one of those cheap Hollywood explosions they tried to pass off as dangerous, only this one actually was. The zombies were thrown into the air and set on fire. I felt the wave of heat hit my face.

Then more zombies came from one of the cargo loading areas just to our left. They were running full bore at us so we started backing up as fast as we could, firing as fast and accurately as we could.

They were almost on top of us when I ran dry. Instead of reloading, I let the FS fall on its single point sling I had rigged up and drew both my Skorpions. There were only six left and I wouldn't need to reload, but I might need a weapon in both hands. Maybe it was a stupid idea and perhaps there were more important things than looking cool. Still, it was the first thing I thought of.

It was point blank range as I got the first shot off. I hit right in the forehead and the thing's head jerked back in a spray of black blood.

Crap, they were close! The things suddenly rushed me faster than I thought they could move.

A zombie tackled me and started biting at my arm. I could feel the pressure of the bite, but the thick leathers stopped his teeth. I used my free gun to shoot it in the head. It's cold, wet blood splattered my face. I definitely made sure to keep my eyes and mouth closed. Still lying on my back I fired both guns simultaneously at one target. One of the bullets hit the last zombie in the head. Its bald dome burst open and it dropped like a sack of rotten apples.

I was breathing heavy as I stood up. That had been way too friggin' close.

"Alright, I think its time to get out of here. I'm done playing CSI."

We went back to the Humvees and explained everything that happened. I showed them the footage of the explosion, but then I saw that we had filmed the zombie attack. It showed me whipping out two Skorpions and firing.

Nice. My awesomeness was preserved. I finally got one up on the universe. It was too bad that there wasn't anyone left to see it.

As cool as it had been, I didn't want to get that close to death again. I planned to survive all this crap and getting bitten wasn't in the game plan.

Then we went back into Salt Lake looking for signs of survivors. We drove around for a long while, retracing our "steps" through the city.

That was when I saw a white bed sheet hanging out a window with the words "Up Here" written on it.

"I guess we have to go to them," I said.

"Damn," Kevin said.

We pulled up to the hotel and dismounted. One of the guys with a Saiga 12 gauge came with me this time. Me, Kevin, and the Saiga entered through the revolving glass doors and tested the elevator. It didn't work. That meant more stairs. Next time the world ended I'd prepare for it by buying a Stairmaster or something.

We climbed all the way to the eighth floor. It was almost as bad as climbing to the top of St Peter's Dome. On the top of St. Peter's roof there was a small cafe for the people that attempted the climb. The view had been worth it, though. I saw all of the Vatican and Rome. I saw the Pantheon, the Tiber River and Coliseum from up there. I'd never see those places again.

When we got to the seventh floor, the door to the stairwell above us burst open and three zombies came in, looking around. One of them spotted us about the same time I raised my FS and fired. In less than one second the three of us took out the three of them. Black blood sprayed across the walls beside and behind them.

"I guess they heard us coming," I wheezed.

We made our way into the eighth floor hallway and looked around. We didn't see anything.

"Hello? We're alive and we're here to help you!" I shouted out.

Kevin was much louder than me so he took over the shouting duty. Towards the end of the hall a door opened. A skinny, bald man poked his head out.

"Is it safe?" He asked.

"As safe as a city full of walking dead can be," I said.

We walked over and he opened the door all the way.

"Thank heaven you're here," the man said.

"Why'd you make us walk up all those stairs?"

"Those things have been sniffing around that door for two days! I thought I'd be trapped in here forever."

"Forever? You couldn't make a club or anything?"

As I walked in I saw two suit cases and a girl sitting on the bed. She looked to be about sixteen or so and dressed in all black with messy chin length blue hair. She had bruises on her face and she kept her eyes on the floor.

"Who are you?" I asked.

"I'm Richard and this is my daughter, Karen."

"We came to get you two out. Let's go."

The man grabbed his suit case and hurried out the door. When the girl passed by she slipped something into my hand and ran down the hall towards the staircase.

I looked at the crumpled paper in my hand. It said, " HELP ME!"

THREE

Day 6 part II Zach Salt Lake City

I looked at the note in my hand. "Help Me!" Then I looked back at the girl. The man already had his arm around her shoulder. He had a large silver revolver tucked into his pants. I gave Kevin the note and motioned for him to be silent. After reading it Kevin looked up from the note and gave the skinny man a hard glare that I knew was lethal.

The girl wore large soled combat type boots, black pleated skirt, chain, and a "Nightmare Before Christmas shirt." An iPod hung around her neck. It was the stiff way she walked and the fearful glances at Richard that alerted me to the kind of help she needed.

I walked up to them as we made our way down the stairs.

"So, what are you all doing here?" I asked. I had to get this man's trust.

"We were staying the week here, on vacation. Got trapped up in our room. All this craziness, huh? Say, got anything to eat? We ate the last of our granola bars two days ago."

"As the newly appointed Utah Historian, I'd like to record your stories if you don't mind."

"There's nothing to tell."

"Where you all from?"

"Texas," Karen said.

I noticed the brief angry look Richard gave Karen. Something bad was going on.

Leaning over to Kevin, I whispered, "We need to secure this guy."

"When we get outside, we'll take him," Kevin said.

As we walked to the door, Richard suddenly pulled out his huge revolver and got behind Karen with the barrel pressed against her temple. I instantly had my gun up.

I wanted to shoot him in the face, but I couldn't risk hitting the girl.

"This is crazy, Richard. There's six of us. You don't think we'll let you get away with anything, do you?" I said.

I had my Aim Point's red dot placed right on his head, I knew there was a difference with bore height, but as the adrenaline surged through me and the pressure hit me like a wave, all the cool calculations left me. All I had left was fear of accidentally shooting the girl.

"I'm leaving and taking one of your trucks," Richard said with a manic look in his eyes.

"You're not taking our truck," I said.

I looked at Karen's face. She looked ready to cry. She clutched Richard's arm to keep herself from being strangled. I then noticed the bruises around her wrists. She was some kind of captive; kidnapped perhaps. Who knew how long she had been this sicko's prisoner.

"We're going to kill you. There's no way around that. Give us the girl and I'll make it a painless death," I said.

"Go to hell. There's no rules anymore!"

As the man stepped through the door, he made sure to stay behind Karen. When he passed through the revolving doors he quickly turned so Karen was facing my three men in the Humvees.

I went to the revolving door and slowly went through with my short Bullpup still at the ready. I had never wanted to shoot anyone so badly in my life.

"Give me a truck!" Richard was yelling. The three men looked to me and I nodded.

I really had to think of something. He wanted a truck.

Then I realized that my truck had all the spare gas and an idea formed.

"Give him that truck," I pointed to the one that I hadn't ridden in.

One of the turret gunners got out of his truck and Richard quickly pushed Karen into it while keeping his revolver pressed against her.

"What the hell are you doing?" Kevin asked.

"That truck is low on gas. My truck has the spare gas cans. He'll only have about a half hour, if that, before he has to refuel. It's getting dark. We have night vision. He doesn't," I said.

"We follow him and hit him when he's not ready."

"Exactly. The Art of War my friend. Right now, he has the advantage. We wait until he doesn't."

I watched as our second Humvee drove off. Luckily, the idiot knew nothing about a Blue Force Tracker. I followed him, keeping well out of sight. I noticed that he kept turning around, as if watching to see if we were indeed following him. We were, but not in a way that he'd ever see.

We drove down State Street which ran parallel to I-15. We were all silent. I don't know what the others were thinking, but I knew I was thinking about what was at stake. The life of an innocent: a survivor.

I was the kind of guy that beat himself up for failures and this wasn't something I could afford to fail at. I knew I'd never forgive myself.

It was near dusk when he finally stopped. I knew that intersection. My old Camaro had broken down there once. There were two gas stations there. He had finally ran out of gas.

"How we going to play this?" Kevin asked.

"He'll hear our Humvee if we get close. We have to go in by foot, but we'll have to be quick because he won't take very long to fill up his tank. That's assuming he's smart enough to siphon the gas. There also might be a lot of zeds in the area. He has five or six shots and I don't know how many reloads. One wrong move and he shoots the girl."

"What about that sniper rifle or yours?"

"My PSL? Maybe if we get there before it gets dark. I can't use the scope at night."

"That sucks."

"Yes it does."

We parked the Humvee out of sight and dismounted. This time, everyone was going. I kept my FS slung, but I also took my PSL and bandoleer of spare mags. I liked bandoleers because I could just throw them on and off. I liked convenience.

The sun was setting quickly and with the tall mountains all around us things were getting dark fast. I could hear moaning in the distance and it felt like it was getting louder.

We were a good two blocks away, but we had to hurry. As we kept low and made our way toward the once busy intersection we saw that zombies were coming out of everywhere, like when a young boy kicked an ant nest.

"Crap. This isn't good," I said.

There were at least fifty shuffling zeds between us and the intersection. I had my silenced FS, but the others didn't have silencers. I had my club and the others had machetes and such, but there were just too many of them to take out like that.

I was preferring the FS to the AK right now because we had pallets of army 5.56 from Camp Williams. I'll keep the AK for special occasions.

"Damn. If I could get in sight of him, I can take him, but we have a freaking horde between us," I whispered.

We were crouched low, going along the sides of buildings to stay out of sight.

"Can we make it through?" Kevin asked.

"Not without making a ruckus and alerting that scumbag."

Then one of the zombies saw them and let out a long moan about the same time I heard Richard's revolver going off in the distance.

"Run back to the Humvees!" I said in a hushed, whisper yell.

With that, we turned and bolted back. The zeds were following after us, thankfully slower than I remembered them being. I didn't waste any bullets and we got in the Humvee before the horde arrived. We plowed through them on the way to the intersection. I watched on the BFT as Richard sped out and got back onto I-15. He must have gotten a little gas or had some left.

Near the point of the mountain, where Utah Valley and Salt Lake Valley come together, he turned off towards South Jordan.

Before too long he pulled into a small neighborhood and stopped.

"He stopped at a house. Maybe his house?" I said. The six men crammed in the back were itching to get their ride back and I had to save the girl. I had to admit to myself that I wanted to kill this man. He was a worse monster than any of the zombies out there. He was supremely selfish, arrogant and didn't care who he hurt as long as he got what he wanted.

The world would be better off without him.

We pulled into the neighborhood and shut off the headlights. We dismounted and continued on foot. Kevin carried my silenced AK so we at least had two silenced weapons. We stayed absolutely quiet as we walked through the streets with our night vision goggles. George had taken them from Camp Williams. They weren't the newest design like I had used in Iraq, but they did the job. I could see the shuffling green forms of zombies wandering around the streets. Without the city lights the place was completely black and I doubted that those dead eyes could see better than ours.

One of them was in our way so I pulled out my gunstock club and snuck up behind it and smashed its skull in.

I began thinking of silent night raids to decrease the zed population, but then I snapped my attention back to the present. My mind wandered too often and I couldn't afford to let it. Especially not now.

We got to the house. It was a single story house that looked in bad condition. There was a car on blocks in the driveway and it was missing some shutters. There weren't any lights on, not even candles. I wish I had one of those thermal imaging things from the movies that could see through walls. But, we had windows and we crept up to the house and peeked in. I could see a living room with a couch and TV, but no one was there. I tested the door. Locked.

"Window," Kevin whispered.

I tried it and found that it slid open. I did it carefully so as to make as little noise as possible. Me and Kevin climbed in the window. He was better at it than I was. Even at the peak of my physical condition in the Army I had never been good at this stuff.

Next, I came to the kitchen. There was an open fridge filled with beer and little else. The place was covered in boxes of magazines, mostly porn and smelled of rotten food.

I heard some laughing coming from a room down the small hallway. I motioned for Kevin to follow. We walked into the carpeted hallway and came to the first room. There was a bed that was just a box springs and mattress. Richard was on top of Karen, groping her with one hand and holding a beer in the other.

I placed my sight's red dot on the back of his head and thought for a second. That would be entirely too quick and easy. I placed the dot on his shoulder and fired. Unlike in movies where the hero gets shot in the shoulder and is perfectly okay, a real shoulder hit destroys a lot of bone, joints, and tendons, making the arm completely useless: probably for life.

The bullet struck Richard in the shoulder, knocking him off of Karen. He hit the wall and blood splattered all over.

"Karen, it's us. You're alright," I said.

Karen quickly jumped up and ran towards them. She wrapped her arms around my waist and buried her face in my chest.

"You son of a..." Richard moaned.

I noticed his revolver lying on the ground near the foot of the bed and I motioned for Kevin to go over and secure it.

"What do you want us to do with him?" I asked Karen.

"Kill him," Karen said without looking up.

I didn't want to waste ammo. Every bullet was precious, more so than some lives and I had already wasted a bullet on him.

"You should have listened to me, Dick. I told the truth of a mathematical equation. Me plus you equals your death."

I pulled out my club and the only thing left to decide was if I gave him the blunt end or the end with the spike.

"Break his legs first," Karen said as she cried.

"As the lady wishes."

I started with the blunt edge. I didn't enjoy it, but I didn't feel bad about it either. It was more like putting down a stray dog that had rabies. He wasn't human and I knew he wouldn't be haunting my dreams.

When I finished we took Karen back out to the Humvees and we all loaded back up. I took shotgun with Karen in the back seat.

"I have burritos and Coke for you," I said pointing to the cooler.

She wiped tears away and took out a tinfoil wrapped burrito.

There were many questions I wanted to ask but Karen needed a little more time before I asked them. At least she was safe now. We still had a lot of work to do in Salt Lake so we drove to Camp Williams to sleep. Tomorrow we'd figure out what to do with Karen.

FOUR

Uprising Day 8
Zach Salt Lake City

George's plan was crazy, but it was elegant in its brutal simplicity. You gather the zombies into one area and drop a big bomb on them. Of course, the details were a little more complicated. George gathered riders on horses and had them run around gathering hordes of the infected. Then they'd all meet up at one place. It was a wide open area where they'd be extracted by helicopter. Then a C-130 from Hill Air Force Base would drop a MOAB, a huge air fuel bomb that would wipe out everything within a mile radius.

"Think it will work?" Kevin asked.

"I don't see why not."

"I wouldn't want to be one of those runners."

"What's the matter? You don't want to draw the attention of every zombie in the neighborhood and have them chase you around?"

"Can't say that I do. Not my idea of a good time."

"How long we got?"

"One minute."

We waited around at Camp Williams for the show.

Then we saw a flash and a giant fireball covering a whole section of the city. The sound reached us a few seconds later, a dull 'thwump.'

I watched the mushroom cloud while sitting on the hood of my Humvee. Karen sat next to me sipping on a Mountain Dew Throwback. We had cleared Midvale and Sandy of any survivors and raided the comic book store and hobby store while we were at it.

We toasted to the growing fireball.

"That's what they get!" Karen said.

I looked at the mushroom cloud with my PSL scope. It was truly massive. An entire neighborhood had disappeared.

"We should do that more often," I said.

Karen was flipping through the Dungeons and Dragons "Players Handbook" looking for what kind of character she wanted to play as. When I mentioned that my nephews loved D&D, she got very excited. Turned out she was a huge nerd, maybe as huge a one as I was.

"Alright, let's get back to Vernal," I said to everyone. "Historical Team assemble!" I needed a better name than that, but I figured that could wait.

On the way back to Vernal I looked at the Blue Force Tracker. Fort Sill was still there, though with decreased activity. What I was really curious about was how the modern "10,000" were doing. I found them in central Turkey. What I wanted to know was what they were going to do about crossing over to Greece. They couldn't go through Istanbul because that was an incredibly overpopulated, crowded place that would now be wall to wall zombies.

Heck, I could ask them. I sent them a message telling them to avoid Istanbul at all costs and asked what their plans were.

While I waited I thought of that old song "Istanbul was once Constantinople..." Fun song and highly ironic because my main focus in study was Byzantine history. I only had to wait a few minutes.

"Aware of Istanbul situation. There's a highway north of city that crosses straight. Still risky but better chances. How are things state side?" The message said.

"Not good. Utah came out very well and we've lost about 90% of population. East Coast not a good place to be right now. You guys heading to Ramstein?"

"Yes. We see activity there. Maybe hitch a ride back."

"I'll see what I can do on my end."

"Thanks."

Then I sent a message to Nightcrawler. He was the only Air Force guy I knew with a BFT.

"Nightcrawler, we got lots of Americans heading to Germany. Any way we can help pick them up?"

"I'll ask."

It would be a while before I got an answer back.

It felt like very little, but I had to do something. I imagined myself stranded in the armpit of the world, far away from home. I didn't want any US service member to die out there. We needed them too much back here.

We drove back to Vernal. It was a peaceful ride and had some of the most gorgeous scenery ever. Well, it was peaceful once one got past Heber. Then it was wide open countryside with sparse population and a high percentage of gun ownership. We drove past blue reservoirs, small towns and sprawling ranches. No one really spoke much.

Once we got to Vernal, we went to the elementary school were Rebekah was. I introduced Karen and as I guessed, they got along. Heavy metal can bring people together like few things could. After getting Karen situated there I took her to Ogre Ranch for a good meal and to let her meet my "Nightwish" listening, D&D playing nephews.

One person I didn't see was Rosa. When I asked, Mrs. Ogre took me aside.

"We seem to be short a person," I said.

"I don't know how to break this to you easy, but we caught her cheating on you with one of the guardsmen."

"Oh. That all?"

"I kicked her out and haven't seen her since."

"When?"

"Yesterday morning."

"You're kidding."

"I'm not."

At first I didn't know what to say.

"I guess there's more fish in the sea, right?" Mrs. Ogre said.

"Yes, but it's a much smaller sea."

I couldn't think of anything else to say except four letter words so I went to my room and played X-Box the rest of the day. A few people tried to comfort me, but I didn't want to be comforted. I hadn't been in love with Rosa, not by a long shot, but she had been a great kisser. We had made out but we hadn't "gone all the way."

Still, being cheated on hurt and I didn't like being insulted like that.

Sometime in the night I took a break and went outside to check on the BFT. The field in front of Ogre Ranch was full of military vehicles and now looked like an Army motor pool. Large field tents were set up and I could see soldiers milling about.

George had been busy.

Ogre Ranch had been a somewhat quiet and peaceful place isolated from the world. Now it was a hub of traffic full of smelly vehicles and soldiers talking into walkie talkies.

All I could hear were orders being barked out, engines revving and the sound of welding. The whole place smelled like a mechanic's garage, metal, dirt and oil.

I walked down the steps of the porch and went over to where I had parked my Humvee. I had three new messages from Nightcrawler.

The first message said that they would look the situation over and discuss it. The second message said that they were all in agreement that they needed to do something. The third message said that they were making plans now and would be leaving in two days. They had a C-17 that could make it there.

"How long will it take to ferry them all back to the US?"

"Unknown. It could take one trip, it could take weeks. Ramstein is operational. We're talking to them now to find out the situation."

Then a thought occurred to me. I wondered if I was going crazy. It sounded almost suicidal, but once the thought entered I couldn't dislodge it.

"I'm coming."

"Why?"

Really, I just had to see Italy one more time.

"Europe is full of history and art. I can't let all that go to the dead heads."

Europe was a high population, low guns place. It would be crawling with the dead. It was one homicidal cemetery right now. Zeds wouldn't know what art was. All that would still be sitting there.

I had to break the news to George softly.

"I'm going to Europe," I said.

George looked at me over the maps he had spread out on the dinning room table.

"What for?"

"While they're evacuating Ramstein, I'm going down to Italy and stealing all the art I can."

"Don't you think there's more important things to do?"

I needed a rational sounding excuse.

"I'm thinking about our cultural heritage. We could use that connection to the past. We've lost too much already. I'm not going to leave all that to the dead."

He looked me up and down, considering the plan in his head.

"No."

"We have to save something of our past. This would be a moral booster and we kinda need that now."

"This is a really dumb idea. I mean, really stupid," he said.

"I know, but I think this is important."

"I guess you'll need a team."

"I'd appreciate one."

He just shook his head.

When I went around and asked for volunteers, the only ones that wanted to go were Rebekah and Karen. Not exactly the overwhelming response I'd hoped for.

"We're going," Rebekah said.

"Not a chance."

"You're going to leave us here by ourselves?"

"I think a few hundred soldiers can keep you safe."

"That's not what I meant," Rebekah said.

"What are we supposed to do if you decide you like it there and don't want to come back?" Karen asked.

I knew what she meant.

"I'm coming back."

"Oh? And I suppose you'll promise, right?"

"You want to take your little brother into middle of this?"

"Well…no."

"You want to leave him here then? You want to leave him here by himself to worry about you?"

"No."

I didn't think so.

So much for finding a team.

"It's alright," I told Ogre, "I'll just find my crew when I get there."

"You're crazy."

"Probably."

I told them that I'd be back, but I could tell that they didn't believe me. I drove away with Kevin and Sarah. They'd bring the Humvee back to Vernal. We talked about horror movies and heavy metal. I talked because I was bored. They talked to get their minds off of the idea that I wasn't coming back. I'd come back. This was something I had to do and there wasn't any way for me to explain it to others. When your gut tells you something, sometimes you have to throw logic away and just do it.

This could be my last chance to see the place I had been happiest. Italy was my earthly heaven and I had to see it for myself.

Though, even I had to admit to myself that this wasn't the brightest idea I'd ever had. In fact, if I thought about it more, I'd probably talk myself out of it.

Outbreak didn't like leaving his C-130, but the C-17 could bring back more Americans and their equipment. Nightcrawler said I was either insane or an idiot.

I told everyone that I'd bring them back souvenirs and waved as the ramp of the C-17 closed. Once the ramp closed and I felt the enormous plane taxi and take off, I wondered if I was making the biggest mistake of my possibly short life.

I had traveled across the pond many times, but never in a military aircraft. However, I had flown from Iraq to Afghanistan and back in a C-17 before and knew one thing that could make the trip pleasant; power outlets. On the walls of the giant plane were normal outlets. So I plugged in my laptop and played "Dawn of War." I had my cooler of food and soda and played video games, drank Dew and watched movies during my flight.

Except for the pilots I was the only one in the aircraft. All this space would be taken up with returning military folks.

I tried to sleep but I never could sleep on airplanes, let alone utilitarian military ones. So I powered through campaign mode and the first few episodes of "Jericho."

FIVE

Uprising day 10 Zach Hill Germany Ramstein Air Force Base. History Art Reclamation Team. (H.A.R.T.) Yes, I just made that up.

We arrived at Ramstein sometime before midnight. It was a rainy, beautiful night and the airbase looked like it should, soldiers and people with guns everywhere. Old M113's rolled around along with Strykers and armored Humvees. There were even some German armored cars driving around. The place was like a fortress. I had seen this place before and always at night so for me the airbase existed in this dark, worldless dream-state. I saw troops from all over Europe, Polish, Romanian, Aussies and even some Brits.

With me I had my FS2000 and lots of ammo on a chest rig and thigh rig. I had my PSL with a bandoleer and as much ammo as I could carry. I also had a couple of M4's in case I needed a backup and needed to arm my H.A.R.T. volunteers. I wanted to bring my AK, but Europe, at least the parts I planned on seeing, used NATO 5.56.

Outbreak and his crew connected with the local leadership to find out what the situation was. While he did that I went around looking for volunteers. I found a small unit of Brits sitting around a computer. They were watching pod casts from England.

"Hey, Mate, where you heading?" One of them asked.

"Italy," I said.

"What the blazes for?"

"Saving people and art."

"Sounds like bloody suicide to me."

"I get that a lot."

"You got an M4 there, eh? Want to trade?" The one asking had an LA-86, the squad automatic/DM version of the LA-85.

"Trade? Your gun broken or something?" I asked skeptically.

"No, I just love carrying this big beast around all day. It's quite relaxing."

George had always wanted one, so I guess I had found his souvenir. Also, I thought they were dead sexy weapons.

"Alright, you got a deal."

He had six mags so I traded him for six mags. He kept his ACOG though. That was okay because I had military issue ACOG's and Aim points to spare.

I asked around. The place was full of homeless units camping out in hangers. It seemed that a lot of Americans were staying there in order to help out the stranded Europeans. There were also a few thousand civilian refugees, mostly Germans. The place was a fortress. They said that the first few days were barbaric. All their armored vehicles had fended off a massive wave of undead. Even with automatic grenade launchers and 25mm cannons the battle had lasted all day. The hordes were smaller now, but the armor kept up their patrols and skirmishes. Eventually they'd run out of ammo and gas, though, and I hoped that they had a plan by then.

Then I found gold. There was a small platoon of Italians. They were sitting around on army cots talking. They didn't look happy. They were easily recognizable by the long peacock feathers in their caps. I walked up to them and asked if any of them spoke English.

"I do," one of them said. It didn't look like he really wanted to be bothered.

"I'm heading to Italy. Anyone want to come?"

The officer translated to the others. Two of them raised their hands. I had hoped for more.

"There's no point to go there," he said in a thick Italian accent. "The place is dead."

"Well, I want to see if there's anything I can do to help." That was only half the truth.

"There's no helping the place."

"Won't know until I try."

"Take the Centauro. You'll need it."

Having been an avid reader of Jane's armored vehicle guide, I knew what a Centauro was. It was an armored vehicle with a 105mm cannon. The thing was sleek like a shark. It had an operational range of 800km and could go over 100km an hour. That thing would get me to Italy without a problem. However, once there, I'd need something with a larger cargo capacity. I was there to steal a whole lot of stuff.

Before we headed out I had to find Outbreak. I found him standing by a whole gaggle of officers. Back in my army days I wouldn't step foot near officers. Now, however, I didn't even have to salute. There was a not-so-small satisfaction in not saluting officers.

"Hey, what's up?" I asked.

"We're discussing an evacuation. A massive one. They can't hold out here indefinitely," Outbreak said.

"A plan would be nice."

"Once our boys from Iraq show up, we'll start moving everyone out. It'll take a long time to organize this and get everything ready. I'm guessing about three weeks."

"Good. That'll give me plenty of time."

"You're sure about this?"

"Yup. I wasn't an art major because of the pay."

"You were an art major? I thought that was a joke."

"No, sir! I'm a hippy, good vibes, painter. Alright. I'll see you in about two weeks."

We shook hands and parted ways.

On the way back to the Italians I came across a hanger full of civilians.

"Hey! Anybody want to go to Italy? Good food, historic sights and lots of art!" I shouted out.

A large man stood up. He wore a tight black shirt that showed off his massive muscles. He had a long blond beard braided like a Viking and a shaved head with sunglasses parked on top. He had tattoos on his arm that looked like Viking runes. An iPod hung around his neck.

"What you go there for?" He said in an almost unintelligible Swedish accent.

"Kill zombies, see what there is to find."

"Sounds like fun. I come with you."

"My name's Zach."

"I'm Stig."

Then he picked up a giant Medieval two handed sword and followed behind me.

We went to the Italians and they took us where the black painted Centauro tank killer was parked. One of the Italians got in the driver seat and the other took the gunner seat. I got in the commander seat and Stig got into the loader's seat.

The Centauro purred like no American military vehicle could. The seats were actually designed for humans and were comfortable. No Italian would give up his comforts just because they were at war! The Italians had their Beretta rifles and I gave Stig an M4, but he didn't seem impressed. He put his earphones in and sat back.

We drove out to the gate. .50 cals were roaring into a crowd of zombies that were swarming toward the fence. I had never seen so many. It was an ocean of undead and the constant roar from their collective moaning was almost deafening.

I thought Salt Lake was infested; I had no idea. There were thousands upon thousands of them and the moaning shook the ground. I was standing up, looking out of my small cupola and taking in the horrible sight. The moon was clear and bright overhead and I could see the horde with frightening clarity.

I've seen what the .50's did to people and they did the same to zombies. You didn't need a head shot with them. The power of the .50 tore the zeds apart like Grendel in a Viking mead hall. They opened the gate on the condition that we used the 105mm cannon. That wouldn't be a problem.

The gate opened and as soon as it was cleared the cannon fired. The shell hit and blew a huge hole in the swarm. The coaxial machine gun opened up while the cannon was reloaded. We fired again and tore a huge gash into the crowd like a slow motioned bullet through ballistic jelly.

I was glad I couldn't see it all and I didn't want to think about the smell once the sun came up. How messed up was I that my main concern was the smell? Was I so numb to it all now?

I should probably be worried.

Then the driver gunned the gas and we tore through the zombies like we were four wheeling through mud. We did figure eights and drove around until the crowd had been thinned down considerably. Once our duty was done, we tore off down the highway, heading south towards Italy.

We had a full tank and we wouldn't have to stop the entire way. Of course, we did though. Around dawn we saw a small roadside café in what used to be a quiet German town. The IR didn't pick up any zeds so we decided to risk it.

Stig jumped out of the top hatch and rested his giant sword over his shoulder. His head was bobbing as he listened to his music. The sword seemed like a bit of overkill with him. He was large enough to rip zombies apart with his bare hands. I jumped out and stretched.

"Where are we?" I asked.

"A small town called Nerishiem," the Italian driver said.

I looked around the area scanning for zeds. The place was a small, German town with old Bavarian looking buildings. There weren't any lights and the air was disturbingly still.

Me and Stig went inside. He had his giant sword and I kept my FS at the ready. I turned on the tac-light and looked around the cafe. Nothing.

Suddenly a head popped up from behind a counter and I saw two large, dead eyes looking at me. Instantly I fired and hit it in the forehead. Black blood sprayed the wall behind it and it fell back down.

"Whack-a-mole!" Stig said.

There was a cooler of sodas and water, but nothing really edible. I looked around and found a back room. Stig got to the side and opened the door.

A zombie shuffled out of the door, half starved and weak. Stig attacked first with the giant sword held over his head and literally cleaved the zombie straight down the middle in a spray of gore and congealed blood. He stepped away and wiped some blood from his too tight shirt.

There was nothing edible back there either. We grabbed the sodas and went back outside. The sky was turning purple and the skyline of the small town was becoming visible. It was a shame. This place seemed like it could have been beautiful at one time.

A half hour later we came to a bridge that had a roadblock. Three trucks had crashed together blocking access to the bridge.

"Push our way through?" I asked the driver.

"Maybe. I got a better idea," the Italian said.

We fired the 105 and blew the trucks apart. We then drove over the wreckage and continued on our merry way.

"Why you really going to Italy?" The driver asked.

"We're all evacuating Ramstein. Europe is dead. I'm going to rescue people and as much art and history as I can. I'm with the provisional government of Utah. I think it's the only government in the U.S. right now."

"Okay." He didn't seem to care one way or another.

I knew when we were near a town because there were zombies everywhere. I had no idea that there were that many. We were constantly hitting them like potholes on country roads. Occasionally, they were in larger crowds and the driver hit the gas for those occasions.

It was heartbreaking to see everything dead. The Alps came into view and I prayed that those roads were open. My first stop was going to be Venice. If it was dead, then there would be a lot of stuff to steal. If I wished for anywhere to have survivors, it was Venice. I loved no place like I loved Venice. It was my ideal of an earthly paradise and I really hoped it wasn't a death filled hell.

I prayed that something of the old world survived.

Uprising Day 12
Zach Northern Italy:
Operation H.A.R.T.

We had gotten through the Alps somehow. Some of the sections of road were nearly completely blocked off by abandoned cars. The base of the Alps had been an ocean of undead. The zeds from the mountains came down and the zeds from the lowlands stopped there.

Our 105mm cannon plowed through zed and car alike, creating small gaps we could pass through. Having been in the field artillery for several years, I found the cannon very comforting. Stig, up on the .50 cal helped as well with clearing out the zeds. So far the .50 was the only gun he would touch.

In the day it took to finally get to Italy we hadn't come across a single survivor, only hordes and hordes of walking dead the kinds that Utah never saw. In the purple, early morning light I could make out the shuffling forms of thousands of undead as we came down from the mountains. Marco, the driver, stepped on the gas and with the accelerated speed from our Alpine decent we tore through them like a race car through a mud puddle. We could have seen the Venetian Lagoon, but it was a cloudy day and mist clung to everything.

I was tired and Europe didn't have Mountain Dew. For that reason I could never truly call it home. I made do with the Coca-Cola we found, but two days with only tiny naps required at least a Red Bull or a Monster.

I hated seeing Italy like this. I loved the country. We passed by street signs in Italian smart cars, motor cycles and those small three wheeled little pickup trucks. We had to slow down and weave between all the cars. Everything here was much more torn up with burnt cars and buildings, bodies lying in the streets and destruction everywhere.

"Not looking good, Boss," Marco said.

"We'll find someone," I said.

"You really believe that?"

"Of course."

I didn't. I had never seen such chaos before.

"At least we won't have to worry about where we're shooting," Marco said.

"That would be a problem I'd like to have."

Then we came upon a roadblock in the middle of the highway. Wooden barricades with yellow stripes barred the road. It looked like the military had tried to stop people from entering. The wooden barricades had been broken and dried blood was everywhere.

There were some military trucks behind the barricade but what caught my eye was a few yards behind it. We slowly worked our way around the wreckage and pulled up to the object of my attention.

It was a Marine Amphibious Assault Vehicle. A giant tracked amphibious armored vehicle with a turret mounted .50 cal and Mk19 automatic grenade launcher. There were three reasons that the AAV made me celebrate with some serious air guitar. First, the automatic grenade launcher was the most fun thing ever conceived by the minds of men.

Second, the huge thing was amphibious, so I could get to Venice without a problem. Third, it could carry a lot and lot of stuff.

I jumped out with my FS while Stig covered me. The mist made seeing anything beyond fifty meters impossible. There could be a whole crowd of shamblers just out of view and I'd never know.

It was eerily quiet as I ran up to the AAV and found that it was open. All I could hear was the sounds of my own footfalls. Aside from a little dried blood along the rear hatch, there was no sign of its former occupants. There were a few Beretta rifles lying around and some Italian MRE's, so I tossed them and all the spare magazines into the AAV.

Keeping my eyes and ears open I went back and grabbed my PSL and all the M4's and ammo. The quicker this was done the better.

"Hurry!" I whispered to Marco.

I didn't need to explain the reason for haste.

Marco ran over and we got in and closed all the hatches with a sense of relief. He got in the drivers seat and I jumped up in the turret. None of the turret weapons had been fired. What had happened here? Killed without firing a shot?

The giant armored vehicle lurched forward with a sputtering sound and diesel smell and we were on the move again. Too bad none of these Italian units had Blue Force Trackers. I wanted to send a message telling everyone that I was okay.

I thought of Rebekah, Dan and Karen. I wanted them especially to know I was alright. I shouldn't have left them but they'd be safer back there and this was something I had to do.

Why did I have to do it though? Why did I feel so strongly about coming here? I'd seen Italy before and though I loved it, I think I'd rather have let the good memories remain and not have to see this graveyard.

Maybe I was going crazy.

As the sun rose in the sky, the fog dissipated and within the hour the sky was clear and sunny. I opened the top hatch and stood up, looking out at the now desolate Italian landscape. Much of it looked the same, with the Cyprus trees and the small, square buildings. But what was different made the scene all the more horrible. Torn bodies covered in blood lay strewn about the road where they had been pulled out of their cars. Smoke rose from farm houses and corpses walked around looking for something living to kill.

It still held its beauty, but it was now marred with death and destruction that was obvious wherever I looked. The thought of so many people dying destroyed any joy of my return to Italy.

The AAV had a hard time keeping up with the Centauro so we had to slow it down a bit.

Eventually, we came to a marshy beach. It was the Venetian lagoon. Past the half submerged reeds was a green ocean with circling seagulls. We had to avoid the city of Maestre due to highly probable zed activity so we went straight to the water.

One thing I noticed was that the dead avoided the water. Venice had more tourists than locals, so the threat of infection was there, but being surrounded by water gave it some hope. Venice was my favorite place on Earth and I prayed that it was still there and still breathing.

We pulled up on the grassy beach and everyone climbed into the AAV. They drove the AAV into the water and activated the water engines. We chugged along and after a while I saw the skyline of Venice filled with bell towers and church domes emerge from the mist.

I stood up in the turret and watched as the city grew closer. I could feel the salty sea spray and sun on my face and the smell of the ocean filled my nostrils. It felt almost like I was returning home. It all felt so familiar.

Then I saw that the long bridge that led to Venice had a shredded gap in the middle. It looked like it had been blown up. There were a few zombies wandering around the land section of the bridge. That was a good sign indeed.

As our lumbering AAV swam up to bridge I saw moving figures appear. I couldn't tell if they were living or dead.

Then one of them waved at us. I couldn't tell if the wave was friendly or some kind of warning. They shouted something in Italian and I had Marco get up and he shouted back. They talked for a while but I had no idea what the heck they were talking about.

At this point, I didn't really care because I was just too glad to see living people. Then Marco turned to me.

"He tells us to report to the Doge's Palace in St. Mark's Square."

"Anything else?"

"He said not to cause trouble."

"That's not terribly specific. Was he friendly or are we about to be arrested and have all our crap confiscated?"

"Flip a coin?"

"Heads."

We went around the broken bridge and followed its length until we sailed into the entrance of the Grand Canal. The buildings of Venice came right up to the water. The water broke against the buildings like a dam.

There were people all around, standing on the walkways, bridges and open areas. They looked out from the windows of the elaborate houses and from the dozens of smaller boats that plied along the wide canal. I hadn't thought there would be so many survivors crammed into one small city.

It was hope.

We sailed down the uniquely beautiful Grand Canal and past the Rialto Bridge and past the hundreds of beautiful and ancient palaces that sparkled like unique jewels. I began taking pictures of everything I saw. This remarkable feat of survival had to be documented.

Some people stared at us and others waved. Still no clue on what awaited us at St. Mark's Square.

As we came up to the landings and piers of St. Mark's Square I saw a lot of people in lines while people handed out fish. We did our best to pull up to the docks without breaking anything.

Only ancient Venetian flags were flying from the poles. There were no more Italian or European Union flags, just the maroon and gold lion of St. Mark.

Four men in suits walked up with six soldiers behind them.

"Here we go. Be on your best behavior, gentlemen," I said.

I carefully took the safety off of my Beretta.

I was standing up on the top of the AAV, feeling it rock beneath me. I had the FS slung in front of me, but kept my hands in the open where they could see them.

"You guys speak English?" I shouted out.

"Yes, I do," a distinguished, middle aged man with an expensive suit and thick hair said.

"Greetings from America! I'm Zach Hill, official representative from the Governor of Utah. That might not sound like much, but I guarantee that it's the best show in town."

"I'm Antonio DeCanali. Welcome to Venice. You're a long way from America."

"It was a long flight and I hate airplane food. I must say that you guys are doing remarkably well here."

"We were lucky. What brings you to our city?"

Well, I couldn't save the art from the living so my mission here was scrapped, but wasn't terribly eager to be on my way. I loved this city and was overjoyed to see it still alive. I wanted one last time to wander its narrow, ancient streets.

Already my senses filled with the sight of glistening water, the sound of seagulls and the smell of the ocean. The buildings here all had the unmistakable feeling of antiquity. Each building was ancient and held thousands of stories. Always the feeling of death and inevitability lingered over Venice and was punctuated by a deah's head relief peering at us from a nearby building. It was a city that was very much aware of its own death and expected it at any time. Now, however, the city of morbid death was a beacon of life and the refuge for the living.

"I don't need anything, but is there something I can do for you?" I said.

"I can't think of anything. Our problems are too large for a man and his tank."

"You may be surprised what a strong dose of violence can do. Then, may I stay here for two days? Give me one last chance to see Venice?"

"Of course."

There was literally no other city like it on earth. No picture or film can capture everything I love about the city. There's the smell of the sea, the feel of the salty wind on your face and then the indescribable feeling the place has that's ancient and unmovable and yet fragile and mortal. There's a celebration of life but, a realization of death at the same time. Every corner and alley has long held secrets.

Then I looked out into the lagoon and saw a cruise liner.

"What's that?"

"There's a group of Americans that want to sail back to the States. They were stuck here on vacation when the plague hit."

"Did you have a lot of sick?"

"Not many. We put all our infected on the island of Poveglia."

"We have room. If anyone wants to come with us, they can."

I also wanted more people that could hold a rifle.

"I'll spread the word. Fewer mouths to feed would be nice."

I spent the next two days wandering around Venice. Many of the tourist shops were closed with metal shutters. Like we had done in Vernal, unoccupied buildings were used to house refugees who seemed to fill the city.

The faces of the people there seemed empty and hollow. They sat in groups, huddled together, hopeless about their future. They had seen the destruction of their world so I couldn't blame them too much. Still, there was a lot to do and moping around wouldn't help. They were alive when others weren't. They needed to realize that.

I went to the nearly abandoned island of Torcello and found the place to be as quiet and isolated as ever. I went through St. Mark's Cathedral and saw the glittering gold that covered the entire inside of the magnificent church. The Doge's Palace was once again the center of government action. People were sleeping everywhere they could and the old rooms in the palace had refugees from the nearby city of Meastre. I continued to take pictures so I'd have proof that Venice still lived.

Venice was founded by refugees fleeing the collapse of the Roman Empire. Now it was again populated by refugees fleeing the collapse of civilization. They would grow strong here and would one day retake the mainland.

We only found one American, a former Marine that volunteered to come with us. He looked like a Marine and thankfully acted like one too. His T-shirt had a bulldog wearing a Marine uniform. The rest were going to take their chances with the cruise liner. After all, it was safer than trekking across a dead infested Italy with me.

The morning of the third day, we reluctantly headed out. We gave them Governor Ogre's contact information, and such, and I got a radio frequency to contact them on. Our AAV waddled back across to the beach and we retrieved the Centauro armored car.

Next stop: the central mountains of Italy and the gorgeous rural valleys where Assisi and Spelleto were.

SIX

Uprising day 15. Zach Central Italy H.A.R.T.

After leaving Venice, we went south. I really wanted to go to Ravenna because my favorite mosaic of all time was there in the Church of San Vitale. It was the famous mosaic of emperor Justinian and empress Theodora. However, unless I planned on taking the entire wall, it was impossible to move. That was one art treasure I couldn't do a thing about. The Venetians owned Ravenna for a long time, perhaps they'd do so again.

Instead, we went down through the mountain valleys of central Italy to the Umbrian region. Umbria had by far the best food in Italy. The wild boar sausage was the most delicious thing I had ever eaten. Unfortunately, there would be no boar sausage this time.

Going towards Umbria we passed by small town after small town, all of them completely infested with the dead. They apparently heard our vehicles rumbling down the highway and came out to investigate. I saw one fall from the train station's balcony and crack its head open on the tracks.

These were unprotected towns on the valley floors, near the highway that ran along ancient Roman paths. I saw olive groves lining the hills and in its peacefulness it all seemed almost normal.

When we saw trucks we had to stop and syphon gas. Gas stations were not nearly as common in Italy as in the States and no where near as convenient.

We drove up into the mountains and the towns grew much thinner. As we drove through a narrow mountain pass surrounded on both sides by thick bushes, a man jumped out from the thin wood line. He was waving and carrying a long over and under shotgun. We slammed on the brakes and Marco stood up out of the top hatch.

Again there was a long conversation in Italian which consisted of shouting very fast and waving their arms about.

It turned out that him and his father had a hunting lodge up in the mountains. We were the first living humans they had seen in ten days. They loaded all their food and supplies in the AAV and we were under way again. Both of them had done their mandatory service in the military and were avid hunters. They hunted boar and their supplies included a lot of cured boar meat. It wasn't juicy sausage, but I could definitely use some boar jerky. Neither of them spoke English but through Marco they asked what a yank was doing there. Marco had a hard time answering that question. I didn't mention that I was there to steal art.

I needed a bath and I was tired. Seeing Italy crawling with dead was a little depressing. I had no idea how everyone was doing back home. I wished I knew how my twin was. He was traveling across the entire United States.

We entered Umbria and it was bright and sunny. The roads were clear until we passed by the towns. For the most part the towns were off the highway and up on a hill. Some of them had medieval walls, but not all of them.

Then I saw the familiar hilltop town of Assisi. The giant convent that took up a whole side of the hill was a distinct landmark that told me exactly where I was. Assisi had a medieval stone wall complete with gates and battlements.

"Take the exit. We're going to go check up on Assisi," I called down to Marco.

The streets that led up to Assisi were narrow and winding and we had to slow down. The town at the base of the hill was full of zombies. They came up and hit our vehicles as we passed by. They chased after us, but we were still faster. They no longer ran like raving berserkers, but shambled at a trot that someone could easily outrun.

As we came to the small park in front of the main gate of Assisi, we saw a large crowd of zombies pushing and shoving to get in. They were banging away on the stone walls like the idiotic grail knights in Monty Python's Holy Grail. It was a small grassy park and there were hundreds of zeds there.

"Open fire?" Stig called over from the turret of the Centauro.

There were a lot of zombies. Sure, we had enough bullets, but what about the next horde or the horde after that. I didn't like it, but we just couldn't shoot them all.

"Save the ammo. Let's just run them over."

Stig nodded and we secured all the hatches. Then we began to Grand Theft Auto-style the horde of zombies and went around in circles, figure eights and the classic back and forth. As the horde that we had attracted on our way up the hill came into the small park, we ran them over as well. The narrow streets were in our advantage for once.

The few stragglers that tried to climb onto our APC's we picked off with our side arms.

Once the horde was cleared away the gate to Assisi opened and twenty men in chain mail, swords and shields came out in a tight cluster. A man in a military uniform and a Beretta rifle followed them.

I got out of the hatch and stood on top the AAV.

"Anybody speak English?"

Five of them said they did, including the military officer.

"Can you good people use any help?" I asked.

"I think you just did," the Italian officer said. I had no idea what rank he was.

"How many survivors you have here?"

"Almost everyone living here and a few tourists," he said.

That was good news indeed. The Dark Ages didn't get everything wrong after all. Stone walls around towns turned out to be a good idea as well as chain mail and swords. It made me wonder about the other small walled towns I had passed by.

"I'm sure there are still plenty of zombies around. Let's take care of them," I said.

"Take this," one of the men said and handed me a tourist map.

"I'm here to kill zombies, not see the sights."

That wasn't entirely true.

"I marked the gates. We have undead at each gate. Too many for us to handle."

"Ah, I get it. We got more work to do."

We went around to each gate, smashing zeds under our treads and wheels. Then we drove through the city looking for any pockets of resistance. I was up in the turret and picked off the stragglers with my FS.

Once we finished we went back to the main gate. There was now a crowd of living people there cheering and waving. Some had medieval looking banners and some had Italian flags. We were greeted with a hero's welcome. Hot Italian women with long, black hair kissed me on the cheek after I had dismounted and somehow a sandwich ended up in my hand, a prosciutto panino with fresh tomato. Delicious!

A group of Americans surrounded me: tourists that had been trapped there since the beginning. It was nice to see some families intact. It made me wonder about Josh and how George and Musket were doing. But most of my thoughts turned to Rebekah, Dan and Karen. They would be completely alone if I didn't return.

I explained to everyone my story and they wanted a ride back to Ramstein and back to the US. There were English and some Germans that also wanted a ride out of Europe.

Assisi was doing well considering the situation. There were no art treasures here either, just beautiful, large, very decorated churches that were highly ironic considering that St. Francis spoke out against beautiful, large, very decorated churches. So to remember him, they built a giant, expensive cathedral. They couldn't 'not get it' any more than that. Still, I loved this place and was glad to see more survivors.

I told them of Venice and they cheered at the news. Aside from the wall around the city, there was also an ancient fortress at the very top of the hill. They had people with telescopes and signaling mirrors to communicate with the nearby town of Spello. Spello was a less famous town, but was even more charming in a picturesque Italian, countryside kind of way.

I got a few volunteers that were going to follow in a civilian truck and then we went to Spello to GTA the zombies there. It was a smaller town and took less time. My biggest worry was the fuel gage. Sure, we could run over as many zeds as we wanted, but once that fuel ran out, we'd be a large metal hot pocket for the zombies.

I popped out of the hatch and looked around. There were still a lot of zombies near the town. The town outside the old section with its stone walls was a cemetery and weaving between tightly packed houses wasn't as rapid as I'd like.

The map showed that we had half the wall to go and I really hoped that most of the town's zombies were by the wall because I did not look forward to clearing the town out on foot.

Then I saw a parked cargo truck.

"Marco, look there."

I tapped him on the shoulder with my foot. He looked up and nodded that he understood.

"You keep them off me while I refuel," I said.

I couldn't ask Marco or the former Drill Instructor to go out in my place. So I hopped out and ran over to the truck with the pump in my hand. Zombies shuffled towards us by then they were at least two blocks away.

I heard the Marine fire a few shots with the M4 from up on top the AAV. I didn't have the luxury of seeing what he was shooting at. All my attention went to the pump. Being out in the open felt like one of those dreams where you're giving a speech and you realize you forgot your pants. I preferred the safety of an armored vehicle.

I inserted the tubes and began pumping as fast as I could. One eye was kept on the zombie stumbling down the street toward me. Apparently, he wasn't the only threat because the others were still shooting off in another direction.

I continued pumping and the zombie continued to get closer. Only now, he had two friends with him. He was only a few houses away and I could see he was wearing a soccer jersey. Already that was too close.

Then the tank ran dry.

"Done!" I called out and scrambled back up onto the AAV.

I didn't realize how heavy I was breathing until I started to relax.

We circled the town twice and once we were sure the main horde was long gone, we knocked on the door.

Two local police poked their heads out and wouldn't believe us until we showed them all the mangled corpses that had been pounding at their gates, until minutes ago.

They were so thrilled that they even brought their mayor out to see us.

I had met the mayor of Spello before during one of my prior trips to Italy. He was just one of the men there in the town piazza chatting with anyone passing by: typical of older Italians. It was the kind of small town that used to exist all over the place and now didn't exist at all; except for this one last exception. The mayor was the sort to greet visitors with a smile and a handshake and knew everyone's name. Unlike Assisi, there were no tourists.

The people gathered in the town piazza to celebrate. There was a live band and dancing. Someone was throwing around red flower peddles.

"You go do this at other towns?" The mayor asked.

"Do you know of any other town that survived?" I asked.

"Spelleto," he said.

"Spelleto's alive?" I asked.

"Yes, yes it is! They're held up in the castle. We got word of them before we lost contact. The castle is strong. They must still be there."

"We don't know? We need to find out if they need help right away." I turned to Marco. "Get the armor ready to go. We're rolling out."

"Right!"

"Mayor, we need some volunteers," I said.

He raised his eyebrows and then smiled. One thing about the small towns of the Umbria region was that they loved their festivals. Their festivals often had everyone dressing in Renaissance costumes which sometimes included armor and weapons. Halberds turned out to be excellent weapons against zeds.

After loading up the Medieval pikemen into trucks, we went back down the hill and toward the highway that led to Spelleto. I had been to Spelleto once before and found it to be a beautiful town. It was also on a hill with a castle up on top. Unlike Assisi and Spello, however, it didn't have a wall. I knew that if the people didn't make it to the castle they'd be dead already. There probably wasn't much food or water in the castle either. We had to hurry.

We took the exit to Spolleto and began slowly making our way up the narrow, ancient streets. The going was slow due to the smallness of the streets and the largeness of our vehicles. One advantage it gave us though was that there was no where for the zombies to go so we smashed them under our armored tracks.

"When do we get out and have some fun?" The large Viking asked.

"You'll have your chance," I said. So far we hadn't encountered very many zombies in town. That meant they were all where they thought they could get food and that meant they were all chilling at the castle.

I ducked back down from the turret and looked at the brightly colored halberdiers in our rear crew compartment. They looked somewhat goofy, but every last one of them had seen more death and killing than anyone should be allowed to see. They were grim-faced and determined. That meant that they stood a chance of having a future. They were willing to fight as long as they thought they had hope.

It took us a half hour to creep and wind our way up the steep, winding hill town. The castle which had at one time been a prison was in good shape and modernized. Maybe they still had power and water?

When we finally got up to the top of the hill it opened up and I saw the parking lot of the castle. It was filled with the dead. They were funneling toward the front gate of the castle which looked to be smashed open.

"Open fire!" I shouted out.

I pressed down the turret's trigger and the .50 cal machine gun roared out a long stream of destruction. The thumb sized bullets tore into the horde popping them like darts against balloons.

Some of my guys jumped out with their M4's and began firing at the crowd. The Viking also leapt out of the top hatch and waded into the horde like he was wading into the ocean. His large sword cut through zombie in a way a sharpened baseball bat would; messily.

Our halberdiers and pikemen filed out of our AAV and trucks, quickly got into a phalanx and began moving toward the gate. They rolled over the zed horde like they were sweeping a floor and were soon at the main gate.

I hopped out of the AAV with my FS and followed behind them. Inside was a courtyard with makeshift barricades made out of tables, beds and every other scrap of metal and wood. The defenders were using bats, table legs and anything else to stay alive, but stay alive they had.

I stayed back and watched. Not only did I have no desire to be treated like a hero, I also didn't like crowds of people. The Italians deserved the credit here, not me.

Over the next two days we worked our way down Umbria, lifting the sieges of the old medieval towns. Then, with the survivors that had weapons we began clearing the valley. I told them how we in Vernal blocked off the narrow passes and were able to defend the valley like that. I stayed in a hotel in Assisi and even got a bath. Cold, but it was good to feel a little cleaner.

The mayors of the towns gathered in Assisi to discuss how to secure the valley and keep everyone alive. Whatever they decided, it wasn't my problem. This was their country and they'd take care of it.

As happy as I was to be there and helping those people, it felt empty in a way. I didn't have any of my friends or family there. I took plenty of pictures and wrote my thoughts in a notebook so I could tell them all about it, but that just wasn't enough. I was eager to head back to the states and be with the people I cared about. It was difficult to face such hardships and accomplishments without anyone there that I cared about.

Our next stop was going to be particularly annoying. We were about to head to Rome where it had been peak tourist season. It would have been packed with people and would now be packed with zombies. However, there was the villa Borghesse museum that was filled with art. If the Vatican Museum was open, then there would be even more there.

I needed to save as much of my ammo as I could in preparation for Rome. I had a feeling that we would need every round for the .50 and MK19 that we had.

There were too many civilians to take to Rome, so I left most of them there in Assisi and promised to come back within the week. The two hunters were left there in Assisi to help secure the valley and get food. I gained about ten people that could use firearms, some of them were Italians who had done their mandatory military service. They were eager to help clear their country of walking dead. I issued them the M4's and gave a brief class on how to use it.

We continued on down the empty highway towards Rome. I could always tell when we neared a small city because abandoned cars started appearing. A sign said "Terni." I wasn't familiar with that town.

I watched from on top the turret as we passed by a train that had stopped between stations. Luggage and bodies were scattered everywhere.

Houses started growing closer together and small shops began to grow more common as we made our way closer to the town.

"How's our gas?" I asked Marco.

"Not good."

"I see a truck up ahead. We better gas up while we can."

"Keep eyes open."

I let my new volunteers handle the syphoning of the gas while I dismounted to pull security and stretch my legs. I scanned the nearby buildings for movement. When a corpse walked into view, I put a bullet between its eyes. With my silencer I attracted far fewer zeds.

It was a beautiful place, even in death. The tall, thin Cyprus trees and the old but cared for buildings were all a part of this scene worthy of a painting. It made me itch for my paints and canvases. It had been too long since I thought about anything creative. My soul hungered to paint and draw, but I was in survival mode and had to keep my thoughts and eyes focused on the immediate and the practical. One day, though, I would paint again and create art of my own instead of stealing it.

Then I saw movement out of the corner of my eye. I shouldered my FS and scanned around, but didn't see anything. I was about to turn away, but then I saw it again. Someone down a wide street was darting from parked car to parked car. They were still far away. A zombie wouldn't worry about cover...would they?

I pulled the PSL off my shoulder and looked through the scope. As I watched I saw the person get up and run into an alleyway. Whoever it was,

was definitely female. She ran in an awkward, girly kind of run with her hands out to the side. She was wearing mostly black and gray and had a large backpack. I didn't see any weapons, but she was wearing what looked like a nun's habit.

"Is that a nun?" I asked out loud.

"Huh?" Stig asked and swung his .50 cal over to take a look. "Yeah. Looks like a nun."

"You got to be freaking kidding me."

I waved at her and the next time she ran closer she quickly waved back.

"What is this chick doing? Why doesn't she just run for us?"

Then I saw about ten zombies shuffle out of a side street and into the main street. They were between us and the nun.

"Stig, hold fire."

I kneeled down behind the railing of the highway and propped my PSL and the rails. I judged the distance using the scope's built in range finder, assuming the zeds were mostly average height. I clicked the scope to 200 yards and took aim. I fired and one of the zed's heads splattered like a melon. Instantly the others turned toward me and began moaning as they trotted closer. I aimed again, making sure that the nun wasn't in danger. I fired again and blew the whole side of a zombie's head off. One by one I took them out. When I quickly changed mags, using the same technique I used for my AK, I looked up and saw that they were all dead, but for real this time.

Then the nun stood up and began running full tilt toward us. Two more zombies came out of the alleyways behind her, but she was much faster.

When she got to the highway railings, I reached out my hand to help her over. She quickly took it and still managed to fall over onto her face.

"Grazie, grazie," she said between gulps of air.

She was a young woman, maybe early twenties. She was thin and just a little shorter than me. She had a sharp, angular face, but still fairly pleasant and wore rectangular, black rimmed glasses that were so popular in Italy. She had ugly, but sensible shoes and a long black skirt, gray buttoned up long-sleeved shirt and a black habit that fell down to her shoulders. She had some dirt on her, but was surprisingly clean of blood.

"Prego. You're welcome," I said.

"You American?" She asked in that Italian accent that drove me crazy in a good way.

"Yeah, I'm American. Sister, what are you doing out here?"

"I was hiding in bell tower and saw you coming. I took chance and ran for you."

"How long have you been hiding there?"

"Two days. Got trapped up there."

She was still breathing hard and probably needed a rest. I led her inside the AAV through the top hatch. I wish I could say I was a big enough man to not check out her legs as she climbed up, but I most certainly did.

Inside I sat her down on a bench and gave her a bottled water which she hastily drank down. I took out my private stash of Assisi cheese and cut her a large slice along with some salami. She nodded her thanks and ate like a starving person.

"You must be quiet like a ninja or really lucky," I said.

"Both," she said with a smile.

"Have you seen any other survivors around here?"

"No. None. My whole convent: dead. City is dead. Where you come from?"

"I'm with what's left of the American government. We have a base alive and well in Ramstein Germany. I'm collecting survivors and works of art that need saving."

"You first people I see alive in many days. Ten I think. Thank you."

"I'm only glad to help."

When we began to roll again I let someone else go up in the turret while I sat and talked to our newest guest.

"I'm Zach Hill," I said.

"Sister Cecelia."

"Very pleased to meet you."

"You rescuing art and taking it back to America?"

"That's the idea."

"I always want to go to America. Italy not safe."

"You're welcome to come along."

"I should have known you are American." She then pointed to my black cowboy hat or "tactical taco" as it's known in certain circles.

"It's kind of a give away," I said.

We continued to talk. It turns out that she had done her two year service in the military as a clerk and studied history in the university. We talked Roman history all they way to Rome.

The circular highway that surrounded Rome was covered in abandoned and burned cars. We had to push our way through, ignoring the zeds as we went. We carefully planned our route to the Vatican first because it had a bigger haul. The caution was because some of the streets in Old Rome wouldn't accommodate our vehicles.

We came over a hill and saw Rome before us. I climbed up in the turret to take a look. There were a few columns of smoke rising in places. Bodies, trash and abandoned vehicles were everywhere. In the distance I could see the coliseum and the tops of many church domes and bell towers.

As we drove closer, we came to what was once a government roadblock. There was another Centauro armored car and their equivalent of a duce and half, though not as big and had a flat nose.

I sent over a crew for each vehicle. We'd need the Centauro for its guns and protection, but the truck I'd need to haul art and possibly people.

With our new friends we rolled into the city, coming in north of the

Vatican. It was the neighborhood that I used to live in. I knew it and I knew what streets to take and even where a grocery store was, a horror novelty shop, and even where a model store was.

As we came off the highway near the rear of the Vatican we waded into what was literally an ocean of zombies. I could see the five story tall walls of the Vatican and it seemed the zombies were trying to get in. I knew that there'd be a lot of them, but I had no idea. All I could see were the heads and flailing arms of the shambling dead. We couldn't drive through that. There were so many that'd be able to push us over, gum up our tracks or even climb on top of each other to get in. The wide street in front of me was literally packed with the animated corpses of the dead. So many people. I hadn't seen anything like this before. Utah just didn't have a concentrated enough population for this kind of obscene horror.

For a moment I sat there in my turret, dumbstruck and wondering what the hell I had gotten myself into.

SEVEN

Uprising: Rome Day 15
Zach H.A.R.T.

Rome was a sea of zombies and the collective moaning was almost deafening. I had seen concerts with less noise and far less stink than this. The sun was setting and the tall buildings on each side of us cast all the zombies into a massive shadow that hid their distinct features.

We were near the rear of the Vatican and the brown wall rose up too high for the zombies to ever get into, but they kept trying. If they were trying to get in, that meant there was living flesh inside.

This was just the rear of the Vatican. Up ahead and around the corner was a piazza that would be loaded with people and behind that was St. Peter's Square. St. Peter's Square was literally full of people at the best of times. Now it would be full of zombies. As bad as it was here, we'd have to conserve ammo just to make it there.

Sister Cecelia squeezed up into the turret with me to look out at the Vatican.

"There's people still alive there," I said.

Her eyes squinted and she got an overly exaggerated look of concentration.

"We have to help them!" She said.

"That's the plan."

"When the Holy Roman Empire invaded Rome, people fled to the Castel Sant' Angelo. There might be people there," she said.

"We'll check if we get a chance. I just didn't know there would be so many of them!"

"We're going to blow them to hell."

"Damn straight sister."

It was awkward having a young attractive nun pressing up against me. She had no idea what that was doing to me. (Not that I was complaining.) After getting her back down, though I had enjoyed it, I got the Mk-19 grenade launcher ready. The belt of grenades was ready to rock and roll.

"Okay, Centauros, make every shot count. We don't have ammo to waist. Centauro 1, you fire, then Centauro 2," I said over the radio.

"Understood," someone said in a thick Italian accent.

"Once we open up on them, they won't like us. They'll come at us. Keep aiming for the thickest concentrations. I'll keep them off of us the best I can. Your .50 cal gunners will take care of anything else. Ready?"

"Ready."

"Fire!"

Centauro 1 fired its 105mm cannon. The shell hit right in the middle of the crowd and exploded, sending shredded corpses flying in all directions. A second later, Centauro 2 fired and blew another hole into the horde. As soon as a hole was created more zombies flooded in and filled that hole up.

The ocean of zombies began to slowly ebb our way. A massive wave of undead was surging toward us. The Centauro's fired again and again, tearing apart what must have been hundreds of zombies. The shells were flying nearly horizontal so they would shred a whole line of zeds before finally impacting into a huge cloud of dust and flying body parts. I was used to the 155mm, but I had to admit that the 105's were doing a great job. I had never actually seen what they would do on the receiving end. I could see the circular waves of concussion tear through the crowds, breaking bones and smashing skulls.

As the tidal wave of walking dead grew closer I knew it was my turn. I began firing in short bursts of only two or three. The grenades tore through the crowd. I didn't waste any rounds and made each one count.

I heard Stig and the other Centauro open up with the .50 cals. We were laying down a hail of death like I had never seen before. All I could see was explosions and broken bodies. Still the horde swarmed forward and they were getting closer. Despite the onslaught we were throwing down, they were gaining ground.

"Back up! Give us some space between us and them!"

We began a fighting retreat. As long as they couldn't get to us and drown us in their numbers, we could live. I let loose with another burst of grenades and the two Centauros fired again and again.

When the smoke cleared, there was little more than craters and mangled corpses. There were still plenty of zeds left though, but they were now thinner in number and spread out.

"Let's run them over boys!"

We plowed into them, running them over like prairie dogs on the road. Our team came around the corner to the piazza and we came to another crowd, though surprisingly this one wasn't as large as the other one. Then I remembered where we were; the entrance to the Vatican museum. Here there was no entrance. We ran these shamblers over and moved to St. Peter's Square, the place I had been dreading ever since I thought of coming to Italy. My nightmares did not disappoint me.

As we entered the square through the open gates in the ancient wall, it was as I had imagined. I had the opportunity to see this place during Easter Sunday and this was just like that, except now instead of devout Catholics, they were murderous, cannibalistic, walking corpses.

There was a narrow corner we had to navigate to get around and into the square. The place was surrounded by a gigantic colonnade that blocked our shots. We had to get around it and my AAV led the way. I switched to the .50 cal and opened fire, tearing a path for us. The colonnade blocked our shots but it also blocked the ocean of dead. Once the piazza was open to me, I let loose with my Mk-19 and began blasting huge holes into the crowd.

I had never seen so much death before in so many guises. Stig kept the .50 cal roaring and as soon as the 105's were clear, they began pounding away.

Still, the horde surged on us and the wave of undead hit the AAV and the two Centauros like a tsunami. I could feel their pounding fists on the armor of the AAV. Their moaning and stench was almost unbearable. The sure mass of bodies was tipping the armored vehicles slightly, but not enough.

We kept moving and kept firing. The hatch next to me opened up and Cecelia popped out with one of the M4's.

"Aim for the head!" I shouted.

I couldn't believe I just said that. I was there in the zombie apocalypse and I actually said to aim for the head. I didn't know if I deserved cool points or a slap on the head.

She clumsily readied the weapon and began firing at the zeds that were close to us. Despite everything that was going on I stopped to take a picture and admire the scene. A nun with an M4 was firing down from an armored vehicle at a crowd of zombies. That was going to be on the cover of my zombie history book...in black and white of course.

Our constant, but controlled fire, eventually thinned the horde out and we began driving through the masses while keeping up our fire.

"Look!" Cecelia shouted. I looked where she was pointing and saw the front doors of St. Peter's opening up and what looked like a platoon of clowns came out. They were the famed Swiss Guard, but instead of halberds, they were carrying automatic weapons. P-90's by the look of them. They began to lay down controlled fire that tore into the crowd.

I switched back to the .50 cal and began firing at the now scattered clusters of resistance. I also was running low on the Mk-19 and wanted to save it for a special occasion.

Fifteen minutes later we were picking off the isolated stragglers with small arms.

"We did it!" Cecelia shouted and gave out a victory shout.

We drove up to the Swiss guard, who despite their clown outfits, I had to admit were pretty intimidating. One had to be the best of the best to join and these guys were armed to the teeth. One guy had two P-90's and two guys had SAW's.

They said something in Italian, but they were smiling.

"Sorry guys, I don't speak Italian," I said.

"What? Who are you then?" One of them asked in a near perfect American accent.

"I flew over from the States and wondered if you fellows could use some help."

"Thank you for the assistance. Without you we never would have been able to kill them all."

"I don't know. Looks like you guys know what you're doing."

"We simply didn't have enough ammunition."

"That's what we're here for. I'm just glad I can be of assistance!"

"You certainly have our thanks."

"I'm Zach Hill and I'm on an official mission from the government of Utah."

"Please, come inside. I'm sure they'll want to talk to you."

I left Stig and a few others to guard the now torn up piazza while I entered St. Peter's. Simply put it was the most impressive building I had ever seen. I remembered climbing to the top of the dome and it felt like climbing a mountain. The whole thing was on a scale built for giants.

Cecelia was right beside me.

"I've never been to St. Peter's," she whispered.

"What?" I've been several times and I'm not even Catholic...or Italian."

"You're not Catholic?"

"Nope."

"But I..."

She cut off when we entered and saw the hundreds of people that filled the inside of the cathedral. There were refugees wall to wall and priests, monks and nuns were going around handing out bread and plastic cups of water. All their eyes were on us however.

"You all caused quite a ruckus," the captain of the Swiss Guard said.

Then the refugees began clapping and cheering.

A man in a snappy red uniform came up to us and shook our hands. The only thing I understood of him was "Grazie," which meant 'thank you.'

Soon we were surrounded by several cardinals and bishops, all thanking us and shaking our hands. Cecelia almost fainted from so much attention from the Catholic hierarchy.

"I'm glad I can help. What can I do for you?" I asked.

"Rome," a living mummy of a Cardinal said. "We need to take back

Rome."

"Yes, street by street if we have to," one of the Swiss Guard said.

"We have people in the Castel Sant' Angelo. They're surrounded by the dead."

"We'll get them out," I said.

"What can we do to thank you?" The Cardinal asked.

"Let me choose a souvenir from your museum."

Uprising Zach Day 16 Rome, Italy H.A.R.T.

They allowed me to take two things from the very extensive Vatican museum. I would have loved to take a statue or two, but they were too heavy, too big and too fragile. I had to limit myself to paintings. There was a painting I loved and I went right to it…after wandering around lost for a while. The place was enormous.

I finally found it, a painting of Judith holding the severed head. There was something about this painting that made me unable to tare my eyes away. Maybe it was the serene, almost pleased look in Judith's eyes. Maybe because she was a babe. I don't know, but I chose that one and another one of the resurrected Christ appearing to Mary Magdalene. I loved the theatricality and drama of the old Baroque paintings. They could make simple scenes seem a matter of life and death and every gesture held pages of significance.

I loaded the paintings into the AAV beside a rack of guns.

"Now what do we do?" Sister Cecelia asked.

"We help them out the best we can. I can only stay a few days because I have a plane to catch."

"Then you're heading back to America?"

"You sure you want to come?"

"Yes."

"It's going to be a rough ride."

"I can handle it." She raised her M4 as punctuation.

Since she was going to be rolling with me for a while, I figured she could use something a little more. I gave her one of the Aim points I had been saving. We used up a 30 round magazine to zero it and give her a little practice.

"Once my prizes were loaded up, us, the Swiss Guard and a few of the now M4 armed survivors rode over to the Castel Sant' Angelo. The castle and the Vatican were connected by a not very secret passage so there was no urgent need to raise the siege except for killing more zombies.

We rolled out at night and had our NVG's on. As scary as zombies were, we were the ones that went bump in the night. A 105mm cannon made an awfully big bump.

"Sir, we found something!" One of the Italians said. He was a surviving carabineiri and he still wore his flashy uniform and had his male model looks. Women tourists were always having their pictures taken with them.

"I'm not a sir. What did you find?"

"In the back of the Centauro: canister rounds for the 105!"

"Wait…did you say canister…as in a giant shotgun shell?"

"Yes, that's what I mean." His smile grew huge.

"A giant shotgun, eh? I like," Stig said from the turret of Centauro 1.

This day kept getting better and better.

"You got room for one more?" A voice asked. I turned to see a man in a dark uniform and a huge peacock feather sticking out of his hat. I shook my head and laughed; not at them, but at how typically Italian it was.

"I always have room for a fellow cav trooper."

Our small army rolled up to the massive crowd that surrounded the round castle. There wasn't a lot of space in front of the castle due to it being right near the river. The bridge of angels that led to the castle however was covered in the dead.

"One shot from each Centauro of canister, then we move in. I'll take the bridge."

The Centauros fired in unison. The shot canisters ripped through the crowd like nothing I've ever seen. The crowd turned into fine chunks of dead flesh and blackish mist. At once, the crowd seemed a whole lot smaller.

We moved out and ran the crowd over. The dead were too stupid to move out of the way. I took the AAV down the bridge. It was almost too easy. Zombies were extraordinarily dangerous in vast numbers like this, but given the proper tools, their numbers turned against them.

"There might be survivors in the city. There are lots of apartments, sealed off buildings, and secure places that could have held out," the male model policeman said.

"The Holy See has asked our help to clear out the city," I said. "We have the help of the Swiss Guard. This could be their finest moment in history. I want to be a part of it."

"But, why? You're not even Catholic," Cecilia said.

"Because they're people that need help. Nothing else should really matter."

Cecilia smiled a shy smile and looked away.

"Yes, well. Let's get started." Then she lowered the NVG's down.

We drove across the bridge of angles and into the Old City. The problem with having a city this ancient was the narrow streets that could barely fit a single car, let alone an armored vehicle. We took one of the few navigable streets to the Piazza De Venezia. I never understood why Rome had a piazza named after Venice. They had never been friends until about 1900's when Venice was forced to become a part of Italy.

"This is where Venice had their embassy," Cecilia explained.

"And because Venice was the economic powerhouse of the day, they got a piazza named after them?"

"Correct!"

There were scattered shamblers around, but nothing like the Piazza of St. Peter's. We shot the few wandering dead and jumped out of our vehicles to have a pow wow. We huddled around a map and made a plan. A group would run through the streets, luring the zombies into one large mass and then bringing them down a narrow street.

"I'll be bait," I said.

"No, you're the leader," Cecilia said.

"I said I'd help them and I will. I'm not a douche REMF who sits back and does nothing while everyone else works their butts off. I'll go the first time."

"I'll go too!" Sister Cecilia said.

"I just rescued you. I don't want to see you get hurt," I said.

"And I don't want to see you hurt. I go too."

With that accent I couldn't resist.

We planned our rout and got our hand held radios ready. I left my PSL in the AAV and made sure all the magazines for my FS2000 were topped off. Sister Cecelia was wearing a tac-vest that the Swiss Guard had given her. The Guard and the Cardinals were impressed that a nun was fighting back. Some of them thought it was shameful, but the Guard approved to a man. I certainly approved.

"Ready?" I asked.

She took a deep breath and nodded. I was about to run, but her slender hand shot out and stopped me.

"What's wrong?" I asked.

She pointed to one of the large scooters that would actually look kind of cool and mean if it wasn't for the fact that it was a scooter. It could definitely hold two people.

"Okay, so I'll drive and…"

Sister Cecilia just laughed.

"You're American. You drive big car in big streets. I'm Italian. I drive scooters in narrow streets. I drive."

I smiled and gave her a nod.

We jumped on the scooter and she put the large round helmet on. I'd rely on my black cowboy hat. If I was going to die, I wouldn't die looking like Dokakis. Also, with my FS, it'd be easier to use while on the move.

Cecilia started the motor and we drove off going about a slow jog pace.

"Hey! We're right here! Come get us!" I shouted out. It didn't take long before we had a huge following. We continued our way through the narrow streets of the Old City. Some of the buildings there dated back hundreds of years and older. I was surprised when we came upon the Pantheon. It looked completely unchanged even after the zombie apocalypse. There were more zeds there than I would have liked and Cecilia had to demonstrate her scooter proficiency and zip around a few of them.

Once we had our horde following us, we made our way to the rally point. I had the map out and directed her where to go.

A zombie shambled out in front of us and I had to quickly aim and fire. The zombie fell down and Cecelia rode right over it like a speed bump.

"Nice one!" I said.

"No, good job to you," she said.

Once we got to the last narrow street, we saw the Centauro at the end. We hurried and drove past it. Then the sleek, black armored car drove forward and completely blocked the street. The zombies filed into the long alleyway, filling it until it was completely packed full of shuffling dead.

Then the Centauro fired a canister shot and the whole crowd burst into chunks and mist. The entire street was butchered in an instant like they had been in a blender.

"Did you see that?" Cecilia shouted out still holding her ears.

"I couldn't miss it."

She literally jumped up and clapped her hands. There was something innocent and nerdy about Cecilia. How she managed to maintain her youthful cheerfulness I'll never know.

"Again!" She said.

"As the lady wishes."

We did our ride through again. She joined in my yelling and she yelled out in Italian. I had no idea what she was saying, but her voice was simply too soft and too nice sounding to attract anything more than twenty feet away.

"Hey, stop!" I said.

She slammed on the breaks.

"What?"

"There! Pull in really quick!"

We had to hurry because a small crowd was already following us.

It was a store whose window was full of ancient Roman type stuff. Three things got my attention. One, was a Gladius. Imitation, but I didn't' care. Two, was a shining Centurion helmet, complete with red crest. Three was a Lorica Segmentata, the awesome looking body armor of the Roman legions. I weighed my options and decided it was worth the expenditure of ammo.

I turned and began shooting the few that had followed us. Not knowing why, Cecilia joined in.

Once the danger was clear for a few seconds, I took off my tac vest, put on the armor and Gladius and loosely put the tac vest over that.

Cecilia laughed as she put on the centurion helmet.

"Roman holiday!" She said.

This chick was messed up in a wonderfully morbid way.

My gun fire had attracted more zeds and the streets around us were filling up again. We jumped back on the scooter and continued down our path. Her large, crested helmet flying in the breeze. She would look back and we'd share a glance for a second.

Again, we brought our homicidal crowd to the narrow, but long, street. We flew by the Centauro and it blocked the exit. Once the horde was large enough, it fired again. The walls and street were literally running with black, oozing blood.

"One more time!" Cecilia said. I couldn't resist her.

After keeping the Gladius and dumping the other Roman armor in the AAV, we went back out. Cecilia kept the Centurion helmet on.

As we drove through we came to the Trevi fountain and found that it was filled with zombies. They must have fallen in and hadn't bothered to climb out.

"Can we turn around?" She asked.

I looked back and saw the crowd we had brought with us.

"Not a good idea."

We hastily went to one of the side streets, but saw it was also filled with zombies.

"I think we in trouble," she said softly.

"Agreed," I said.

EIGHT

Uprising Zach Day 16
Rome, Italy H.A.R.T.

There were a whole mess of zombies in front of us, behind us and to our left. Sister Cecilia reached back and grabbed a hold of my hand. Normally I wouldn't mind, but right now I had

more things on my mind; a whole lot of shuffling moaning things.

"There's an alley to the right! Move!"

She turned the scooter and narrowly missed two zombies as she drove into the small alley. The handle bars were almost scrapping the brick walls to our sides. A few zombies blocked the exit so I took aim and fired. They went down and we neared the exit.

As we drove out, we came face to face with another small crowd, maybe ten of them. Two of them reached out and grabbed the scooter and we toppled over onto the street. I covered my head with my arms and rolled to a stop. My elbows and knees screamed in pain, but I couldn't worry about that right now. I was out in the open and surrounded by zeds.

While still on the ground I began shooting the zombies. Cecilia scrambled to her knees and followed my example.

Those few zeds were dropped easily, but our gunfire was attracting unwanted attention. More zombies were swarming into the street filling the small piazza we found ourselves in.

I quickly reached into one of my pouches and pulled out my silencer. I screwed in on and took aim.

"You got one for me?" Cecilia asked.

"Sorry."

"We need to run. Can't fight all of them," she said in a whisper.

"Where to?"

"Inside."

She pointed to a church on the far side of the tiny piazza. It was one of the small, triangular piazzas scattered about that wasn't found on any tourist maps. There were zeds in the way, but I took a deep breath and began popping them one by one. Once a small path was cleared I grabbed her hand and we sprinted to the church door.

It opened. We quickly went in and slammed the door. Inside was dark, but we had our NVG's on. There wasn't a person in sight, living or dead.

"Hold the door. I'll get a pew."

I dragged a wooden pew over and propped it against the door. Just to be sure I pulled over two more.

The zombies were pounding away at the door, but it was holding.

"Please tell me there's a back door or something."

"Of course. This is no dead end. Follow."

She led me back to a small side door that led to a bunch of offices and class rooms. I got on the radio.

"Hey, Marco, Stig, you guys read me?"

"Yeah, boss," Stig said.

"Um, we ran into some difficulty. We're stuck in a church right now."

"Like, on foot or something?"

"Yeah, exactly like that. Where's a good pick up spot?"

"Let me look at map." I waited a minute. "Yeah, south, between the forum and the Coliseum."

"That's a bit of a walk. Believe me, I've done it before."

"Hey, it's best we can do, boss."

"Alright, we'll be there."

"Tell us when you get close and we come right there."

"Will do."

We found the back entrance and we peeked out. There were shamblers in the street: three of them.

"I take them out, nice and quiet. Then we head south."

She nodded and checked her M4.

We crept out and I fired one shot per head.

"Okay, it's clear."

We walked out into the street and realized that I had no flippin' idea which direction was south.

"Which way?" I asked.

"I don't know. I only been to Rome once."

"We'll pick a direction. Believe me, we won't have far to go before we run into something famous."

We made our way as silently as we could through the dark, narrow streets of the old quarter. I know south of here was that huge monument to some famous Italian guy during the Unification, but couldn't see it to get my bearings.

No matter where we went, there were zombies. I didn't have enough bullets to possibly kill all of them so we had to sneak the best we could.

It reminded me a bit like the old Spanish horror movie "Tombs of the Blind Dead" where blinded zombie Templars could only find you if they could hear you. When one did notice us, I dropped them quietly.

If we did make too much sound, I didn't want to be there to see what happened. There were a freaking million of them. That was probably literal.

It seemed like forever, but we eventually came to a large open piazza. It took me a moment to recognize it.

"Bernnini's four fountains," I said.

The giant fountain in the middle of the stretched out oval shaped piazza had statues representing the four major rivers of the world. The only one I recognized was the Nile because its head was covered with a veil. That was to show they didn't know the source of the river. One of them was the Danube and another was the Amazon, I think. Hell if I knew what the fourth one was.

More importantly, I knew exactly which way was south from here.

"That way," I said.

"You sure?"

"I'm sure. I used to live here."

"You're not Italian or Catholic, but you know Rome better than me!" She had to take a hand off her M4 so she could gesture wildly like I've seen so many Italians do. I used to think that it was just a made up stereo-type, but when I came to Rome I saw it with my own eyes. It's totally true. They speak very loud and with a lot of gesticulation. Even now Cecilia's whispers were almost like other people's talking and she had to open her mouth really wide when she talked. Her skinny arm flailed around wildly and I loved it.

I wondered if she could also cook like an Italian.

"Well, if you're coming with me, you can become an American. You'll find our immigration laws a bit more lax than they used to be. I know people."

"We talk about that later."

"Speaking of that, did they ever say where the Pope was?"

"He is safe. Some island I think."

"I guess it pays to have your own helicopter."

We continued to slowly make our way down the streets, but we had to check every way at the intersections. It was slow going.

Then a zombie came out of a door we had passed and began moaning. She quickly turned and shot him, but I began to hear more moaning.

"We better hurry!" I said.

We ran down to the intersection of the street and saw zombies coming toward us from all four directions.

"Which way?" She asked, grabbing my arm.

"That way," I pointed south with my FS and fired at the two zombies in the ally.

As we entered the ally, four zombies stumbled out of a doorway that used to be a restaurant. I fired and suddenly my gun clicked dry. I didn't have time for a reload and my Beretta would be too loud.

So I pulled out the souvenir Gladius and thrust it into the eye socket of the nearest zombie. It stumbled back into the others buying me enough time to do a quick reload and shoot the others.

As we passed by the non-moving corpses I retrieved my Gladius and re-sheathed it.

"Hey! You! Up here!" I heard a whispered shout. I looked around for the source. Up in the window of an old hotel I saw three figures waving wildly at me.

"Cecilia, look." I pointed up.

"They might need help," she said.

I had to restrain myself from commenting on the obviousness of her statement.

I nodded and we found the door to the hotel. We went in and went up to the floor we had seen them. Like many old buildings here, the stair case spiraled around an ancient elevator that wasn't safe during the best of times. We took the stairs.

The fourth floor door was blocked, but I heard voices on the other side and the sound of moving objects.

When the door finally opened, I saw the frightened figures of four Japanese girls.

"Any of you speak English?" I asked.

"O Italiano?" Cecilia asked.

"I speak a little," one of the girls said. She had pigtails and a brightly colored shirt. When Rome was alive I could always tell where the Japanese tourists were in a crowd. The Romans all wore black (one of the reasons I love Italians) and the Japanese all wore bright colors like a nation of Rainbow Brights. They looked maybe about fourteen or so, but I was always bad at guessing ages. One of them looked maybe about nine though.

"How many here?" I asked.

"Just us four. You first no dead persons we see in two week," the girl said.

"We're here to help. We're here killing zombies and looking for survivors. You should come with us. There are trucks waiting for us."

"Okay. We go."

They went and got their backpacks shaped like pandas and anime characters and then they all fell in line.

"We ready now," the spokes-girl said.

"Okay, follow me," I said.

"I guard the rear," Cecilia said.

"Okay, but be careful."

"I will," she said with a smile. She lowered her NVG's back down. Then we were back in the dark streets of Rome.

Uprising: Day 17 Rome, Italy H.A.R.T.

I checked my watch. It was now after midnight. I had the Japanese students behind me with Cecilia taking up the rear. We slowly and very quietly moved through the narrow streets of Rome.

I loved seeing the large square sewer grates marked with S.P.Q.R.

"Senatus Popolusque Romanus," Cecilia said when she saw me looking at it.

"Senate and People of Rome," I answered back.

She smiled that shy, but unapologetic smile. I wished we weren't wearing the NVG's because I liked looking at her. She had a very pretty and very typically Roman face. She had small and subtle mannerisms that were also very cute and very uniquely her.

Then I saw a light out of the corner of my eye. I looked over and saw a flash light turning on and off in the high up window of one of the many buildings that were all unique but somehow blended together. It could be a business hotel, or house for all I knew.

"Sister, look," I said, pointing to the light.

She looked over and lifted her NVG's up and squinted.

I tried something. I waved and the light waved back and forth.

"They're alive, whoever they are," I said.

"We have to help them."

"Of course, sister."

I loved her talent for stating the obvious.

I moved up with my silenced FS and peeked around the corner. There were three zeds shuffling around aimlessly. One of them was a caribinari and his pistol was still in his holster.

In a quick, one, two, three, I put the zeds down and moved up to take the pistol and magazines. I waved for the others to come up.

Then the door to the building opened and a man waved us over. He was a middle aged man and smartly dressed in a tie-less suit that still looked clean.

We all ran over and inside. The man and a woman, probably his wife, quickly closed the door and bolted it shut.

The man said something in Italian, but he was smiling. Cecilia busted out with her rapid fire Italian and the two were soon engaged in a conversation. After a while Cecilia turned back to me.

"They been here the whole time and had run out of food. They have about twenty survivors up the stairs."

"Tell them that they have to come with us because our vehicles won't be able to come here."

"I already did. They agreed."

"Excellent."

A few minutes later and the twenty other survivors were coming down and preparing to leave. They were all types. Some looked like film students, others looked like manual laborers. At least three of them were attractive young ladies so I felt pretty good about that.

"Ask if any have military experience," I said.

Cecilia asked with a flourish of her hands. She made gestures an art form. As she went around and talked to the people I took the opportunity to admire her. Wrong, I know, but I didn't care.

One of the men, a younger man with glasses and a beard had been in the boarder guards so I gave him the carabiniri's pistol. I had Cecilia explain that he shouldn't fire unless it was absolutely necessary.

When we were ready we went back out.

In only a few turns we found ourselves at the large stairs that led up to the piazza that had the city's old government buildings. They were museums now. The piazza was designed by Michelangelo and had an equestrian statue of Marcus Aurelius. In the silence of the dead city, he seemed remarkably unmoved. This statue had seen very bad times for Rome: plague, war and revolution.

"Emperor Marcus Aurelius," Cecilia whispered in my ear as we came up the stairs.

"The only reason the statue wasn't melted down was because they thought it was a statue of Constantine the Great, first Christian…well, sort of, emperor of Rome."

"Aurelius was a pagan and persecuted Christians," Cecilia giggled.

An Italian girl that dorked out about history as much as I did. I was weak in the knees.

Down a side alley there was a staircase that led down and over looked the Forum.

"Cecilia, let's go through the Forum. Might be less zombies down there," I said.

"Sounds good. I always wanted to see the Forum."

"Just past the Forum is the Coliseum. We'll meet up with the others there.

Normally one had to go all the way to the south side and buy a ticket that led to the Forum and Palatine hill where all the 'who's who' of Rome used to live. Now we just hopped the fence.

One of the great triumphal arches was the first thing we passed through. I don't know how triumphant our little group was, but I hoped for survival at least. I took it as a good omen.

Then I saw something in what would have been the 'main street' of Ancient Rome. Between what used to be two large basilicas, was a large man fighting zombies with a large sword. We hurried down the small hill toward the man.

It was Stig. He had his ear phones in and was dancing around in a crazy techno rave kind of deal. When a zombie got close he'd take a pause from his dancing and chop the zombie cleanly in half.

"Hey, Stig!" I called out.

He looked over and waved, but kept dancing.

"Where's the trucks?" I asked.

"That way. I'm just having little fun here, boss."

"Come on Stig, we got to get these people to safety."

"Okay."

He danced as he led us back to the vehicles.

"Whoa, boss, you picked up a few people," Marco said as we came up to the parked vehicles.

"Survivors. I'm willing to bet there are a whole lot more. Those small staircases are easy to barricade and zombies don't like to go up hill."

"I'm glad you made it. It seems pretty hairy in there," Marco said.

"Get everyone loaded up into the AAV."

Once the people were safe we drove back to the Vatican were people were starting to barricade St. Peters Square. To save space in the troop hold, Cecilia rode up in the turret with me. She didn't seem to mind at all being close to me. She gave a holler of victory and shouted something in Italian.

The head of the Swiss Guard approached us as our AAV came to a stop in front of the barricades.

"How did it go?" He asked.

I lowered the back ramp where the survivors were.

"See for yourself. We also managed to wipe out a lot of zeds, but I don't think we put a dent in their population. You folks have a lot of work ahead of you."

"You're not staying?"

"Sorry, I can't. I have to get back to the States. Maybe I'll be back."

"You'll be very welcome. You will be mentioned in the stories and history of the Swiss Guard."

"I'm honored," I said.

"And of course, the fighting nun, Sister Cecilia," the Swiss Guard said.

"Grazie," Cecilia said.

We relaxed and they brought some food out for us, chocolate filled croissants they had scavenged from a nearby grocery store. They were the individually wrapped ones so they were still fresh.

"Sir? You go to America, yes?" The oldest Japanese girl asked.

"That's right."

"Can we come with you? Much safer there than Japan."

"You are more than welcome. I think I know a few American boys your age that have similar interests."

George's sons would have to thank me later.

They giggled with their hands up to their mouths and went back inside the AAV.

By the time we dumped the survivors off and rolled out, the sun was coming up. We stopped by the Castel Sant' Angelo and greeted the survivors there. While Marco and Cecilia occupied them with the story of last night, Stig and I snuck up to the castle museum where they had an armory. I grabbed an old Italian rifle that looked like a single shot Mosin Nagant, a few swords and two halberds. If my arms weren't full I'd have grabbed the full plate armor.

Screw it. I went back and grabbed the armor as well.

Next we drove to the Villa Borghese where they had hundreds of priceless works of art. They even had a whole room full of Caravaggios which were priceless. Caravaggio had a way with light and shadow that no one else except Rembrandt could touch.

I stood there in the large, marble room looking at the masterpieces that were some of the finest accomplishments of the human race.

I knew what I had come here to do, but it felt wrong to take them. Italy wasn't dead. There were still survivors fighting for their homes. I couldn't take away their cultures accomplishments.

So, instead I wandered the historic villa and marveled at the Bernini statues and lifelike quality he had managed to give the marble. The marble leaves on Daphne's hands were carved so delicately thin that one could see light through them.

I heard Cecilia come up behind me, but I didn't turn away from Apollo and Daphne. We stood there for a long time. I wanted to soak in the image of these masterpieces while I could. I would never see them again. Few people living would.

"Why do you want to go to America so bad?" I asked.

"I always wanted to go. Been dream of mine."

I could understand that. Italy had been my dream.

We walked back out without taking a single work of art.

We left Rome going north towards Assisi. There we'd pick up a truck of survivors and head to Florence and the greatest collection of art I had ever seen. The whole trip I wondered what I was doing. I needed to rescue art, but the Romans would take back their city so I had left their art in place as their reward.

Again, Cecilia rode up in the turret with me. I couldn't decide if she really liked the open air, the scenery or me. Probably the second one because that was why I rode in the turret. I loved the Italian countryside.

"I'm going to miss Italy," she said.

"We'll be back, I promise."

"You promise?" She asked and looked me right in the eyes. Her gorgeous brown eyes burrowed into mine. I could tell that she had a shining light of intellect behind those brown orbs.

"I do. I can't go my life knowing I won't be back. Besides, I love the people of Rome, Umbria and Venice."

"I love Venice. Most beautiful city in the world."

"Agreed. After Florence, me and you are taking a vacation to Venice. We have to pass by there anyway."

She smiled that huge, honest smile of hers and she put her hand in mine.

NINE

Uprising Zach Day 17
Rome, Italy H.A.R.T.

We got to Florence about noon.

I looked through the binoculars at the city in front of us. From the hill I could see the pillars of smoke rising from several spots and the enormous dome of the Duomo like a scale miniature of a city with an out of scale cathedral placed in the middle.

"What do you think?" I asked.

"I think it's lost some of its charm," Marco said.

"Is different than I remember," Cecilia said.

Florence was dead. Unlike Rome and Umbria, there weren't any large pockets of survivors. Apparently some of the Italian Army had used Florence as some kind of last stand and the place was torn apart. Fires were raging all over and burnt out cars littered the streets.

We drove through the narrow streets calling out for survivors, but no one answered us. The whole place was disturbingly silent. It could be a while before any Italian comes here. This time it wasn't stealing art, it was rescuing it.

I knew exactly where to go. There were two amazing museums in Florence, the first one we went to was the Ufuzi. While Marco and Stig stood guard on the outside, the rest of us went and grabbed what we could. We got Bottecelli's "Primavera" and "Birth of Venus." Both very large paintings. The gallery was filled with so many paintings that I loved, but weren't famous so most people didn't know about them. One was called "Fortitude" and showed a woman in armor. I digged chicks in armor.

Then we went to the other museum by the Duomo, the Academia. There was an old shield painted with Medusa's head that I wanted to mount on the front of the AAV, but we had a lot of zombies to get through first. Aside from a few more paintings, there was a statue I had to get. It was by Donatello and was of Mary Magdalene.

Unlike most statues from the Renaissance, this one wasn't marble or bronze. It was wood. Simply, and almost crudely carved wood. The statue of Mary Magdalene was rough and showed an aged and bone thin Mary covered by her own long hair. She was physically wretched but her hands were clasped together in prayer and her eyes gazed upward. It showed that physical beauty was temporary and only the spiritual mattered.

"I love this statue," Cecilia said.

"Most people will think its ugly," I said.

"And what do you think?"

"I think its one of the most amazing works of art ever. I don't mean that as an exaggeration. He defied all norms of the time and created a work that was outwardly ugly, but showed an inner spirit and beauty that goes beyond worldly concerns."

"Can we keep it?" She asked.

"If you want it, it's yours."

We hauled it to the AAV. Once we were full, we left Florence, plowing through the hordes of zombies that infested it.

Our convoy stopped by Assisi and picked up the truckload of survivors and continued on our way.

Next, was Venice.

Outside of Florence was smooth sailing. We had open highways with no traffic and no ghouls.

"Stop!" I shouted down.

"What is it?" Marco asked.

"I see something."

Marco radioed for the Centauros to stop.

"Cecilia, come with me," I said.

We climbed down from the AAV and Cecilia instantly got her gun up at the ready. She was learning quickly.

Once we got stateside I'd have to give her something I liked more, maybe my ACR I had in my closet back in Vernal. She would look good with my PSL. I'd have to train her up on it a bit first.

"What did you see? Movement?" She asked in a whisper.

"No, better."

Then we came upon it. In front of us was a bright red Ferrari. The door was open and the keys were inside. Blood stains on the road gave a fair clue what had happened to the former owner.

"Is that a…" She began to ask.

"It is indeed, Sister."

"Are we going to…"

"Indeed we are, Sister."

I climbed into the driver's seat and she took shotgun. She eased the door closed and we both sat there soaking it in.

"I've never been in a car like this," she said almost reverently.

"Me neither."

As I started the car I heard the engine purr and roar at the same time like I've never heard a machine sound before.

"Whoa," she said.

We buckled up and we were on our way again. This time, I was driving in comfort, style and speed. We could only go as fast as the slow convoy, but it sure felt nice.

Me and the nun cruised down the road and got to the shore by Venice just before nightfall. We parked all the vehicles on the beach except the AAV which we then took over the lagoon to Venice.

The mayor, which people were calling "Doge" greeted us and I presented him with more gifts of M4's and ammo. I also told him that we were leaving one of the Centauros for them; just in case. I gave him all the news of Assisi and Rome and the radio frequency to get in touch with them.

As thanks they gave us a great feast of fish and rooms in the fanciest hotel that over looked the Grand Canal.

They even gave us a gondola ride over to the hotel. Me and Cecilia shared a gondola. This was something I had always wanted, a gondola ride in Venice with a pretty girl.

"I love this city," she sighed.

"Me too," I said as I let the waves of the canal rock me into relaxation.

"No other place like it. I came here two years ago to visit one of the convents. I've always wanted to come back."

The next day I went around with Cecilia to all the famous tourist spots. We visited St. Mark's the Rialto Bridge and just walked around the city. We managed to get lost, which was very easy to do there, and we found ourselves in a narrow, crowded part where the tourists usually didn't go. Those were the kinds of hidden corners that I loved.

As we walked she took my hand again. I looked over and saw that she was blushing and smiling. I gave her hand a squeeze to show that I didn't mind at all.

Someone lent us a boat and we went over to the semi abandoned island of Torcello. It had a few desolate houses, a silted up green canal, two of the oldest churches in the Lagoon and a tall bell tower. We went up into the bell tower and marveled at the view. We could see Burano, Murano and even distant Venice. This was as good a place to hole up for the Apocalypse as any. Despite the world ending, the Venetian lagoon was full of life. The glass blowers would continue their trade only instead of art they'd be making glasses, telescopes and microscopes.

"Thank you for finding me," she said as we stood in the bell tower with the cool breeze coming in from the sea.

"That's what I'm here for."

"Before you arrived, I had been praying for someone to come and rescue me. I didn't know what to do. I had prayed for a miracle. Then you came."

I honestly didn't know what to say. Nothing came to mind, so I did what I felt like doing. I wrapped my arms around her and gave her a large, but not too tight hug. She returned the embrace and we stood there for a long time.

We made it back to Venice before dark and had another fish dinner. Then we went up to our hotel rooms.

I couldn't sleep. I hated sleeping in Venice because I didn't want to miss a second of experience. So I stood on my balcony over looking the dark, quiet Grand Canal. It was quiet, but not silent. I could hear the gentle lapping of the waves.

There was a knock on my door.

"Yes?" I called out.

"It's me, Sister Cecilia. Can I come in?"

"Of course."

She came in and closed the door behind her. Then she joined me out on the balcony. We both leaned on the rails and soaked in the ancient essence of Venice.

"There's something romantic about this city," she said in a near whisper.

"The history, the layers and layers of culture."

"It's more than that though."

"Much more."

"It would be a shame to be here and not be with the one you loved."

I put my arm around her and drew her in closer.

"I know that I'm not supposed to be here with you. But things are different now. You know about the history of the nuns in Venice, no?"

"I've heard a few things."

The convents in Venice were once said to have done more "business" than the brothels. I wasn't about to say that.

She chuckled lightly.

"Please, kiss me," she said without looking at me.

I used my free hand to turn her face toward me. Her eyes were closed and I kissed her lightly on the mouth. Her lips were far softer than I imagined they could be. She was warm and full of life and intellect. I wanted her and I knew that she unreservedly wanted me.

We kissed and caressed on the balcony over looking the Grand Canal.

Uprising Zach Day 19
Rome, Italy H.A.R.T.

When I met Cecilia in the morning for breakfast, she had an embarrassed and very happy grin on her face.

"Good morning," she said, barely able to contain her laughter.

"You're in a good mood," I said.

"Why would I not be?"

"It was amazing," I said.

"A little, yeah. A first for both of us?"

"True, I don't exactly go around kissing nuns on a daily basis."

We sat at a table of the only outdoor restaurant I knew of that sat on the Grand Canal of Venice. I was seriously considering staying there. There were two things that Venice didn't have though, my family and Mountain Dew. Those were two things I couldn't live without.

"What's it like in your home?" Cecilia asked.

"Mountains, rolling, red desert, farms and open sky like you wouldn't believe."

"I want to see the open space of nothing America has. I want to see the wild west."

"I'll even get you a six shooter to go on your hip."

Her face lit up. You will do that?" She leaned over and gave me a peck on the cheek. Then she quickly looked around to see if anyone had seen that. No one else was around.

"Before we leave Venice, there's something I want to get first," I said.

"What's that?"

"A Venetian flag and a carnival mask."

"Let's go shopping then."

After my gift of M4's and an armored car I pretty much had a carte' blanche. I picked up one of the masks that I've always wanted, one with a swooping head crest that had a painting in it. The serene white face of the mask was artificially aged with fine cracks, artistically placed blemishes. I also got two styles of Venetian flags, a small one and a large one.

"Can we stop there?" She pointed to a closed up shop that had high fashion clothes that would normally cost more than I made in a month.

"Of course."

I shot the lock with my Beretta and opened the gate. The fact wasn't lost on me that I was using an Italian gun made by a company that sold its first blunderbusses barrels to the Venetian Arsenal.

That made me wonder about what happened to the Beretta and Benelli factories. I knew they were close to Milan, but I didn't know where exactly. I also wondered if anyone was there. I had helped get Rome, Venice and a few towns communicating, but I also wondered if perhaps my job wasn't done.

No, right now my job was to get me, Cecilia and the art back to Vernal. No one knew if I was alive or dead.

"Look at these!" Cecilia said. She was sitting in a chair and wearing a new pair of black leather, calf length boots. They were a far cry from her ugly but "sensible" shoes.

"I think you should have them."

"This is very selfish of us. We should really be thinking of what we need."

"Well, you need those boots. Besides, we have everything we need in Utah."

"Are you sure?"

"I've already spoken to the Doge and if we can get planes here, we can open trade with them. They make the best glass around. We could use that. They can use something besides fish. If that's what you want, let's check out and get out of here. We have to hit the road."

After picking up souvenirs for my brothers and nephews, we went up to our hotel room. I put on all my gear and slung my FS across my chest. She came out with her black tactical vest that matched perfectly with her black habit, dress and boots.

She straightened her rectangular glasses and asked; "How do I look?"

"You look like a certifiable badass."

"I look tough?"

"Very much so."

I drew her in close and kissed her deeply. We kissed for longer than we should before going out to meet the others by the AAV. The AAV was parked along the docks by St. Mark's Square. The civilians we had gathered from Rome and Assisi were there as well.

I shook hands with the Doge and we departed. Our AAV slowly swam down the Grand Canal while the boaters and gondoliers waved at us. Cecilia was up in the turret with me and this time I had my hand around her waist.

On the far shore we had a welcoming party for us. A crowd of zeds had gathered around the Centauros we had left. We couldn't use the .50 or the MK-19 because we had to save the ammo for getting through Germany and we didn't want to damage the Centauros.

As we came ashore the zombies turned to us and began that awful moaning of theirs. There were at least a hundred of them. I didn't exactly count them or anything but there were a heck of a lot of them.

"Ready?" I asked.

"Ready," she said.

We opened fire and our wall of well aimed bullets tore into the horde.

Then, to my surprise, the zombies, as one whole, stopped moaning, turned around and ran off into the marshes and suburbs.

We looked at each other at the same time.

"What was that about?" I asked.

"Never seen that before."

I looked around for anything that might have caused them to run, but I didn't see anything.

"Also, what were the doing around the Centauros? There's no food."

"I don't like this."

We jumped down, keeping our rifles to the shoulder and scanning the trees for movement. Stig and the crew of the Centauro jumped out after us and ran over to the armored car.

Then a massive horde of zombies jumped out from the trees. This didn't make sense! I didn't see any shuffling or hear any moaning. It was as if they were lying in wait for us.

"What the hell is this?" I asked out loud as I opened fire and began to fall back to the AAV.

As the crowd of undead cannibals charged toward us, I saw that one of them stayed behind. It was a man. And though he stayed in the shadows of the trees, I knew he was looking at me. If I had time I would have fired at him, but as I was, I was a little too occupied.

As the charging horde got closer, my fighting retreat turned into a full out run. I sprinted toward the AAV and Cecilia followed behind me. I jumped up on to the AAV and clumsily climbed up. Once at the top I reached down for Cecilia.

The zombies were on top of us and they began trying to grab Cecilia's foot. I aimed one handed with my FS and began firing at whatever zed was dumb enough to try to hurt Cecilia. I blew a couple of their brains out, firing down right into the tops of their heads.

Cecilia managed to get up on top of the AAV and I quickly looked up to find that man who had been standing still. I didn't see him. Good for him because I would have put a bullet in his brain even if he hadn't been a zombie.

Then the attack suddenly dispersed. The zeds turned and ran away. I fired at them and brought down two of them before they disappeared as well.

Cecilia was breathing hard and I was looking for zombie "survivors."

"What the hell was that?" She asked.

"I have no idea, but I have to tell my brother. He'd know what to do."

TEN

Uprising, Day 19, Zach Northern Italy.

We drove at full speed until we got to the base of the Alps. That was one place I wouldn't want to run out of gas. Much too cold, too remote and surrounded by zombies. We topped off the tanks before hitting the base of the mountains. Like last time there were thousands of zombies around, but they were more spread out now. We plowed through them without much problem.

"It's sad the Ferrari couldn't come," Cecilia said.

"I thought nuns were supposed to turn away from such worldly desires."

"I think the car is the least of my sins," she said.

"We just kissed."

"Yes, but that is big 'no no' for me."

Last time it was dark when we passed through the Alps. This time I stayed in the turret to take the sights in. I've seen the Rockies before and this was just as breathtaking. It was a sight I could never get accustomed to.

"Goodbye Italy!" Cecilia waved.

"I hope it won't be for good," I said. "There's a fountain in Rome where if you drop a coin in it, you're destined to return. I should have dropped a coin."

"Pagan superstitions," she said, laughing and straightening her glasses.

"Speaking of fountains, I wish we could have grabbed some Bernninis."

"Too big. Too delicate. Marble statue is hard to move. But yes, I wish we grabbed one."

"Apollo and Daphne," I said.

"Ecstasy of St. Teressa," she said.

That statue got my imagination going places it definitely didn't need to go.

I hated leaving Italy. It felt like I was abandoning someone I loved. I wanted to stay and take the country back from the dead, but I had my own home and my own family.

We crawled back inside with all the art and the Japanese and American survivors. The rest were in the backs of two Italian Army trucks.

"How long till we get there?" The oldest Japanese girl, Sakura, asked.

"We'll be there tonight. Take off tomorrow and be in Utah by that night. Or something like that."

"You promise that it safe?" The youngest girl, Hitomi, asked.

"Yes, I promise. The whole area is locked down tight. Also, we have a large percentage of people with guns."

"I want gun!" Sakura said, raising her hand like it was school.

"Eventually you might get one," I said.

"I got a gun," Cecilia said.

"You'll get more. I'll train you up on this baby," I said, patting my PSL.

"Ooooh. I like bigger," she said.

I wondered if she had any idea if she realized the implications of what she said.

We drove through the ruins of Austria and Germany. Things only got worse the further north we got. It was after sunset by the time we got near the Air base. When I looked out with my NVG's, I saw everywhere, the shambling corpses that filled the towns and streets.

Ramstein was easy to spot because it had the only lights around except the dull, soft orange glow from distant fires. As we got close I saw that there was still a field crawling with the dead. The occasional, casual gunfire coming from the fence told me that everything was still alright.

I began to unleash with my MK-19 and again I laid waste to the horde of zombies. As many as I killed there were always more waiting to take its place.

"I want to try," Cecilia said. She squeezed up into the turret and I watched as she rocked with the automatic grenade launcher. When it finally ran out of ammo, I switched it over to the .50 cal and she began to blast away with that.

The Centauro fired the last of its canister shots as a parting gift. With the path clear we rode into the Air base and the gates closed behind us. The place looked markedly emptier since the last time I left it.

A few Marines approached us with hands on their weapons. I opened the top hatch and waved.

"Hey, I'm a friendly. I got a bunch of refugees from Italy. Is Outbreak around?"

They led me to where the air crews were. I found Outbreak lying on a cot listening to head phones and reading what was probably the last issue of Stars and Stripes. I recognized his 'combat stache' from across the hanger.

He almost dropped the newspaper when he saw me approach.

"You must be kidding. That isn't Zach walking up on me. Last time I checked he was heading towards suicide in Italy," Outbreak said.

"Unfortunately, it is me. Mission accomplished and then some."

Outbreak lowered his aviator glasses and looked at Sister Cecilia.

"Clearly," he said.

"When's our flight out of here?"

"Tomorrow morning. We're taking the last two C-17's. They're mostly empty, but we felt bad about leaving them here."

"You'll be glad to get out of here and back to your C-130. Oh, and back to America. In that order?"

"I ain't telling. So tell me, what did you get?"

I took him to the AAV and opened up the back. It was full of paintings wrapped in blankets. Antique weapons and a shield were there as well. The wooden statue of Mary Magdalene was standing at the opening.

"Isn't that the ugliest thing I've ever seen," he muttered.

"I think it's beautiful!" Cecilia said, waving her hand wildly.

"Alright, alright. I didn't mean any offense by it."

The Japanese girls introduced themselves with bows and giggles and I showed him the Centauro and the two trucks of American refugees.

We found a few cots off to the side and me and Cecilia grabbed two army sleeping bags from a pile of equipment that was being left behind.

We peeled off our vests and holsters and tried to get comfortable. In spite of being achingly tired, my eyes wouldn't close.

Around midnight someone shut off the lights to the groans of the airmen that were playing cards.

"We made it this far," Cecilia whispered in the dark.

"We'll make it the whole way," I said.

"I know."

A few seconds later I heard her quietly sleeping. I didn't fall asleep till long after that.

As per military custom we were all awakened much earlier than necessary and waited around chowing down on MRE's.

"How do you eat such food?" Cecilia asked.

"Aren't nuns supposed be eating bread and water?"

"Please. I am Italian. When we get to America I will make you the best cannoli you've ever had."

I almost chocked on my "jambalaya" MRE. My prayers had been answered.

"You know how to make cannoli?"

"Of course. My mother's recipe. I'm an excellent cook."

"If you make me cannoli or gnocchi, I'll worship the ground you walk on."

"Deal."

The Marines set up claymores to cover their retreat. They'd be the last ones boarding the second C-17. We loaded up both the Centauros and the AAV. Everything else useful had been flown out by then.

"Hey, Outbreak, let me know when we reach the States, will you?"

"Sure, I'll bring you up to the cockpit and give you little pilot's wings. You ever watch movies about Gladiators?"

I had to laugh at the cheesy reference to the movie "Airplane." Cecilia was confused.

We took off just after dawn. I plugged in my laptop to the outlet behind my seat and I showed Cecilia photos of my family, when I was in Italy when it was alive and of Vernal, where we were heading.

I told her of mine and George's daring rescue/raid into Salt Lake and our eventual dropping of a MOAB onto Sandy Utah. People were going to have to hear about that. I took pictures and it was definitely going into my history book.

She fell asleep leaning on my shoulder. Everyone else was asleep as well. The Japanese girls all had their iPods charging while they slept and the rest of the refugees were probably still tired from the early wake up. Also, there just wasn't much to do on a long flight in a C-17.

An unknown time later Outbreak came and woke me up.

"We're passing over land now," he said.

Me and Cecilia went up to the cockpit and looked out. The daylight was growing dim, but we could see the land beneath us.

"We made it," I said.

"I told you so," she said.

"That's Virginia below us," Outbreak said.

That made me think of my twin brother. I wonder if he and his little convoy made it to Utah or not. The possibility of the biggest tragedy of my life still awaited me.

We watched until it grew dark and then the land beneath us was just a blanket of darkness. No lights, no anything.

We arrived at Hill Air Force Base, dropped a few things off and then took our C-17 straight to Vernal.

It was around midnight when we arrived. I was tired and Cecilia definitely looked tired.

We drove the Centauro and AAV the twenty minutes to Ogre Ranch. When I got there the whole place was completely changed. It now looked more militarized than Camp Williams. There were LAV's, MATV's and Apaches everywhere.

"This is your brother's house?" Cecilia asked.

"Umm…yes. It's a bit different than I remembered."

We were stopped by some soldiers, but they waved us on when they saw me.

"Sorry Musashi," one of them said.

They thought I was my twin. That meant he was here and alive. I could feel the tension leaving my back.

Everyone at Ogre Ranch was asleep and someone was sleeping in my bed. It was dark and I couldn't see who it was. So we took our sleeping bags and I brought everyone to the school.

I woke up Rebekah, Dan and Karen and hugged them with a giant bear hug. I introduced them to Cecilia and told them a little about my trip.

"Is she your girlfriend?" Rebekah asked.

"Yes I am," Cecilia answered.

That made me pause to say the least. I hadn't thought of her in those terms, but certainly wasn't going to argue.

We got comfortable in our sleeping bags and fell asleep. I didn't think I would due to the excitement of my reunion with my brothers and parents. But I slept soundly and very content that night.

Uprising, Day 21, Zach, Vernal UT.

Me and my brothers sat there in Uncle Musket's pub talking and laughing. I told them of my adventures in Italy and some of it probably wouldn't have believed it if Cecilia wasn't there to confirm it all.

My twin, Musashi was the first to find me and wake me in the morning. We played it off like it was no big deal, but we each knew how close we had come to loosing everything.

The sight of a pub in the middle of the field was rather odd to say the least. I had no idea that my brother 'Musket' had a supernatural ability to have beer and wenches wherever he went. It was THE gathering place so we gathered there.

"You found a bunch of Japanese girls that are about the same age as my boys?" George asked.

"You can thank me later. There's also a whole lot of refugees that were tourists in Italy when this whole thing broke out."

"What a minute. Can we get to the part where you have a nun girlfriend? Isn't that supposed to be impossible; like that's the whole point of them?" Josh asked.

"The world is different. I believe the Lord has different plans for me now," Cecilia said.

"You be a right honest Catholic then?" Musket asked from the bar where he was cleaning glasses.

Cecilia shrugged.

"I think so. I been doing a lot of questions lately," she said.

"You're a lousy nun," Josh said.

"What gave you that idea? Maybe because I'm your brother's girl friend?" Cecilia asked.

"Just stating the obvious I suppose," Josh said.

"So, you are all Mormon then?" Cecilia asked.

I heard a laughing snort coming from Musket.

"Is he not?" Cecilia asked.

"We honestly don't know what he is," George said.

"Oh, hey, I got something for you Zach," Josh said.

"What's that?"

"Hold on."

Josh left the pub in a hurry.

"I guess I brought back souvenirs. I got glass from Venice, masks and tons of priceless art. Hey, Musket, how would you like a Botticelli to go up in your pub?" I asked.

"A what's it?"

"Botticelli. Famous Italian painter."

"Is it a picture of a fair trollop?"

"Probably not."

"Then I have no use for it."

"I did get an old Italian musket from Rome."

"Aye! That'll always be welcome here in me pub."

"I'll bring it on over later."

When Josh came back he was carrying a real Russian SVD.

"I found it and thought that you'd appreciate it," Josh said.

My jaw fell open and I reached to take it, scarcely believing that I could touch it.

"Zach, what is that? I like it. It's pretty!" Cecilia said with eyes almost as wide as mine.

"It came with a few mags," He said.

"Josh, you've gone above and beyond the call of duty," I said.

I took them all out to the AAV and opened the back.

"Guys, listen. I have here some of the greatest art treasures in the world." When I pulled out the giant painting of Botticelli's 'Primavera' it was their turn to drop their jaws. "Please, be gentle with these and treat them with respect," I said.

"I'll have these moved to the museum in Vernal. We can move out some of those ugly quilts they have there," George said.

"Guys, this all together is worth more than Vernal. Or at least it used to. I suspect it will again one day. We need to protect these. This is our history, our culture and will be an inspiration to the people that come after us."

George assigned some of his best people to take the AAV to the museum and sent his wife to get her family to start arranging it all. They were the artistic ones here.

Josh and Ruth went out to walk their three basset hounds, Musket went back to his pub carrying his new antique musket. George went off to do whatever it is that post-apocalyptic governors do.

"So, what now?" Cecilia asked. She had the SVD slung over her shoulder.

"How would you like to go learn how to shoot that?"

She smiled.

I grabbed my AK, PSL, FS2000, ACR, Benelli Super Nova, a bunch of ammo and threw them all in the back of my Camaro.

"It's no Ferrari," I said.

"Nothing is," she said.

When we got to the "Ballistic Laboratory One" - a clearing up on top of a hill where me and Ogre go shooting a lot - I set up a target and began her training. It was ironic that the target I was using was one of George's old, cartoon 'zombie' targets. I went over the basics first, then how to load, clear jams and engage the target. I switched her over to the ACR because…well… I simply didn't like M4's. They work just fine; I just have an emotional resentment to them and no girl of mine was using an AR. Uncle Musket had his aversion modern firearms and I had my aversion to AR's. Carried one during my second deployment and found it very handy. Good gun and all, but reason doesn't always fit into my train of thought. I would make a lousy ancient Greek philosopher. Of course, I was also straight so that was two strikes against me.

I spent the morning running her through drills, practicing malfunctions, speed reloads, tactical reloads, quick and accurate target acquisition and weapon transitions.

She wore the black tac-vest with a black thigh holster for a Beretta. She was still wearing the habit, skirt and boots. We'd have to look into getting her a better wardrobe. Neither of us had bathed in a while.

At noon I got her practicing a little medium range shooting with the SVD she now treated as her own. I had no problem with that. As a twin the idea of personal property had always been a vague notion to begin with. The idea of being an individual was far stranger to me than being part of a whole.

So we were there with my PSL and her SVD, shooting at a paper zombie target.

I heard some dirt bikes approaching and turned to see two of George's sons, Echo and Bravo racing up to our position.

"On patrol?" I said.

"Nah, just having fun. We heard you were back," Echo said.

"Bring us anything back from Italy?" Bravo asked.

"As a matter of fact I did. In the Elementary you will find a group of Japanese girls your age. I need you to go there and start showing them around the place. Have Rebekah and Karen go with you. You all show them our strange culture and customs. I know it's a rough assignment, but I think you can do that."

I don't think they heard anything past "Japanese girls."

"Really?" Echo asked.

"Yes, really."

As they raced off one of them shouted, "We owe you Zach!"

We went back to target practice.

"It's so beautiful here. No trees, big sky, red rock cliffs. I love it," she said, taking in a deep breath.

"A little different, isn't it?"

"I think I was meant to be here. Destiny, you know?"

"Believe me, I've felt it too. I think we've done enough. How about a shower?"

"What? You got showers here?"

"Plumbing, electricity, the works. Heck, we can even play my X-Box 360 and watch movies."

"I need a shower. Now."

We quickly packed everything up and went back to Ogre Ranch. She rushed into the shower.

I went out and sat on the porch where Josh and his basset hound "Leonidas" were. The handsome basset hound was lying down next to him while Josh scratched behind his ear.

"You seduced a nun?" Josh asked.

"I didn't seduce her. She sort of seduced me."

"First George's bimbo squad and now this."

I told Josh exactly how we met and what she thought.

"So, you're some kind of chosen one?" He asked with a laugh.

"Not quite like that."

"You got an impressive haul."

"It was all I could carry. Believe me, I wanted a whole lot more."

"You probably wanted to stay in Italy."

"I did. But the food wasn't as good this time around. Neither was the hospitality."

"Couldn't be worse than freaking Alma Kansas. Cappello, Hardcore and Ullu will want to see you."

I laughed at the thought of a reunion with them. I went through two deployments with them. They were practically kin.

When Cecilia came out I went in and took my shower. I had forgotten how good they felt. After my shower I found Cecilia playing with all three goofy basset hounds in the front yard. The rows of armored vehicles and Apache helicopters were a strange sight. It now looked like a military base.

"She's sweet, in a naive, innocent kind of way," Josh said.

"She's an odd one, but she comes by it naturally. I've heard people talk about George nuking Salt Lake? Was that after the MOAB?"

"Nah, it was the MOAB. But he did Nuke Arizona."

"Wait…what?"

He told the story and I shook my head.

"I guess George is an optimist; trying to make lemonade out of lemons."

"That's one way to put it. More like trying to make lemons out of lemonade."

That evening Cecilia pushed everyone out of the kitchen and she began cooking. I was the only one permitted to be in her presence. I don't know what she was making but it smelled good. She was there all evening and we talked. She told me about how she liked it there and she felt good about coming here. I said that we'd watch a movie after dinner.

When dinner was ready my family gathered around two tables and we had simple pasta and bread. Simple, yes, but also delicious. It was strange to have such a domestic scene, like something out of a Norman Rockwell painting, but we had rifles stacked in the corner, cases of ammunition, and rolled up sleeping bags for people that slept on the floor.

After dinner I took Cecilia to my room where we watched 'Invader Zim' and talked most of the night. We talked about the make up of the Roman Republic's legions and how it differed from the legions during the Pax Romana and the late Empire. We talked about history that only nerds would find interesting. She was the only girl I've met that knew who Empress Theodora was.

Days like this I had to sit back and enjoy. No one was trying to kill me. I didn't have to kill anyone or anything. I wasn't worrying about the life of my brothers or other people I cared about. I was content and maybe even happy and I had to be thankful for that.

Of course, the making out with a beautiful woman part didn't hurt at all.

ELEVEN

Uprising, Day 22, Zach, Vernal UT.

I watched as the Governor of Alaska and her security detail got back into their helicopter and took off. She had come down to Alaska to talk to the Ogre that had nuked Salt Lake and was now the leader of the strongest military force in North America. The whole conversation had me thinking about defense. Utah and the surrounding states had a whole lot of artillery. We also had a whole lot of choke points and high ground. What we needed to do is train more of the men that were standing around doing nothing and get them on the big guns. Artillery couldn't win a battle alone, but you couldn't win a battle without it. Put enough of those big guns up on the high ground and we could stop whatever force that tried to come through.

Right now, the world was in a state of nature and we had to act accordingly. It was no longer about right, wrong, or who has authority, it was about who had the power. We needed more power.

Then I remembered the Tooele army depot. By most internet rumors it was a new "Area 51" type of place. There was a whole lot of security there for just a few bunkers. I think it was time to find out what resources we might have there.

"Cecilia, you want to take a shopping trip? We can get new clothes and I can use a new car. My Camaro is on its last leg."

"Shopping? Yes. I need new clothes. I'm no longer a nun and don't want to look like one."

"Well, maybe you can at certain times…"

We went to find Ogre. He was still in the pub talking to a few of the officers. I noticed how one of the girls from his hoochie squad was clinging awfully tight to him. That wasn't good at all. I'd have to have words with her.

"George. I want to take a detail to go over and check out the Tooele Depot."

"I assume there's a reason."

"We haven't heard from them and I want to know what they got. I'll take my car and the Centauro."

"Alright. Take it safe. If you find anything useful, let me know immediately. I'd like to know exactly what cards I have in my hand."

"Depot or shopping first?" I asked.

"Work, then pleasure," she said.

One thing I loved about the 3 hour drive from Vernal to Salt Lake was the scenery. Once we got into Salt Lake the scenery changed. Instead of mountains we were now looking out for zeds and possible choke points. The Centauro led the way and we followed close behind.

Kevin and Cappello were in the Centauro. Cappello was well versed in convoy action from our two deployments in Iraq and Kevin needed to get out and get more combat experience.

The path to Toole was all along the highways and such, so it was relatively smooth sailing. We had my MP3 player hooked into my car's stereo and we listened to "Lacuna Coil" most of the way. I had been massively relieved to find out that she liked hard rock. She had been a bit of a gothy rocker before her rich parents pushed her into a convent. She hadn't taken her last vows yet so she said that it meant she could still say 'no' to being a nun. It was fairly obvious that she had.

I told her the history of Utah, the pioneers, the 'war' against the United States and what the heck "Temple Square" was. She loved history lessons and despite not wanting to take vows, she loved talking religion. In Utah the two things were intertwined.

We drove past Saltair where I had seen Rob Zombie perform live. Best concert ever. I wondered if Rob Zombie had survived the zombies. I hope so. I'd like to see him perform again.

When we got to the sign at the turn off for the Toole Depot, I noticed a white SUV parked off in a field. I had seen the white SUV's pulling security here before. Normal army bases don't have unmarked SUV's with men in civilian clothes and P-90's pulling security. I had always known something was here and it was about time I found out.

"Cappello, you got the tank. Go check it out," I said over the walkie talkie.

"You know a Camaro isn't a good choice for a patrol vehicle, right?"

The Centauro pulled up next to the SUV and after a few moments, Cappello got out and looked around.

"Nothing but a chewed up body, some bottled water and a P-90," Cappello said.

"That all?"

"Oh, and a security card. No biggie, right?"

"Grab it all."

When we finally reached the collection of bunkers we saw the slots for the keycards. Me and Cecilia dismounted and we approached the door. She kept her ACR up at the ready and I had my AK and was scanning the area for movement.

I swiped the card and a green light came on. A few seconds later the door began to open up.

Inside was a garage for the SUV's and a small office off to the side. Another door led further in. Inside the office was a soldier who had blown his own brains out. Maybe he thought he was the last man left alive or something. The stench was unbearable and we hurried on.

I swiped the card again and the small door unlocked. I was about to open the door when the door was knocked open and about twenty zeds in military uniforms came pouring out. Some wore dress uniforms, some looked like civilian contractors and others were wearing ACU's.

Me and Cecilia quickly backed up, firing away. I was impressed. She kept her cool and kept her gun leveled at their heads. She burned through a magazine and did a quick reload like I had taught her. She fumbled a bit, but she was a quick learner.

My AK pounded away and within seconds all the zeds were dead.

"That's a lot of brass to be hanging around a few bunkers," I said. Most of the military personal were officers.

She was breathing hard and looked around in quick, jerky movements.

"Relax," I said.

"Right," she said with a hesitant nod.

We went through the door and turned on the lights.

"Holy, s…!" Cecilia said.

We were in a room full of yellow chemical suits. There was a computer that was on to a glowing green screen. It showed the layout of the bunker in a 3-D map. This was bunker Alpha 3 and had two large storage rooms full of all kinds of chemical weapons. There were enough chemical warheads here to destroy the eastern United States.

What the heck was in the other bunkers then?

We didn't spend much time there. I was far from an expert in such matters and knew it would be better if George sent people here who actually knew what they were doing.

So Cecilia and I packed up and followed the Centauro back into Salt Lake.

Cecilia was underwhelmed by the clothing selection at the mall.

"All these clothes are ugly."

"Sorry, Salt Lake isn't known for its high fashion."

The Camaro and Centauro were parked outside the mall and we only had to clear out a handful of zeds inside.

"Where do you think the zeds are off to?" I asked.

"Looking for food somewhere else?" She shrugged.

It made sense. They were off to greener pastures.

She settled on a black skirt, black T-shirt and black sock hat.

"You look hard core," I said.

"I am hard core."

Then my radio crackled to life.

"Um...Zach, we got a problem out here," Kevin said.

"Alright, I'll be right there."

We ran outside and saw that the streets were filling with shambling corpses. They weren't charging at us, just walking slowly and neat and orderly as a Roman legion would.

"What the heck is this?" I asked.

"The freak back in Italy. Maybe he like that?" Cecilia said. Her English got sloppy when she was scared or under a lot of stress.

"Maybe. Look for the controller. Take the boss down," I shouted.

I got out my camera and made sure to document all of this.

We quickly climbed up onto the Centauro. I wished I had the AAV with the Mk-19 right about then.

Cappello opened up with the Ma Deuce and began tearing the zeds into chunks, but that caused all the zeds to rush forward. Me and Cecilia, up on the turret were firing with our rifles, her ACR and my AK.

"I'm low on ammo!" Ceppello called out.

The horde kept coming. An unstoppable tide of undead shuffle-charged us and the sound of their moaning and feet filled the air.

The zeds were almost on top of us so we all climbed inside and slammed the hatch down.

"Start this thing up. Let's get out of here!" I said.

The Centauro's six wheels spun and we sped out of there, running over dozens of zeds.

"Should we come around and hit them with the cannon?" Kevin asked.

"No, I have a better idea. We're going to come back at night and find that controller," I said. "I'm not going to have some undead king of Salt Lake on my watch."

We drove to Saltair to rest because there wasn't any zed activity there. We waited, listened to our iPods and relaxed until nightfall. Then we put on our NVG's and rode back out.

Day 24 Zach Salt Lake City

Cecilia, Kevin and I made our way through the dead city. The world was a grainy green through our NVG's and there wasn't a sound to be heard. We'd see the occasional shambler roaming around, but their night vision wasn't nearly as good as ours. As long as we kept quiet they didn't know where we were. I was glad that it wasn't like the old cheesy Spanish movie "Tombs of the Blind Dead" where the dead Templar nights could hear a person's heart beat.

We were all dressed in biker leathers neck to toe but if we got swarmed all they would do was delay the inevitable. I wished we had fully enclosed helmets though.

I led them back to where we were attacked by the organized zeds led by a "red eye," as George called them. I kind of preferred the term "Zombie Lord", but I didn't think that term would stick.

"If you were an undead king of the city, where would you stay?" I whispered to the others.

"The nicest place I could," Kevin said. "There's a lot of nice houses right near downtown."

"Let's start searching the mansions then," I said.

We made our way towards the ritzy part of town where the rich once had their homes. The whole time we had to sneak. One alerted zombie and the whole city would be after us. I saw how many zeds a city could have while in Rome. I really didn't want to go through that again.

It was a warm summer night and I hated walking. Crossing the streets was the hardest part. If we couldn't sneak past I would have to put a zombie or two down and even that was risky because a silenced weapon still wasn't silent.

We found the mansion much easier than I had anticipated. It had candles or lanterns glowing orange in the inside and what looked like hundreds of zombies milling about outside. It was at the top of a hill surrounded by thick trees.

"I think we found our man," Cappello whispered.

"How do we do this?" Kevin asked.

"We go ninja."

"Bro, I don't care how quiet we are, they're going to see us. We can't sneak past a hundred zombies," Kevin said.

"You're right. We have to get rid of them."

"You have a plan," Cecilia said.

"I do."

We back tracked to ZCMI Mall and went to the electronics store. I got a boombox that took batteries and a CD of Disturbed. It was the loudest one they had.

Kevin volunteered to be the bait man. He gave us a half hour to get into position, then he placed the CD player two blocks away, pushed play, turned the volume up and ran like hell.

As the sweet sounds of Disturbed began wafting in through the streets, the horde of zombies began jogging towards the sound. Unfortunately, not all of them left.

Me, Cappello and Cecilia crouched down with me leading the way. We dashed across the street and into a row of bushes. There was a large lawn to cross before we got to the house and there were only a few bushes and trees to hide us there.

We watched to make sure no zed had seen us, then he peeked into the window. Inside was a room with a few bookshelves and a black, upright piano. No sign of movement. I tried the window, but it was locked from inside. We carefully made our way to the next window. It was a kitchen, but it was locked as well.

Next up was the back door. I looked back to check on Cecilia and she gave me an affirming nod. It was a glass double door/french window kinda thing. It let us see in and with the lanterns inside, they'd have a hard time seeing out.

Again, I peeked in and didn't see anything. I tried the door and it slid open. Making sure my Kalashnikov didn't bump anything as I entered we got inside and closed the door.

My feet landed on a soft rug and I quickly got out of the way for the others.

I could hear music playing upstairs; Blink 182 or some other useless, crappy music. Cappello stayed on this floor to secure our position. Cecilia was cutting the pie like I had taught her and we cleared the lower floor. There wasn't anything. She pointed upstairs and I nodded.

I hated stairs. Well, I hated stairs for many reasons, but stairs were the hardest thing to do while clearing rooms. I hadn't really gone over this with Cecilia so I hoped she was good with improvisation.

I was glad the crappy music was playing because it would mask what sounds we made.

My AK was at the ready as I went up the wooden stairs. Pictures of people from recently to the 1800's lined the staircase walls. It made me wonder if this red eye actually lived here or was just squatting. Chances are, the latter, but it had to have had family somewhere; a life before.

I wondered if they could be reasoned with, but I didn't have the luxury of finding out. Whoever it was, was in the habit of attacking living folks and I couldn't tolerate that.

We made it up the stairs without anything happening and found ourselves in a narrow hallway. More pictures lined the walls like you'd find in an old person's home. One door was open and the music was coming from there.

Cecilia and I stacked on the door, ready to burst in and I peeked around the corner. I saw a frail, thin looking man sitting at a desk, writing in a journal or something like that. There was a bloody corpse of another man on the ground beside him. It didn't look fresh. This creep didn't mind rotting bodies hanging around him.

I counted down from three on my fingers and then I went in, cut to the left and fired. Cecilia came in and cut to the right.

The corpse dodged as if he knew we were coming. I know I hit him, but a few bullets in his body wouldn't stop him.

It turned around and I could see its dried, curled up lips and taut skin. Blood stains covered his face and the front of his clothes and those red eyes that I could swear were glowing. Before I could get another shot off, it raised its hand and I was knocked backward like the creature was a freaking "thunder punch He-Man."

The force of the blow hit my SAPPI plate but it still knocked the wind out of me. Then it reached out like it was Darth Vader and grabbed Cecilia by the neck with an invisible force.

I fired and hit his shoulder. His arm jerked and he dropped Cecilia. I grabbed Cecilia's hand and ran out of the room.

Walls weren't cover. So I fired into the room at where I thought he was. My shots tore through the wall sending wood and torn bits of wallpaper flying everywhere. The muzzle flash of my AK caused a strobe-light effect and the hall filled with the cordite smelling smoke.

A blast like an explosion burst through the wall toward us, but missed us by a good foot or two. It created a hole the size of a beach ball.

I stopped, turned back, and went to the hall. The emaciated corpse was standing there with both hands ready to use whatever witchery it had. As soon as I saw him, so did the sights of my AK. I leveled it at his head and fired. My first shot went straight into his right eye and my second one entered at the bridge of his nose.

It stood there, not moving for a second, then it slumped as if tired and finally fell over. I didn't want to risk a horror movie ending where the bad guy gets one last scare, so I put three more rounds into its head, just to make sure.

"What the hell was that?" Cecilia asked, trying to catch her breath.

"I don't know, but I don't think a bad case of the flu explains it."

I got on the radio and gave Kevin my report. We then hurried out of the house and to the rally point. Cappello and Kevin were waiting for us.

"So, you fought a sith?" Cappello asked.

"I don't know what it was," I said.

"The zombie dude had magic, huh?" Kevin asked.

"I swear it," I said.

"It's true," Cecilia quickly added.

We slept in a fancy hotel and in the morning we finally got our shopping done. Kevin and Cappello raided grocery stores and another gun store that had been missed.

Cecilia came out of the changing booth wearing a long black dress, tight black leather biker jacket, combat boots, and without her habit. It was the first time I had seen her hair. It was raven black, parted simply down the middle and hung to her chin.

"My head feels naked," she said and looked around for a hat. She settled on her black sock cap.

She grabbed armfuls of clothes, mostly black --I love Roman sense of fashion -- then we got back in our vehicles and began our drive back toward Vernal. We didn't get very far before we stopped.

I saw a car dealership up ahead.

There in the parking lot was a brand new Camaro, black with chrome trim and tinted windows.

Neither of us had to say anything. We both jumped out and began throwing all our stuff into the new car. I grabbed the keys from inside and we headed out. I bid farewell to "Slow Ride" my old Camaro. It had served me well, but it was time to move on.

Cecilia plugged in her iPod and we cruised back to Vernal in style.

TWELVE

Zach, Washington State.
Day 40

"Where were we supposed to meet this guy?" Cecilia asked with a few unnecessary wild gestures of her hands.

George had sent us up here to Washington State to retrieve something very important. I used to live in Washington when I was a kid and it was a bit different than I remembered. One thing that was the same was that it was still rainy and over cast, just how I liked it.

We turned a corner on the highway that was lined with massive, green trees all around and saw a roadblock up ahead. It was manned. By living humans.

I stopped the Camaro and got out with my hands up.

"Zach Hill?" One of the men wearing a badge called out.

"That would be me."

"Took you long enough. We got work to do."

The deputy showed us on the map where to meet with MacLean for the Football. I didn't know what the "Football" was, but I was sure it wasn't something that could be found at a sporting goods store.

"Tacoma?" I asked, not sure if I read it right.

"Yes, sir," the deputy said.

"I'm not a sir. Dang. I used to live there."

"I've never seen so many trees," Cecilia said, shielding her eyes from the sun with her hand.

"Alright. We better head out," I said.

I looked over our three armored cars and the dozens of spare gas cans that were strapped all over the sides of them. Most of them were empty now.

I took a bite of my pizza hot pocket and chugged some of my Dew.

It was a cool, gray, rainy day, the kind that I loved. If there was one thing I loved about Washington, it was the weather.

We moved out and drove to Tacoma, near the Tacoma Narrows Bridge. I drove by what used to be my old home. The windows were smashed in and a burned car sat in the driveway. The 7- Eleven was still there, but it had been looted. Shuffling corpses wandered around, but we ignored them. Tacoma was now a quiet death zone with nothing living.

The long, slender bridge over the Narrows was completely empty except for two pickup trucks. We drove up and stopped about a hundred yards away. A man got out and waved them forward.

I drove forward and climbed out.

"Zach Hill?" The man asked.

"I am. You MacLean?"

"Unfortunately."

We shook hands and his men put the "Football" into the back of the Camaro.

"I believe I have something for you," he said.

"It must be a potluck or something because I also brought something for you. A promise of supplies. It's going to be a long winter for you and whatever survivors you have here."

"The survivors are mostly in the east and on the islands. Seattle is crawling. We have barricades and road blocks and we put up signs to warn people, but it seems someone keeps taking them down. One of our men said that he saw a zombie take it down."

"He saw a zombie take it down?" Cecilia asked.

That wasn't good news.

"A red eye," I muttered.

The more MacLean told me about the situation in Seattle, the less I liked it. I had to return the Football back to Ogre, but I couldn't leave them defenseless.

I got on the horn with Outbreak and cleared something with Ogre.

"I need a vehicle you won't mind having destroyed," I said.

MacLean thought for a second.

"It's a little out of the way, but I think I have just the one."

We drove clear out practically to the coast. It was a long drive and I wondered what could possibly be so important about this specific vehicle.

"You know, it's just going to get blown up," I said over our walkie talkie.

"I know. Trust me on this," he said.

The man did just give me the keys to the kingdom. The least I could do was trust him on this one thing.

We passed a sign that said "Welcome to Forks."

"Forks? As in glittering vampires?" I asked.

We pulled up to a house and out if front was that stupid truck that had become a tourist attraction.

"Bella's truck? We're going to blow up Bella's truck?"

"Bella's stupid," Cecilia said dismissively.

"I told you it was worth it," MacLean said.

We spent the night and had some really good fish from some of the local survivors. In the morning we went back to Seattle prepared to do some damage.

It took a few hours to get everything together. I made sure the helicopter was ready and that Outbreak was on his way. MacLean found a volunteer and we loaded the truck with rotten meat and a stereo pumping out Hannah Montana.

I was in the helicopter and watched the whole thing. It was one of those small, glass dome helicopters. I preferred the ones where I couldn't look down and see nothing between me and the ground, but a flimsy clear plastic.

We followed the truck as it drove passed the barricades and into Seattle. It wasn't long before the rickety truck had amassed a huge following. We had chosen a football field for the ground zero.

Our Coast Guard heli swooped in and picked him up before the zombie hordes could close in on him.

I could already see the C-130 as a distant dot approaching fast.

Then I saw something strange. Suddenly the zombies began scattering as if running for cover.

The bomb slid out the rear cargo hatch of the plane and fell down like a lawn dart. A parachute opened up to give the plane time to get out of Dodge. The large missile shaped bomb detonated right above Bella's truck. The truck, football field and most of the zombies disappeared in a massive fireball.

"We have confirmed red eye activity," I radioed to Cecilia.

"We'll have to come back, honey. We have this football to deliver."

"I know. I just really want to do something."

"I'd call that something."

I told MacLean that I would deliver the football and be back to help out the best I could."

We left the armored vehicles there and caught a ride on the Herc.

I delivered the football to Ogre in Uncle Musket's pub. Musashi, Cecilia, Musket and a bar wench were the only witnesses to the historic event. I would write about it years later, but I'd glorify it a bit and make it more dramatic. Two years later I also did a painting about it. I made everyone look like total badasses, standing there, posing like super heroes.

George now had the ability to use the nation's nuclear weapons.

Zach, Vernal Utah

I sat back on the porch of Ogre Ranch sipping my Dew and listening to music. Me and Cecilia were relaxing before something else horrible happened that would require our attention. We were cleaning our weapons and just talking.

We heard the report that one of Ogre's girl squad had been killed. I hated to admit it to myself, but I wasn't upset about it. They were a bunch of home wrecking hoochies that cared nothing for Ogre's real family or reputation. He was better off without them. I didn't like being so cold and apathetic, two things I usually detested. Still, she had been a human being and those were in short supply lately. Maybe she had actually been a decent person.

"Are you sure Uncle Musket is your brother?" Cecilia asked as she watched Musket in the distance. He was throwing hatchets at a tree stump with a group of soldiers while holding a bar wench in one arm.

"Reasonably sure."

She took the cover off of her SVD and removed the spring and bolt. We had done some target practice with our PSL and SVD that morning and were now doing a cleaning party.

I glanced over to her. She was wearing her nerd glasses, black sock hat, tight black hoodie and long gray dress.

"This is a strange place," she said.

"What do you mean?" I asked.

"So many soldiers running around, but kids and normal people too"

"That's the world we live in now. It has to be like this until we clear out the dead and get a stable government going."

"How long that take?"

"I don't know how long it'll be before they have schools and factories, but I guess a new normal will rise up."

"Normal. No such thing exists."

Two days later we were back in Provo. We were up on top of a building taking 300 yard shots at zombies with our SVD and PSL.

Ogre wanted Salt Lake and Provo cleared out completely.

A group of National Guard soldiers were held up behind a barricade and we were providing support.

"I got the one in the white jacket," I said as I looked through my scope.

"Red hat," she said.

We breathed and fired. Both zombies went down.

The zombies had started their attacks that morning, probing our defenses. We were on top of a UPS truck and the Guardsmen had the streets blocked off.

It started off with light skirmishes and we made one area seem purposefully weak. Maybe they were being controlled by an intelligence, but that didn't make them great strategists.

We let them break through into a blocked off street where we had explosives planted. We had the squad of National Guardsmen making what looked like a last stand.

Then I saw something. I looked through my scope to verify.

"Cecilia, look in the center of the horde. There's a zombie with a shotgun."

"What?"

She looked through her scope and gritted her teeth.

"I see it. Maybe…its just holding on to it?"

There was a group of zombies walking along with the shotgun wielding zed like a personal protection detail.

"Bodyguards," I said.

As we watched the zombie raised its shotgun and fired.

"Okay, he's probably under direct control of a red eye. We take him out."

We both fired. My shot took the top of its head off and her shot blew the bottom jaw off.

Then, on the captain's signal, three Bradley APC's came rolling in firing .50 cal and 25mm into the enormous crowd. The soldiers jumped on and they tore out of there. Once they turned the corner MacLean pushed the button. The entire street blew up as thirty claymore's went off, shredding the zombies into fine chunks.

"Now all we got to do is find where this red eye is and cut the head off the snake," I said.

Zach, Vernal, Oct 2nd.

We had gotten back from a hellish time in Provo and were now relaxing in Uncle Musket's pub. Our convoy had come in about midnight, but neither of us felt like sleeping so we trotted over to the pub because we knew it was going to be open. It was always open. Musket was asleep in his hammock, but there was still one serving wench awake.

"Got any pasta?" Cecilia asked. The wench looked at her as if she had asked for a severed baby head. "Never mind. Something with meat then."

The wench nodded and hurried off.

"I'd kill for some real pasta right now," Cecilia said.

"I'm afraid the only way you're going to get real Italian food is if you make it yourself and fresh ingredients are going to be a little hard to come by in the winter time."

She sighed and leaned back. She took off her knit cap and scratched her head. Her chin length black hair was as messy as I've ever seen it.

"I don't like Provo," she said.

"No one does, but it was much better when it was populated by the living."

"I have to take your word on this."

Then we heard some snorts and throat clearing.

"Brother Zach! What are ye doing here at this wee hour?" Musket asked, scratching his stomach and yawning.

"Wanted a bite to eat."

"Came to the right place ye have."

He crawled out of his hammock and sat down at our table.

"How are things at the pub?" I asked.

"Lots o' strange folk coming and going from parts unknown. We have some kinda strange whirly bird like a helicopter and airplane's bastard child. Strange times indeed."

"Strange times."

We ate and had a relaxing conversation with Musket. He brought us up to date as much as Musket could be "up to date" and I had to use creative interpretation to understand some of what he said.

After eating we went back to the house and crawled into our beds. I lay in my dark room and listened to the sounds outside. Guards did patrols and mechanics were up late working on the helicopters and Humvees. This place had once been quiet and remote. Now it was a military base. Strange people were always running around. Helicopters were taking on and off and trucks were always driving around at all hours of the night.

I didn't recognize any of it anymore.

In the morning I went out onto the porch in the increasingly chilly fall air. Sarge was out there holding a mug of hot chocolate. He had come all the way from one of the Carolinas. I could never tell the two apart. Or was it Georgia?

"Sarge!" I said.

"Ah, back from Provo, eh?"

"And glad to be so."

He came up onto the porch and looked out at the military base Ogre Ranch had become.

We talked and chit chatted for a while until we saw one of the girl squad walk by. We both grew silent until she had gone out of sight.

"I can't stand them," I said.

"Neither can I."

"It cheapens his whole image," I said. "I'd love get rid of them in a peaceable manner," I said.

"I don't think we can," Sarge said.

Another girl squad hoochie walked by and waved. I didn't wave back. Sarge made a point to not even look at her.

"All we can do is tolerate it, I suppose," I said.

Sarge shrugged.

Then a nearby radio squawked. I picked it up.

"Zach Hill here."

"Mr. Hill. We have a real situation here at Roadblock Alpha."

Roadblock Alpha was the first choke point guarding the Uintah Basin from the undead of the Salt Lake and Utah Valleys.

"What's wrong?" I asked.

"Sir, we have a whole lot of freaking zombies heading our way. Our scouts said that it looked like the entire damn undead population of Salt Lake is heading right at us."

I looked up at Sarge.

"Alright, we'll be right there," I said.

"Crap," Sarge said.

"Crap is right," I said.

"What's wrong?" Someone said from the doorway.

I turned back to see Q standing there, also with hot chocolate.

"Undead army heading towards our barricade. Thousands of them."

"Where?"

"About an hour west of here."

"We'll take the Osprey."

We grabbed several copters full of soldiers and I got some armored vehicles to head out and they'd meet us there when they could.

Our flying cavalry took off and we arrived at the barricade before the sea of undead got to it. The soldiers there clearly looked frightened. Most of them had been oil workers, farmers or students just a few weeks ago.

"Don't worry fellas, the big guns are on the way," I said.

"Unless you got a nuke, I don't think its going to be enough," a dirty, ragged soldier said. He handed me a digital camera and I flipped through the pictures. The canyons leading to the Uintah Basin was literally filled with zombies.

Musket let out a stream of curses that would cause a drunken Irish sailor's ears to turn red.

I looked out at the fifty or so soldiers that I had brought with me. They now seemed completely inadequate. Between all of us we simply didn't have enough bullets.

I quickly got on the horn and called up Ogre.

"George, we got a really freaking big problem here!" I said.

"Calm down bro, what's wrong?"

"The entire Salt Lake Valley is heading right for the first check point. I'm talking more than I've ever seen. We need air support. Get the Air Force flying now or we're all dead."

"Right. I'll send the gun ship and the F-15's."

"A-10's or B-52's would be nice. Either way, you better hurry."

Already I could hear the distant, dull collective roar of a million zombies.

It grew louder by the minute.

There were two 105 howitzers, but they only had ten shells each. I wish I had the Centauro with the grape shot. I wish I had a hundred of them.

As the zombie army came into view, coming around a bend in the canyon I heard the sound of jet engines over head. Three F-15's streaked over head and let loose their ordnance. The bombs fell in a staggered line along the canyon. Large fireballs erupted in the center of the zombie army. Napalm. I didn't know we still used that.

"George, get us some Willy Pete for the 105's!" I said into the radio. White Phosphorus would burn these shamblers to charred bones.

The fighters came back and did another pass, burning hundreds of them, but too soon they turned back.

Still, many zeds survived and shuffled right for our position.

We began firing. I had my PSL, Musket had his Brown Bess, Josh had a Cetme with some strange optic on top and Kevin had a Crusader Broadsword; a custom AR-10. We wanted to take out as many as we could from long range. Long range wouldn't last very long.

Between all of us, we began to mow down hundreds of them, but they were making ground without even noticing their losses. The guards were firing quickly and accurately so I had to give them credit for that. They at least knew how to shoot.

Then I heard more jet engines and looked up to see ugly cross shaped planes.

"What are those?" One of the soldiers asked.

"A-10's!" Musket shouted out. For someone as primitive as he was, he really was up on modern war gear. He knew all about modern weapons and equipment and theory, he just chose to reject it.

The Warthogs streaked down and opened up with their enormous Gatling cannons. Their giant mini-guns began to cut large gouges through the horde, turning the zombies into red mist and then they dropped their bombs on the rest.

The troops around me cheered, but I had seen the photos and I knew that there were still too many left. After a couple of lethal passes from the warthogs, they turned back and next up was the C-130 gunship. It flew in circles raining death down upon the undead horde.

The gunship didn't fire at the first ranks of the zombie army. It left them for us.

We kept firing. The zeds were looking larger through my PSL's scope, but they weren't on top of us yet.

The howitzers opened up and blew holes into their ranks.

All around me was the chaos of battle. I hadn't seen so much going on since April 2, 2005 at Abu Gahraib. All that was lacking were the Apaches.

I spoke too soon. The Apache helicopters flew over and began opening up with their chain guns and firing hellfire missiles.

"Zach, you down there?" I heard Outbreak say.

"Yeah, I'm here."

"We're going to need more. There's still a ton of them left."

"Agreed."

"Hold on for a while longer."

"I will certainly try."

We kept up our rate of fire, killing as many zeds as we could. The problems were that we weren't killing them fast enough and our ammo would run out soon enough.

A while later the armored vehicles rolled up. Just seeing armor made me feel much better. Cappello popped out of the hatch of the Centauro.

"Cappello in an Italian vehicle, I'm shocked!" I said.

"I roll with style, fool," Cappello said.

The LAV's and Centauro came onto the line and began firing with their big guns. With their support I knew we could hang on for at least a little while.

My PSL finally ran out of ammo and I switched to my AK. It didn't matter because they were getting close enough anyways. I put the red dot on their heads and fired again and again.

It wasn't long before I started running too low.

"I'm almost out," I said.

"Me too," Josh said.

Then I heard the slow humming of a distant C-130. I looked up and saw the plane coming.

The slow plane flew over head and let drop a bomb...a very large bomb.

"Everyone duck down!" I shouted.

I didn't see the bomb go off, but I heard and felt it. It felt as if the entire ground heaved up under me. If I hadn't been behind the sand bags I knew I'd be knocked off my feet at best.

I peeked up from behind the barricade and looked. Shattered and burning zombie bodies lay everywhere. The concussion from the blast was probably enough to liquefy their brains.

"Brava!" Cecilia shouted while she clapped.

The bomb had air bursted and had disintegrated most of the vast horde. The massive concussion had pulverized most of them and the shockwave had traveled down the valley, smashing and burning what few zeds survived. The few that remained near the rear were easily taken cared of by the guards' trucks and APC's.

I sat down and let out a long breath.

"Like old times," Cappello said.

"No, nothing like old times. Nothing like anything."

"Yeah, that was sarcasm, Zach."

"Sorry, I think my brains gone to mush."

"Maybe the zombies won't want you anymore."

THIRTEEN

Uprising: Day 53, Vernal Utah

I watched George's C-17 take off and disappear into the distance. I knew he wouldn't be back. I hated seeing him go. Even more I hated the fact that I had so much to tell him and say to him than my own clumsy tongue would allow. Still, it was his life and I couldn't run it for him.

"It's something I have to do," George said when he told me that he was leaving.

To say that it was unexpected was an understatement. I thought he'd stay here in Utah and build the country back up. I still didn't understand his reasons for leaving.

"What about Vernal?" I asked.

"Vernal will take care of its self. It doesn't need me. If I stay here I'll be trapped in a role I don't want to play."

"But you have everything you need right here."

"Yes, I know. It's safe and secure. But it'll slowly strangle me, bro. I need someplace I can be more."

"Be more? President isn't enough?"

"I'll be in contact, Zach."

"This doesn't make sense."

"It will."

I wondered if I'd ever see him again.

George then shook his head and walked to the ramp of the cargo plane. His wife, sons and a few others including the Japanese students were boarding. Crates of supplies were also being loaded and Musket was carrying a duffle bag full of muskets. One of his wenches was carrying what looked like a swivel gun from a pirate ship.

Just like that, two of my brothers were gone and I was left by myself on the side of the airfield, watching their plane fade away.

I drove back to what used to be Ogre Ranch.

There was nothing for me here any more. I knew Josh had been talking of going back east. Cappello, Hardcore, Ullu, Sarah and Kevin wanted to stay in Vernal and I certainly couldn't blame them.

"You look upset, what happened?" Cecilia said as I walked in the now empty house. She was in the kitchen trying her best to make hand made pasta. She craved pasta like I craved bacon cheeseburgers.

"They actually did it."

"They'll be back...right?"

"I doubt it."

Rebekah and Karen came into the house after spending their day in school where a pretense of normalcy was going on. It was good that there was still school, that meant education and that meant a future.

"At school everyone was saying that the Governor left," Karen said.

"It's true," I said.

"Why?" Rebekah asked.

"Uncle Musket too? Who'll run the pub?" Karen asked.

"Yeah, they're all gone."

I hated that word: gone.

Over the next two days something became increasingly clear to me. There was nothing left for me here. Everything continued to run as normal without any need of me. I relaxed in the mostly empty house, played X-box and read some books. When I walked around outside the military personal greeted me, but I had no authority over them.

When I picked up a book about Venice I knew exactly what I wanted.

I found Cecilia watching a Magpul training DVD and holding an unloaded Beretta.

"Hey, Cecilia, feel like some real Italian food?"

She went wide eyed.

"What? You serious?"

"Very."

"I could use some gnocchi."

I sat down on the couch in the house that now felt empty. Josh had his own house as did my cousins and friends. They all had a place here, but for me Utah now felt like a dead end.

The next day, Me, Cecilia, Rebekah, Daniel and Karen packed our bags, loaded the Centauro, AAV and an LAV and drove to Hill Air Force Base. We took all the guns and ammo we could find and anyone who would come with us. I left a satellite phone in case someone had to contact me. The LAV also had a Blue Force Tracker.

"Italy?" Rebekah asked with wide eyes.

"Yes, I want to go back to Italy. Would you all like to come with me? You all are family now, but it's your choice."

"Is it safe?" Karen asked.

"Venice is safe. Maybe not quite as safe as here in Utah, but it's safe," I said.

"Then why?" Karen asked.

"Because I believe we can do more good there. They need us more than we're needed here."

Rebekah sat back on the couch and ruffled her little brother's hair. Karen folded her arms over her "Black Sabbath" shirt and stared at the floor.

"I don't speak Italian," Karen finally said.

"We'll learn."

"Will we learn how to fight?" Rebekah asked.

"Yes. There aren't enough people and everyone will have to do their part."

"Good. I want those corpses to pay for what they did," Rebekah said.

"We'll be important over there?" Karen asked.

"Yes. I will be one of the few trained people. I'll be bringing arms and ammunition. We'll be important."

"And we'll be safe from the people, right?" Karen asked.

"Yes."

"Then I'll go," Karen said.

"We will to," Rebekah and Daniel said in unison.

The next day we drove to Hill Air Force Base, convinced Outbreak that Milan had enough jet fuel to make the trip worth it and we were off.

Karen, Rebekah and Dan asked questions the whole time and Cecilia began to teach them Italian. I was on my laptop most of the trip, organizing photos of everything I've seen and putting them into separate folders. I still had a job to do as a historian and I had a lot of work to do.

The two C-17's landed and the soldiers were out the door to secure the airfield. Our little convoy was out of the doors and heading east, towards Venice. We drove the four hours to Venice mostly in silence.

Unlike Utah, this place was still covered in the dead and even at night we could hear their moaning and see their shuffling forms in the darkness. Most of the art I had stolen was in the AAV again. I donated one or two for the presidential office in Vernal, but then figured the rest should go back.

I stood in the hatch of the AAV as it paddled its way across the water to the entrance of the Grand Canal. The guards came out in motor boats and stopped us.

"You don't recognize us?" Cecelia called out in Italian.

The rest of the conversation was a complete mess of confusion for me, but it went well because they were smiling and escorted us down the Canal to St. Mark's Square.

I was escorted quickly to the Doge's palace where the leaders were. I suppose it could be called a government.

The palace was filled with armed men and people with maps and stacks of paper. We went up the Golden Stairs to the Doge's office. He sat behind his desk talking to three different men at once. He looked up and waved me forward.

"So, the American and the nun have returned. Vacation?"

"We're here to offer whatever help we can. I brought a few gifts to help you ease your mind."

"Appreciated, but not necessary. We need you and you know it. Come back tomorrow morning and I'll have your new assignment."

"Thank you."

"And I suppose you'll need a new place to live. How's an apartment over the Grand Canal sound?"

"Sounds…doable."

It wasn't until late at night that we were all finally settled in. The house was a very old one, but it was also a very nice one. We had to share the house, but we had the entire top floor which had all the modern conveniences that could be expected. The plumbing worked, but the power was out. We used flashlights to get around because the government didn't want us using candles. There had been too many fires in Venice's history to risk open flames.

Karen, Dan and Rebekah ran to their new rooms and crashed on their beds. They didn't bother to unpack. I promised them that I'd show them the city tomorrow. Cecilia was eager to go exploring again.

I stood at the window over looking the quietly lapping water of the Grand Canal. A solitary gondola silently glided by far below. The moon reflected off the water as did the lights of the houses. It was beautiful and it was perfect.

It was indeed very strange to be back here. Just the day before I was in Vernal where things were returning to a kind of normalcy. Now I was back here, in this utterly unique, wonderful, unreal city on the water. I wasn't a Venetian. I was just a normal guy from Utah.

Well, I wasn't really normal, nor from Utah. I'm more of a transplanted Virginian. I was a guy whose life hadn't gone anywhere. Two college degrees and I was working as a substitute teacher, unable to find a better job. Now, here I was the official military trainer for the new Venetian government. The people here were surviving by only a narrow margin. They needed help and I was able to offer that help. I was useful here.

I stood at my balcony, looking over my new home and soaked it all in. The sounds, the smells and the sight of the clear sky with its nearly full moon. I felt strange, like that moment of falling where there's no ground or sense of real direction. I couldn't go back and I didn't know what was ahead of me. I just had to close my eyes and trust I'd land on my feet.

There was a knock at the door.

"Yes?"

"It's me, Cecilia."

She didn't wait for my response and opened the door. In the darkness all I saw was her dark form as she walked over to stand beside me at the balcony.

"Think we made a mistake?" I asked.

"No, not at all."

"I wonder if I'll ever see my brothers again."

"I think so. It might be long time, but you will see them."

She leaned on the rail and we fell into silence as we looked out over the dark, moonlit city of Venice.

In the morning I showed my adopted girls the wonders of their new home. I had a family of my own now. I found myself with two amazing daughters, a son and in a city I loved. I knew I was going to be happy here. The world was ending, but at least I could carve out a small piece of happiness for myself.

FOURTEEN

Book II The Serene Republic

Zach Hill, Venice, October 7th

In the morning, after a leisurely, but meager meal of some bread and Nutella, I slung my FS2000 and walked to the Doge's palace which was once again the seat of a government. The new Doge, Fredrico De Canalli, was talking to a group of suits, probably his new cabinet, or whatever the Italian term was. A few armed guards stood by. They had Italian military uniforms on and I was glad that there were at least a few people with military training.

Most Italians serve two years in the army, but the thing about Venice was that at any given time, there were vastly more tourists than Venetians. The outbreak occurred at peak tourist season and most of them fled to the airports in Milan or Rome to try to get back home. The few that stayed were the ones that lived. Not many stayed. Now, once again, there were more Venetians than tourists. When I came last, there had been a cruise ship, but it was gone and had taken all but a handful of tourists that knew they had no where else to go.

I stood off to the side, waiting for De Canalli to finish. Once he dismissed the men in suits, (why bother with such things as suits and ties?) he walked over to me.

"Ah, Mr. Hill. Come with me."

He took me up the Golden Stairs to what was once the office of the Doge and was now again. He sat behind a new desk that looked out of place in the antique room. There were only a few papers on the desk.

"We've been compiling a list of the people, finding out who they are, where they are from and more importantly, what they can do. We have twenty eight sailors from the Arsenal, a dozen former army and one American former Marine and a German former army."

"I was hoping for more."

"Me too. Non-military sailors we have plenty of. We can sail anywhere no problem. You're the only one with actual combat experience besides a few raids to the mainland. Also, you help train people to use guns."

"I was just an assistant trainer."

"I don't even have an assistant's assistant trainer. You're all I have. Also, you know powerful people in America. I need you by my side. I want you to become my general of land forces."

I didn't know what to say. I came expecting an advisory role; maybe some low level officer's position.

"I don't think I'm qualified at all," I said.

"None of us are qualified for the roles we find ourselves in. Least of all, me. You're all I have."

"I want to help, but I can't do something like that."

"Too bad. It's already official...as official as anything can be nowadays."

"Alright, but as soon as we find someone better, I'm out."

"Deal."

I could read on his face that he was confident that they wouldn't find anyone else.

I had really been hoping to avoid any responsibility and danger: two things I didn't get along with.

"First order of business is to talk to your new army. Here's a list of their names and where they're staying. Other than that, I want you to organize them into a fighting force and raid for supplies. We need more of everything. More food, vitamins, medicine, anything else that could help."

"How have your men done against the red eyes?"

"I don't understand."

"The red eyes. The intelligent ones with red glowing eyes that control other zombies."

The Doge looked at me like I was telling a bad joke.

"I'm serious."

"We've seen nothing like that."

The situation was worse than I thought. They weren't even aware of how dangerous the enemy was. I definitely had my work cut out for me.

My first order of business was to get a second in command that I could trust. I went back to my house and told Cecilia about the meeting.

"You're a general now? Very nice!" Cecilia said.

Rebekah and Karen heard that and rushed in.

"You're a general? That's awesome," Rebekah said.

"That means our place here is secure," Karen said.

"We're as secure as we can be," I said.

Secure was a relative term.

"Cecilia, you speak Italian. I need you to come with me and act as translator."

Also, I just wanted her by my side. We hadn't done more than kiss, (though I guess that's like third base for a nun) but I enjoyed her company more than anyone else. She was smart, funny, easy going, relaxed and educated. She was pretty, sure, but not a jaw dropping pretty and most guys would probably pass her over without a second glance.

Together we went to our first recruit, the Marine. Once a Marine... He was an old guy, maybe sixty, with white hair and a white beard. He struck me as an old school M14 type.

"You want me to join the army?" He asked sounding not at all impressed with the idea. His name was Jared Maser and despite being sixty, he looked like he could rip me in half with his bare hands.

"Military. I know you're a Marine."

"That's not what I'm talking about. You do realize that I'm old, right?"

"Yes, but you have knowledge that I don't. I want you to be my chief trainer. Teach whatever recruits we get discipline and how to be a soldier... er...or Marine. I'll teach fire arms and tactics, you teach the rest. I'm not mean enough to shape them into what they need to be."

"You want me to turn a bunch of civilian refugees into an effective fighting force?"

"Yes."

He put his hands on his hips and paced around his hotel room.

"I suppose I do owe them, seeing as how I have a place to live when the rest of the world is dead. I guess my duty isn't over yet. Alright, Master Sergeant Maser is coming out of retirement."

I shook his hand and together the three of us went to visit the German. Freder Diedrich was a young man and had been a lieutenant in the German army. Normally I avoided officers at all costs, but compared to the rest on my list, he seemed like a Godsend. He knew maps, communications and the one thing I certainly lacked, organization. He was tall, brown hair and humorless. I don't think he had ever smiled in his life. Defiantly a Northern German.

I took my two new leaders and we went to the Doge's palace to make plans. I was handed a list of Venice's current armory. Half of it had been the M4's I dropped off on my last visit and they only had about 300 rounds per weapon. Not good.

"Gentlemen, we need more guns," I said.

"What about Ramstein?" Freder asked.

"No good. We cleaned it out already," I said.

"Berettas come from Italy. Where are they made?" Maser asked.

I was stunned by the brilliance of the idea. I had thought of it during my last visit to Italy, but had promptly forgotten it. Northern Italy had some of

Europe's largest gun manufacturing. The world's third largest gun show took place in the northern region around Milan. There was the Benelli and Beretta factories to name only a few. There were plenty of arms and ammo.

"That needs to be our first mission," I said.

"So, what's stopping us?" Maser asked.

"The red eyes."

It took some explaining and Cecilia swearing before they believed me. By the end they understood the situation. We needed those guns urgently if we were to make an army so we couldn't wait to train up whoever we recruit. We had to go now. We decided that we'd head out the next morning.

Zach, Northern Italy, October 9th

We had to bypass Milan because it was infested with the dead. The crowded, industrial north of Italy was completely crawling with cannibalistic corpses. Right now, however, we were outside the major cities.

I looked through the binos at the Beretta factory. It looked more like an old mansion than a factory.

"See anything?" I asked Cecilia who was looking through another set of binos.

"Nothing."

"No dead, no living?"

"Nothing."

Me and my squad moved in slowly and carefully. Maser had an M4 that looked tiny in his hands and Freder had a Beretta rifle that had belonged to The Arsenal. Maser was in charge of one squad of five and Freder was in charge of another. I had Cecilia and three others.

Our squads split up and we moved around the factory/mansion/museum. My team went up to the front doors. Locked.

"Looks like we'll use the universal key," I said, raising my FS2000.

"Why don't we knock?" She asked.

I hadn't thought of that. It had been a while since I last knocked on a door. So I knocked. A few moments later a slit opened up and a pair of human eyes looked out. I didn't see much of the owner, but I could still see a look of surprise. The man said a few very rapid words in Italian and Cecilia rattled off a long speech. While they talked I signaled for the other squads to rally on my position.

A few moments later the door opened and we went in.

The man at the door was wearing civilian clothes and he carried a Beretta storm carbine. There were three other men behind him, all armed with

Beretta weapons.

"Parla Engles?" I asked.

"I speak some," one of the guards said.

"How many survivors you got here?"

"Thirty. A few workers and people from the town."

"Alright, we have armored vehicles out front. We're from Venice and Venice is still alive. However, we need food and guns and ammo. We need the latter to get the first."

"You came for guns?" The man asked.

"We didn't expect to see survivors. You should really come with us. It's much safer."

"Gladly," he said. "We have no food here," the man paused with a desperate grin on his face. "It's good to see living people."

I got my troops to follow two of the guards to the factory section to grab every weapon and box of ammo they could get their hands on and load up the AAV. The English speaking guard took me to where the refugees were. I saw mothers holding children, a few fathers holding wives and a few young people, teenagers and children that didn't look like they belonged to a family. I had the man explain the situation to them, that they were saved and being taken to Venice. I had each of them help load up the AAV with all the guns they could. We didn't stop until the large vehicle was completely full. The refugees were loaded up in the truck we had brought.

More important than the guns was the ammo we found there. There were crates and crates of it. There'd be enough for training and fighting. At least for a little while.

I went in and looked around in case we missed something.

I came upon the museum. The very first official sale of Beretta was to Venice. I found it fitting that her last shipment was again to Venice. The museum had samples of everything they had ever made. In memory of Uncle Musket I grabbed a beautiful musket, a musket pistol and a sword.

"We have zed activity," Maser said over the radio.

"That's okay, we're done loading up. Let's move out."

We locked the doors behind us, jumped in the armored vehicles and tore out of there as a small crowd of zeds came up the road. We couldn't grab everything and I knew that we'd be back. Filled to the brim, we sped our way back to Venice. The Doge greeted us and the new refugees and began questioning the civilians to find out how they could help.

The next day we went back to the region around Milan and this time we hit up the Benelli factory.

Here I found the shotgun I had always wanted. The Benelli Super Nova. It had the most comfortable pistol grip, my favorite sights and it just looked sweet. I loved it. Me, Karen and Rebekah got matching shotties, loaded up crates of 12 gauge shells and shot guns, hit up a smaller ammo factory near by and sped out, popping only a few zeds on the way.

Once back to Venice the Doge gave us a large room in the palace to use as an armory and we began to take inventory of everything we had looted. I had to say that I was impressed with the haul, but as great as it was, it was still finite. We would eventually have to take and hold the factories in order to make what we needed.

That was long term, however, and right now I needed to focus on the task at hand.

"What do you think?" Freder asked. He stood beside me with his arms folded and a grim look on his face. Did he have another expression?

"I think we did pretty good. The city guards can use the shotguns, but our raiding parties will use the M4's, the Beretta rifles and carbines. Once we get our volunteer recruits, we'll need to start training them."

"At least we can arm them now."

"Yeah, but there are red eyes out there. I know they know we're here. They have to be planning something."

"We'll be ready for them," Maser said.

"We will be."

I racked the pump of my new shotgun and loaded it with slugs. When I saw a red eye next, I was going to be ready. They were powerful, but they couldn't stop a 12 gauge slug.

For our training area we would need wide open spaces for Physical Training, aka PT, obstacle courses and of course, target practice. One island came to mind. Torcello.

Torcello was mostly abandoned. A handful of people lived on the island. All that remained of what used to be the largest settlement in the Venetian lagoon were two churches, a few surrounding buildings and some ruined houses scattered around. It had as much open space as you were going to find in Venice. The island of Poveglio was also open, but seeing as it was so haunted, the government wouldn't allow anyone to go there, I passed. I didn't need negative feng shui, or whatever, to interfere with the training.

Finding volunteers had proven easier than I had anticipated. It seemed some of the refugees and trapped tourists wanted payback. Others simply had nothing else to do and wanted to be useful. Me, Cecilia, Maser and Freder interviewed them all and spent all night discussing how to organize them all and where best to put them. The few people I had with military experience, no matter how slight were automatically the NCO's and officers. All together we had about a hundred and twenty armed men and women now. It was a small army, but it was going to be a well trained army. The entire population of the new Venetian Republic depended on them. Unlike the old Republic, I didn't hold any illusions that this would be "Serene."

FIFTEEN

Zach, Northern Italy, October 11th

We ended the second day of training on the island of Torcello. The few remaining buildings were now our training headquarters. Instead of shuttling back and forth everyday, we simply brought cots and sleeping bags with us.

We had our rifle range set up and we used the abandoned buildings as shoot houses to practice clearing and sweeping.

"But, do we have to Zach?" Karen asked. She was dressed in some black gothy clothes that she found in one of the formerly expensive high fashion shops scattered around Venice. She was using my FS2000 for the exercises and I had my AK.

"Yes, you do. You need to be able to defend yourself," I said.

"It's not that, I'm just wondering why I have to train like a soldier. I'm in Venice. They can't get us here and I sure as hell ain't going out there."

"It's better to know it than not know it," Rebekah said.

Karen glared at her.

"We're all learning it," Cecilia said, bringing out her conciliatory nun skills.

We took the two girls out to the field where the other recruits were falling into formation. The NCO's took role and reported to the officers. Today was team drills where one fire team would hold position to let another team advance. It used to be "only hits count". In our exercises, only head shots counted.

Me and my officers watched the training and gave hints and advice when we could. I had Cecilia go through most of the exercises as well. She had a lot of combat experience, but lacked some technique and skills.

On the fourth day of our training De Canalli called up on our radio.

"Mr. Hill, we have a situation," the Doge said.

"What kind of situation?"

"They say that many of the dead are gathering on the northern shore of the Lagoon. They said it looked like they are trying to hide. We see them with infra red."

"Okay, well zombies can't swim, so we're still safe."

"That's the bad news, they are gathering many boats."

"The zombies are gathering boats?"

"Yes."

"Okay, that's not good. Hold on."

I took out my maritime map of the lagoon. There were a lot of marshy islands and sand barges all over the area. Only a local knew the ways to navigate the lagoon safely and I doubted the red eyes in control knew much about sailing.

"Alright Doge, I'm bringing our men back to Venice. Gather all the soldiers at St. Mark's Square. Also, I'll need your most experienced local sailors."

"They'll be waiting for you."

I hung up and called an end to training. They had just graduated.

We packed all our gear and got back on the boat. The girls were happy to be heading back to Venice.

At St. Mark's Square we assembled all the soldiers and sailors we could.

"Alright, we have a possible invasion by red eye controlled zombies. Sailors, I need your expertise. We need to keep them away from Venice so we'll meet them on one of the vacant islands. Are there any islands that get covered during high tide?"

We made our plans with the help of the local sailors. They knew every secret and nuance of the lagoon. Venice had never been invaded by a foreign power and was kept safe by its lagoon. It would protect Venice again.

I hand picked the team lead by Freder to go off and hide on a nearby island and wait for the signal of a red flare.

The rest came with me to meet the water bound horde of zombies.

We made no attempt to hide the fact that we were coming. That would draw them out. I could see them waiting by the shore, shoulder to shoulder like a Napoleonic army.

We landed on a small island that was nothing more than a sand barge. Our squads deployed under the watchful eyes of the Italian officers. I wasn't technically in charge, but since it was my plan the officers turned to me. Karen and Rebekah were safe in Venice where a small reserve force of sailors would defend the city. In the Arsenal was a submarine and a small naval corvette, but both were still in dry dock for repairs. If we could get those two running, we'd have a better chance of defending ourselves in the future.

"How long until high tide?" I asked.

"An hour," one of the Italians said.

I took the bullhorn, walked out in front of everyone and turned it on.

"Hey, pink eyed pricks! I know you hear me. Pink eye's contagious you know. You don't have bodies of your own so you got some stinky carcass to posses? Yeah, that's real style guys. I think that's a step down from pigs. When you possess dogs do you lick your own butts?"

I didn't wait long for their response. The shore was far away and I couldn't make out individual zombies, but I heard the whispering voice as clear as if it had been in front of me. I knew that the red eye or red eyes that controlled this horde were still on the shore. They didn't want to get their hands bloodied. I had counted on that.

"Mock us with your false bravado. We have seen your fate here. You do not have enough soldiers and you do not have enough guns."

"You're not about to give me that 'we are legion' crap. It's been too over done. Why don't you bring your limp, flaccid self over here and we'll finish this," I called out on my bullhorn.

The zombies' boats spilled into the lagoon like an oil stain and as they grew closer my men spread out to cover their sectors of fire. One of the boats we brought with us had two .50 cal machine guns for support. I wished we had the AAV with a fully loaded MK19, but it was too slow and wouldn't have gotten here in time.

It took a while for the undead assault boats to reach our little island, but when they did, they rammed ashore and zeds poured out of them, running at us as fast as their clumsy dead legs could carry them.

Immediately my men began to open fire, the heavy .50 cals barking much louder than the rest. Zombies fell by the dozens, but more boats plowed ashore. We were facing them down the long way of the island. It was narrow and they had to come at us for about 500 yards.

I couldn't signal Freder until the last assault craft was beached. Until then we had to hold them off.

The horde was charging us and we let loose with everything we had. Some of my men had shotguns and they waited until zeds got close enough before they let loose with buckshot. I aimed with the red dot, fired and repeated with my AK. It was methodical as I took aim and fired, while my heart pounded. Cecilia was right beside me with her ACR. Again, she was as calm as a summer morning and having her there helped keep me calm.

Whenever one of us stopped to reload, one of the zeds got closer. There was no way we could hold them off indefinitely. Good thing we didn't have to.

Sometimes being a historian paid off. I got the idea for this plan when the Franks tried to invade the Venetian lagoon. Again, history was repeating itself except instead of Franks we had rotting undead creatures.

The last make-shift assault craft came ashore and I quickly fired my flare.

Freder, who was hiding behind a nearby wooded island, came around in his three speed boats. They drove up to the parked undead boats and opened fire with thrown Molotov cocktails, setting all the boats and more than a few zombies on fire.

"Retreat!" I shouted out over my bullhorn and instantly all my men ran back to their boats, splashing in the water while the twin .50's covered their retreat.

We shoved off the small island as the zeds came to the edge of the water. Their vacant eyes stared at us and their hands reached impotently for us. Zombies couldn't swim.

The high tide was coming in and soon the little sand barge would be entirely under water.

"Phase two!" I called out.

Our small fleet of boats turned about and sped toward the shore where the undead masters were.

The two red eyes were arrogantly there waiting for us.

One of the red eyes raised both his hands and the boat next to ours capsized in a geyser of water.

"Open up!" I yelled at the two .50 cal gunners. I really wished I had my SAW right now, but I had left it behind in Vernal. Linked ammo was just too hard to find. So I traded the SAW for a RPK with a drum. The RPK was still back in my room overlooking the Grand Canal. I wished I had that now as well.

The two .50 calls tore up the beach where one of the red eyes was standing. Demonic entity or not, it couldn't take a hit from a fifty. The undead master exploded into dried chunks of jerky and the other red eye almost fell over trying to get away.

Our boats came near the shore and we jumped off the front. I hated getting wet, but I knew that I'd be able to dry off in my comfortable house along the canal. It was stupid that I was thinking of simple comforts at a time like this, but I've been without the necessities of life and now I found that I couldn't go without the luxuries.

We charged the red eye, who thunder punched an entire squad of men and sent them flying backwards, and then turned around and began fleeing. I knew it, they were cowards deep down.

A coward, yes, but still very dangerous and we couldn't let this thing get away. I pushed myself faster up the beach to get a good shot. As it reached the tree line I took aim and placed my red dot on the center of its back and fired.

I hit high and to the left which spun him around and knocked him to the sand. As he began to get up and start running again Cecelia called out, "shoot the legs!"

I aimed and fired at his legs. We all did. His legs shattered into dry, dead chunks and he fell down face first.

"Grenade!" I shouted and two of the soldiers nearby tossed their grenades at the crawling red eye. It was a shame the Italians didn't play baseball because both grenades found their mark. The double explosion left nothing of the red eye, but misty chunks in the air.

I walked over to the smoking mess that had been the red eye. We got him, but what concerned me was this whole leadership thing. I didn't want to be a leader and I didn't want to be in danger and here I was, deep in both.

I had to find a way out of this.

"Bastardo!" Cecilia shouted out and then spit in the thing's direction.

The soldiers cheered and we all got back in the boats. We picked up the capsized soldiers and the medics tended the five wounded men we had. They were bruised from the thing's Jedi force push, but everyone was okay. As we passed the sand barge we saw that the water was up to the stranded zombies' legs.

We went back to St. Mark's Square with our first victory. The Doge and hundreds of people greeted us like we had done something great. I stood back and let the officers take the credit. I had no desire to be in the spotlight.

"Being modest?" The Doge asked as he walked up to me.

"I don't like public attention," I said.

"But you deserve it. It was your plan after all. The men look to you as their leader."

"I don't want to be their leader."

"It doesn't matter what you want. It's what you are."

"Trust me, I'm no leader. I can teach, but leading people on a daily basis is something else entirely. You'd be much better served finding someone that can lead. I'll teach, they lead."

"We'll see," the Doge said.

What the Doge didn't understand was that I wasn't being modest. I really did suck as a leader. I've tried before and every time I attempted to be in a leadership position, I fell flat on my face.

When I got back home, Rebekah, Dan and Karen demanded that I tell every detail. Cecilia had a talent for exaggerating stories and her account made me out to be a super hero.

We had dinner of fish and eggplant, two things I wasn't fond of and knew that tomorrow I had to plan a raid on the mainland for some real food.

I was awakened in the morning by a knock on the door.

"Go away," I muttered.

Apparently they didn't hear me because they kept knocking.

I grabbed my Beretta and went to the door.

"Who is it?" I asked.

"It's me, Maser," the old Marine said.

I opened the door. He was standing there fully dressed with an M4 slung over his shoulder.

"I hope this is important," I said.

"The Doge wants a war meeting."

"I'm tired. What time is it?"

"Eleven."

"What? Seriously? Awesome. I actually slept."

My souvenir insomnia from my first deployment made getting sleep problematic. A good night's sleep was something to celebrate.

"Well, they'll be waiting for us in the council room in the palace."

"Alright, I'll be right there."

I got dressed, put on my boots, tac vest, slung my FS2000 and headed down stairs. I walked out into a bright sunny day with the smell of the salty ocean filling my nostrils. The Grand Canal was filled with small boats plying the emerald green water. The motor boats were less common than before and now most people were using rowboats and the fancy gondolas were now back to more practical work than before.

I made my way to the Rialto Bridge where people had set up shops selling all kinds of things from dental floss, to scissors, to duct tape. Instead of cheap tourist trinkets, the shops here now sold everyday items that people needed. The fishermen would trade fish for such things.

The more I looked at this all, the more I saw that such things were quickly becoming scarce. We needed to start raiding the mainland or we'd run out of necessary items for daily life.

When I walked into the council room in the top floor of the Doge's palace I had to pause to stare at the art. At the head of the room was the world's largest oil painting and the walls and ceiling were covered in paintings depicting scenes from Venice's history. What wasn't covered in paintings was covered in elaborate, gold decorations.

Maser and Freder were there talking to the men in suits. There were a few other people there including one of the American tourists that had decided to stay.

"Mr. Hill. Come on over. We're discussing our immediate priorities," De Canalli said.

I walked over to the table and saw that they were looking over a detailed road map of the area. The city of Mestre was just on the shore and so was the nearest horde of undead. There were smaller towns all over the shore of the lagoon.

"What do we need the most?" I asked.

"Medical supplies," De Canalli said.

"Where's the nearest hospital?" I asked.

"Mestre," Freder said.

"Figures," I said.

Of course the hospital couldn't be in one of the quite towns. It had to be in the dead infested modern city.

I was going to have to bring my camera along. This had to be documented. This was the first push back from Venice to reclaim the mainland.

"I can't lead this. It should be an Italian," I said.

"Yes, propaganda can't be overlooked," De Canalli said.

"I'll tag along, but put someone else in charge," I said.

"Very well. Do you have any suggestions?" He asked.

I looked over to Maser and Freder. We talked it over a bit, but finally came to a decision. There was a sergeant from the Italian army. He would be a great choice with Maser and Freder acting as "advisors."

"Doge, we can plan the raids. In the meantime you all should work out our long term goals."

"We're working on it."

I took my men and left to go plan this raid. There would have to be multiple raids if we were going to even get a fraction of what the city needed. We simply couldn't go into a city with guns blazing (though that would be fun). There weren't enough of us and we couldn't waste the ammo. We had to think this through.

"We need a large distraction," I said.

"What do you mean?" Freder asked.

"Back in Salt Lake, we'd use stereos on full blast. We'd drive around and lure the zeds away from the area we wanted to work with."

Maser nodded his head.

"Sounds good," he said.

"Who's the lucky one that gets to be bait?" Freder asked.

"We'll need a volunteer. Preferably someone that can run fast in case things go wrong."

It didn't take long to find a volunteer. It turned out that everyone in our small security force was eager to prove themselves and take back their country.

So, we held a race. The winner got the honor of being bait.

While they began planning the route of the bait and our route to the hospital, I loaded the highest quality ammo into my PSL. The PSL, the Romanian equivalent of a Dragunov, was a very ammo sensitive weapon. With cheap surplus I could get shot groups around 2.5 to 3 inches at a hundred yards. With good ammo I could get it down to 1.5, easily inside the target area of a zombie's head.

I loaded my vest out with magazines with the good ammo, slung my long PSL and jumped into the AAV. I was the historian and wanted to be in a position to see all the action, but my main reason for hanging back was to take care of the red eye. When that possessed creep showed up, I'd be ready for it. The others didn't have the experience with them that I've had. When it showed its glowing-eyed head, I'd be there to pop it.

"Zach!" Someone called out.

I turned to see Karen, Rebekah and Dan run up to me.

"What's up? We're getting ready to leave. I'll bring you back something good to eat," I said.

"Take this," Rebekah said.

Rebekah held out her hand with a necklace in it. I took it and looked at it. It was a red white and blue Captain America shield.

"Where'd you find this?" I asked.

"We traded one of the American refugees for some spam," Dan said.

"Awesome. It'll protect me."

I put on the necklace and tucked it under my body armor.

With that, we rolled out. We took boats and the AAV over to the shore where we had our motor pool. Our men quickly ran to their assigned armored vehicles and trucks.

Meanwhile, our bait, took a Lamborghini from the parking garage on Venice and drove over a makeshift drawbridge over to the mainland in Mestre.

While he drove around the city, pumping out some Italian techno music, we got into position. There was a small town with a grocery store nearby so while we waited we went to loot the store.

The residential area looked new and fairly upscale. For the most part, we ignored the zeds that wandered around this area. We sped through and went straight to the store.

One of the Italians was in the AAV turret, but I stood up in a hatch and scanned the area myself. The small town was called Tessera and there was a road from Tessera that went straight to Mestre. It was near the airport which we still hadn't cleared out. It seemed that many people had gone to the airport to escape so the place was literally crawling with zombies, abandoned cars and smelled of rotten corpses.

Cecilia was beside me and looking out with binoculars.

"Horrible," she said under her breath.

Several men jumped out of the trucks and broke the lock on the small corner grocery store. Most grocery stores in Italy were quite a bit smaller than what we were used to in America. From the window I could see the dried, salted meats hanging from the window and the large wheels of cheese.

Some zombies began coming out of the dead houses and some came from other streets. There were more of them than I had anticipated, but I didn't see any signs of intelligent control.

I jumped down and went into the store. I saw a plastic bottle of coke and picked it up from the floor. It'd be warm, but it was better than nothing. For good measure I grabbed the wheel of cheese.

It was surprising how quickly they completely cleaned out the store. They shoveled everything into cardboard boxes. It didn't matter what it was, they took everything.

When I came out of the store, sipping on my warm coke, I saw that the streets were getting crowded. The zombies were moving forward and some of the soldiers began picking off the closer ones.

The young man in charge of this raid called out in Italian and waved his hands in an unmistakable sign telling everyone to move out. I hopped up onto the AAV and we sped out, crunching zombies under our wheels and treads.

The amount of zombies even in these small towns was surprising. There simply wasn't any way we could clear them all out with the amount of ammo we had. We'd have to find a better way. Shame we didn't have any MOAB's and C-130's. But…we could make explosives. I'd have to bring that up later.

When it was time, we headed down the road toward the city. Swampland surrounded the city making it hard to tell where the land ended and water began. Short, gnarled trees gave way to tall, bushy ones and the buildings began to grow bigger in a very short period of time.

The hospital, of course, was right in the middle of the city. They had shown me on a street map where it was, but a street map was very different than reality, another reason why I wanted a local to lead this mission. They'd have first hand knowledge of the area that I just couldn't know.

We had to weave in between abandoned and crashed cars, most of them the small European cars that looked like lunch boxes. The scooters crunched easily under the tracks of the AAV.

Zombies peered at us through the windows of shops and apartment buildings. A few began towards us, but we were going full speed and it would be a long while before they caught up.

At least there were very few of them. Our bait had worked well enough. A few zeds were to be expected.

I remembered Mestre from the last time I was here. It was a typical modern and kind of run down city with nothing to make it noteworthy.

When we pulled up to the hospital I was surprised to see that it was a giant, glass, new age looking building that looked like some kind of modern art museum. I would have guessed it to be a square, boring building with peeling paint.

The men jumped out and rushed into the hospital. There would most likely be a mess of zeds in there and I didn't envy them the job of clearing every room as they went.

My job was to watch the outside. The AAV's turret scanned the area and I sat up on top with my PSL. There were zombies about, but I let the soldiers pick them off for target practice. That was good news, but the better news was that I still didn't see any signs of a red eye.

While I waited I took out some dried salami that I had been saving and began chewing on it.

Then I heard the sound of thousands of simultaneous moans.

"Heads up, everyone!"

I put my snack back into my tactical pouch and brought my PSL up to scan the area with my scope. Cecilia brought up her binos.

Down the main, large street I saw a horde of zombie pouring into view from about five blocks away.

"Six O'clock!" I shouted out.

The AAV's turret flipped around and opened up with its Mk-19. A stream of grenades lobbed into the first ranks of the horde and for a moment the whole crowd disappeared into a cloud of smoke and dust.

I adjusted the range on my scope and looked for my target.

My driver was on the radio yelling at the scavenge teams inside.

I really wish I had my SAW right now…or my RPK.

I scanned the horde, but I didn't see any red eye. If it was in there it would be hard to find. We had to thin the herd a bit more before the red eye would show itself.

I put my crosshairs on a zombie's head and gently squeezed the trigger. My round struck lower than I had aimed for, but hit the zombie in the bottom jaw and the back of the head exploded out. It toppled over and the bullet struck the zombie behind it in the neck. The head popped off. The two zeds toppled over and tripped two more behind them.

Not a bad shot if I do say so myself.

The AAV opened up with the Mk-19 again and a stream of explosions tore through the crowd again. Smoke and limbs flew into the air. A steady stream of 5.56 round peppered the crowd from my soldiers. It was whittling away at the horde, but it just wasn't enough.

"How are our teams on the inside?" I called out.

"They're still grabbing supplies," Maser said.

"Tell them to hurry," I said.

I kept looking for the red eye, but in the meantime I could help take a few zombies down. I aimed between two eyes and fired. A hole appeared and the zombie fell down. The zombie behind it lost half its face, but it kept walking.

The fire continued to poor into the horde and the fallen corpses were starting to cause the main horde to slow down. Still, it wasn't enough.

I fired and fired with the bolt throwing my empty casings a good twenty feet away. When the bolt locked back, I brought my PSL up, tore out the empty mag, stuffed it back into its pouch and rocked in a new one. After rocking the bolt again I took aim and scanned for the red eye. The LAV moved into position and opened up with its 25mm cannon. I had to plug my ears.

The 25mm punched long holes through the crowd like a farmer plowing a field. Chunks and black mist exploded up from the paths of the large shells. Brass tumbled out from the turret of the LAV and scattered out on the pavement of the street. One of the soldiers ran with a bag to collect the empty brass for reloading later.

Still, the horde came closer.

Then I saw it. I saw one zombie in the horde that was standing still. It was a male in a too-tight shirt and fashionable scarf and it was standing there like the eye of a hurricane.

"On target," I said to the man in the turret.

I snapped up my PSL and brought the red eye into my scope. I breathed out and started to squeeze the trigger.

Suddenly the red eye disappeared back into the crowd and I lost sight of him. I kept scanning the horde, but I didn't see him and they were getting uncomfortably close. They were now crossing the street to the block we were on.

"We need to roll out," I called down to my driver.

"Rolling," he said and the engine of the AAV roared to life.

Just then a blast of unseen energy ripped through the zombie horde heading our way. Zombies were tossed in the air and out of the way as the force cut through the crowd and struck the LAV. The armored vehicle rocked on its wheels and paused momentarily from firing. The crew must have been shaken up a bit.

It was a great show of power, but it also gave away the red eye's position. I looked through my scope at the area the blast originated and saw the red eyed SOB. Again I breathed out and slowly squeezed the trigger.

I fired. My shot went low and struck the red eye where the shoulder meets the neck. A chunk of his neck was blown out and he jerked backwards, almost falling down, but he was still operational. The red eye turned and looked at me over the 100 yards of flesh eating undead.

I fired again. This shot struck him in the eye and blew out the left side of his cranium. Like a sack of wheat he fell straight down. Instantly the zombie horde stopped and began looking around. I didn't know if they were momentarily stunned from the sudden disconnect from the controller or if they were just smelling around for their next snack.

It only took a few seconds for the first files of zombies to notice us and with a few more seconds, the horde was moaning and heading for us again.

I didn't worry about finding targets and just began picking zeds off as fast as I could. The Mk-19 'thump, thumped' another line of grenades into the front ranks of the zombie horde creating geysers of dirt and rotten body parts.

Given enough ammo, we could hold them off, but that was a luxury we just couldn't afford. We couldn't waste all our ammo on one battle.

Then the scavenge teams came out carrying boxes of supplies.

"Fretta!" I called out in Italian, telling them to hurry.

They jumped into the backs of the waiting trucks and our convoy pulled out at top speed, leaving the now mindless horde behind us.

I could still feel the now familiar surge of adrenaline dying down. The cool autumn air felt great on my face as we raced away from the dead city. We got supplies and hadn't lost anyone. It had been a lucky and successful day.

SIXTEEN

Uprising: Italy, Oct 15th

"I don't like it," Maser grumbled.

"It's not about like it or no. It's about ammunition," Freder said. "We don't have enough."

"No, we don't," I said. "We have thousands and thousands of rounds, but it's a finite amount and with that, every bullet is priceless. We can't continue like this for long. We have to find a renewable supply or we will run out."

"It's mathematics," Freder said.

"Near Milan, where the Beretta factory was, we have plenty of ammunition factories," Lorenzo said. He was the young man that led the raid into Mestre. He was young, but he was sharp and if he were back in the States girls would probably think he was a male model. Here in Italy, he was just a normal guy. "But the problem is, finding the raw materials to feed the factory."

"That might mean recycling metal and some mining," Maser said.

"Then we find a mine and secure it. We have plenty of people that need to earn their keep here," I said.

"True, we have plenty of manpower, but we need to establish a whole new system here," Maser said.

"I'll talk to the Doge," Lorenzo said.

"Please do. Explain the situation and ask if we have anyone with mining experience. Not likely, but if not, we need to find manuals and books about it. Ask if there's any metal recycling plants," I said.

"The Fiocchi factory," Lorenzo said. "Not only would it have all the factory machines we need, it would also have the knowledge. We'll find out how they get their supplies from there. If we're lucky, we might find a surviving worker."

"Excellent idea," I said.

I didn't have a better idea so his sounded pretty good.

After we adjourned the meeting, I went to my apartment and found the girls and Dan reading some books they found in a museum gift shop. Karen was reading a book about ghost stories of Venice. I'd have to remind myself to read that one when she was finished.

"What's for dinner?" Rebekah asked.

"Fish," I said.

"We had fish the night before," Karen said.

"And the night before that," Dan said.

"As soon as we take a farm back from our rude zombie neighbors we can grow stuff again," I said.

"Then do more raids!" Karen said.

"We can't. Not until we get a source of ammunition."

"How long's that going to take?" Dan asked.

"Too long."

The next day I met with Lorenzo and the others in the Doge's office. He sat back in his leather chair, content to just listen.

"Most of their production is in a factory in the city of Lecco. However, their primers are in a smaller facility in the mountains ten miles from Lecco(? Can't make sense of this sentence)," Lorenzo said.

"Fine. We'll take the main factory first. We'll need every man and woman we can get that can carry a gun," I said. "This place is so near Milan that it'll probably be crawling with dead," I said.

"We'll prepare," Lorenzo said.

"This will help our chances of survival, yes?" The Doge asked.

"I think we'll survive for a long while, but this will ensure that we can retake the mainland and retake Italy," I said. "I assume that's the goal."

The Doge nodded in approval and we began to gather our forces in St. Mark's Square for an inspection and briefing. I let Lorenzo handle all that. I hated inspections, formations, ceremonies and uniforms. He seemed to love that stuff. I made sure to take some pictures of it though. Even I had to admit that seeing so many armed and trained people ready to kill the cannibalistic dead was an inspiring sight.

They'd need a name. Right now they were just the "Voluntari," the volunteers. It did kind of have a ring to it, but we'd need something more suitably epic for what was the first organized military force in Venice's new history.

New history.

This was a new beginning for the Republic. It seemed that history had reset itself and now I was participating in the second founding of the Serene Republic. The founding of such things were usually covered in layers of propaganda and legend; something that always infuriated historians like myself. I was one of the few historians that actually got to witness such things first hand.

The original founding was done by refugees from the barbarian invasions that tore apart Rome. Eventually, Venice grew powerful and claimed her own empire. Now it would do so again.

I took more pictures.

We didn't pack many provisions. We'd raid food markets as we traveled. I packed my PSL, but this time I took my FS2000. I'd be jumping in and out of vehicles all along the way and when we got to the factory we'd be clearing rooms.

While they held a mass in St. Mark's to ask for our protection, I went to a small chapel and prayed in my own way. Karen, Rebekah, Dan and I were the only Mormons in Venice. There were a few in Rome, mostly the survivors that had held up in the LDS temple there. I'd have to get in touch with them later, but for now I prayed for my safety and more importantly, for the success of this mission. If we couldn't find a way to make more ammunition, we'd be down to bows and spears eventually.

When I was done praying, I snuck into St. Mark's to witness the solemn ceremony. The priests were decked out in their finest robes and I could see the thick clouds of incense hanging over the crowd. The place was lit by candles and lanterns that caused the gold mosaics all over the walls and ceiling to glitter and come alive, like the ancestors of Venice were watching this new history unfold. Hopefully we'd have their blessings as well.

It was an impressive sight. If there was one thing I had to say about the Catholics, it was that they had style.

After a while of the chanting which I didn't understand, I went out into the night time streets of Venice and wandered around by myself. I passed only a few people and heard very little except the water lapping against the sides of the canals.

I liked being alone, free to walk around. That was when I did my best thinking. I thought about my future and the future of this city. It was a small pocket of humanity in an ocean of undead.

Ocean.

Islands.

Zombies didn't swim or even wade. If there were survivors, they'd be out in the many islands. The Mediterranean was full of thousands of islands; each one would be a pocket of humanity. Maybe we didn't need to retake the mainland. We could form our empire on the ocean. Thousands of gardens, orchards and fields could feed us all.

I went back to my apartment where I found the kids sleeping already. Without TV or electricity to keep them awake, they actually went to bed at a decent hour. I'd have to find something more for them to do.

I sat down at my desk and wrote all my ideas down and also wrote in my journal about what I saw and thought about that day. My journal was going to be the seed of my history book I was going to write about the Uprising.

Cecilia eventually came in a little later and we snuck off to her room for some alone time.

After making out for a long, very nice while, we lay there talking.

"Will things get better?" She asked.

"It's hard to see how they'd get worse."

"But I want world to be better for children."

"It will be. We still have bacon. Besides, I think God figured that we've lost enough."

"We lost more than enough."

"It's a little late to start worrying about that now."

"Now's the perfect time to worry."

"That's what we're doing."

"But what if its end of world? Red eyes might be devils from hell."

"If they are then we'll send them right back."

We left early in the morning just as the sun came up. I hated getting up so early. Apparently Maser did as well because I found him, grumbling in the corner holding a thermos of hot coffee. I was always amazed at some people's ability to find hot coffee even in the middle of the apocalypse.

The highway didn't give us much of a problem. It seemed that the zombies figured out that there wasn't anything to eat along the main roads because we hardly saw them.

We passed through several smaller towns, all dead and crawling with zeds. We'd stop to raid a market and continue on. Most of it was canned food, but anything was better than more fish.

The closer we got to Lecco, the closer the tall, snowy mountains got. Freder explained that these mountains, more than an equal to anything in Utah, were just the foot hills of the Alps. After seeing the Alps first hand, I knew he wasn't exaggerating.

The place was beautiful; absolutely gorgeous. We passed a few resorts along the riverside and the closer we got to Lecco, the more beautiful the countryside became.

We passed a sign that said "Lecco, 5 kilometers."

The towns and resorts we passed near Lecco were full of the shambling dead and the closer we got to the town the more alert I grew in my turret. If a horde was awaiting us, I'd have the Mk-19 ready for it.

Then we came to a roadblock. More surprising was that this roadblock was manned. There were twenty people there with military type rifles and even an MG3 machine gun; complete with cans of belt linked ammo.

"This is surprising," I muttered as I crawled out of the turret and hurried over to where Lorenzo was crawling out of his LAV. Cecilia hurried up beside me and put on her "serious" face. Apparently neither of them liked having guns pointed at them. I couldn't say I was fond of it either.

Lorenzo raised one of his black eyebrows at me and together with Cecilia we walked up to the roadblock.

One of the men at the roadblock raised his rifle and told us to halt.

Lorenzo then began explaining who we were in Italian. I picked up a few words, but basically I stood there completely clueless as they carried on a very long conversation.

Finally, the two men stopped speaking and the roadblock boss turned to his companions and they began speaking quietly to each other.

"What's going on?" I asked Cecilia.

"Lecco is safe. They blocked off the city and have it under control. It turns out, Fiocci factory had a butt load of weapons and plenty ammo to kill every zombie in town. We are not taking over the factory."

Butt load? She was hanging around Karen too much.

"Please tell me there's good news," I said.

"They going to ask the mayor if we can come in and talk to him."

"Wonderful."

"No, not really."

"That was sarcasm."

A few minutes later they escorted Cecilia, Lorenzo, Maser, Freder and me inside the city and to the government building. The people stopped and looked at us as we passed by in the back of a military truck. There were a lot of them. They looked safe, but still desperate somehow and I couldn't put my finger on it. Still, I was glad to see so many survivors.

There were hundreds of them in the streets. Hundreds of living, breathing human beings that didn't want to eat me. I took pictures to remember these survivors. Each one of them had a story and each one of them had lost people.

We arrived at the mayor's office and were ushered in politely, but by armed guards. Again, the mayor was in a suit. What's with Italians and suits? It seemed that even when facing the end of the world, they would not lower their standards of style.

"Greetings gentlemen!" The mayor said with a hint of a British accent over his thick Italian one.

We all shook hands and introduced ourselves. Then I explained our situation and he seemed more than pleased to find Venice and Rome still alive.

"So, my new friends, what has brought you to Lecco?" The mayor asked.

My friends were looking at me.

What for? I wasn't the leader and I definitely didn't want to be, but since we were beginning a negotiation we had to look at least half way competent, so I spoke up.

"Honestly sir," I said. "We came here to take over this factory and get it making ammo again, but that's not possible now. However, we would like to make some kind of arrangement with you."

"Food and medicine," the mayor said. "Can you get them?"

"I'm sure we can manage something."

"You bring those and we'll talk. Consider it a gift."

"And then you'll trade with us?"

"Yes."

"Thank you, sir. There's more. We need some kind of mutual defense agreement and an open line of communication. Us, you, Assisi and Rome, we all have to stay in contact and organize our efforts."

"Understood. But I want you to keep in mind that we are in no way beneath Venice. Equals, partners and separate," the mayor said.

I had been hoping he wouldn't say that. That meant we were relaying on what was basically a foreign government for our supply of ammo. Something else had to be done. However, this was good for the short term. Still, it was better than nothing.

That was my problem. My "short term" was years, decades and generations. Down the road these surviving cities would be their own governments and with that, they'd be fighting one another. There had to be a way to unite them before they turned into squabbling city-states. That was a part of history I did not want repeated.

The mayor gave us some crates of ammo as a gesture of good will. As long as we kept the food and supplies coming, we'd continue to get our ammo.

We'd have to find another source of ammunition, a source we could control ourselves. There were dozens of smaller companies near Milan. I didn't know them, but the Venetians could find them.

I sat inside the AAV as we drove home.

"This isn't good, right?" Cecilia asked.

"No. They have too much of a hold over us," I said.

"But we can bring them food and medicine."

"Until next year when their own crops start coming in. Still, we'll have the medicine, but how long will raiding hospitals last? We need long term solutions."

"Well, our short term is fixed now. We can be happy about that, yes?"

"Of course."

She curled up beside me and wrapped her arm around mine.

SEVENTEEN

Uprising: Italy, Oct 17th

Apparently the Republic thought I needed to get around faster or stop bumming rides from everyone because they gave me a swanky speed boat that looked like something Mr. Howell from Gilligan's Island would use. It had a little Venetian flag fluttering from the rear and polished wood paneling. Cecilia and I went to Torcello and looked around. Technically we were there to see what we might need to improve our training grounds, but really I was there to do some house shopping.

The few people that lived there had moved to the neighboring island of Burano. There was safety in numbers and nobody wanted to be isolated in a zombie apocalypse. So, I had a few choices. There was a highly over priced bed and breakfast that could serve as my new home or three houses that I could choose from.

The old piazza had the two churches (was two churches side by side really necessary?) the old government building, (now a museum) and an old house. (Also a museum.)

There was no really wrong choice because the whole island was beautiful. Green fields, ancient trees, ruined houses and of course, the ancient churches. The bell tower would make a great observation post because you could see almost the whole Lagoon from there and could signal to the bell tower at St. Mark's Square.

Torcello was now my island and I'd do with it what I want. It was my home now.

"I like that house," Cecilia said, pointing to the two story house nearest the ancient town square.

"Settled. We'll take that house."

"That was quick."

"I trust your instinct."

"And yours?"

"My first impressions are almost always inaccurate."

"And your first impression of me?"

"Like I said, almost always."

The house had a small restaurant on the ground floor, but four bedrooms above. Only one bathroom though. We'd have to loot some beds and other comforts from the mainland to make it perfectly 'homey.' The previous owners had taken all their stuff with them.

"That will be my bedroom," she said pointing to one of the windows on the second floor.

"I'll take that one." Mine over looked the canal and bridge that led to the piazza. Every morning I would wake up to the view of silent Torcello.

We still had our apartment in Venice for those occasions where duty made us stay there. So I had two homes now. Not bad.

"This is a nice island. I wonder how long the Doge will let me keep it," I said.

"There's the old church there. It has some buildings attached to it. Barracks?" She asked.

"No, I'd feel wrong about using a church for barracks. Maybe a place for refugees."

She nodded.

"That church there, not the round one, but the tall long one, is one of the oldest surviving churches in Italy. It dates back to the 600's," she said.

"Let's go look."

We walked out and over to the church. It was padlocked, but I used my universal key and shot it off. Inside the church was dark with a few rays of dusty sunshine coming through the narrow windows.

I took out my flashlight and the golden mosaics flashed as they caught the light. In front of us on the other side of the church, in the large round apse, was the mosaic of the Madonna and Child staring back at us. I've seen a few mosaics in my life including the magnificent mosaics of St. Mark's, but this simple one, with the lone, tall figure of a humbly dressed Mary was perhaps the most striking.

"Think they'll let me convert this into a Mormon church?" I asked.

"I think I doubt that."

"It won't hurt to ask."

"Maybe we could use it as a convent?"

"I'm sure that there are other displaced nuns such as yourself."

"No, not like me."

"True that. No one's like you."

"And you wouldn't have it any other way, yes?"

"I wouldn't."

I'm not proud of this, but we did make out in that ancient church.

The next day we brought the AAV to Torcello as its permanent base of operations. I wanted to find more AAV's so we began to plan more raids.

Over the next few weeks we looted Mestre and the small towns nearby. We began to get secure the port of Marghera with its huge industrial complexes and we began securing all the shore line around the lagoon.

Then we raided army and naval bases and within weeks we had a small fleet of modern warships. They were light frigates, but we could only operate one of them at the moment. Once we got more knowledge and fuel, we could also get one of their destroyers up and running, but until we got a refinery working that would have to wait.

I stayed busy training our slowly growing military. A few survivors trickled in from Italy and Slovenia: mostly by boat.

The weather was getting colder and our raids also began picking up winter clothing for our people. The former tourists had come with only a few summer clothes to their name. It was easy to tell who was a native Italian. They wore scarves. Cecilia wasn't immune to this and her black ensemble was usually punctuated with a bright red scarf.

When I wasn't training the official military, I trained with my family. I ran them all through drills such as weapon malfunctions, moving from cover and working in teams. I almost always hated training in the military, but it turns out that if you can set your own pace and not have idiots yelling at you the whole time, combat training could actually be fun.

I heard the quiet motor of a small boat coming up the canal and I waved for everyone to stop their reloading drills. On a small metal boat with a tiny motor I saw Maser and the Doge himself coming up the lone, green canal of Torcello.

"What brings you here?" I asked as I tied them off near the small bridge in front of our house.

"We have a plan," the Doge said without ceremony.

"About what?"

"Long term. You said we need to think long term. We have."

I ushered them in to what used to be the restaurant. Now it was our oversized dining room. They sat down on cheap plastic chairs and Karen and Cecilia made them some hot chocolate over a wood burning stove.

"We are going to search all the islands. Rome is taking southern Italy. Assisi is taking central Italy and Fiochi is taking northern Italy. It's an…informal agreement."

"That doesn't leave us much."

"No, but it leaves us the islands and the ocean. I was thinking we go to Sicily first then perhaps the hundreds of Greek islands."

"I was thinking, we also might want to check Cugir Romania," I said.

I had been thinking of this for a while. I wanted a way to manufacture guns and lots of them. I hadn't figured out the ammunition part yet, but the guns I think we could do.

"What in blazes for?" Maser asked.

"Cugir is where Romania makes AK-47's and other guns. Fiochi may make bullets, but we could make guns. The only problem is that it's pretty far inland."

"Sounds…little difficult," Doge DeCanalli said.

"It is, but I don't know the location of any other firearms manufacturing other than Beretta and I think Fiochi's going to get that in their land deal. It's not like I can look up any other places on the internet."

The Doge nodded as he thought it over.

"There are a handful of Romanians in Venice. I can ask them best way to Cugir?" The Doge said.

"It's an idea."

"A dangerous one that will use a lot of ammo and fuel," Maser said. "But it would be nice to be able to build our own weapons."

"We're still looking into the mine and processing. In Porto Marghera, there is much industry. Make metal. Make fuel."

"Sounds like we have a lot to do," I said.

"We always have a lot to do."

June 17th

I leaned out over the rails of the frigate and looked out over the stunning, blue sea. It had taken all winter to get the fuel refinery up and going. We had to secure the refinery and the oil wells. They were still working on the coal power plant to get the lights back on in Venice. Maybe there'd be power by the time I got back. There was no telling when that would be.

The water of the Mediterranean was the clearest blue I had ever seen. The smell of salt and the sound of the ocean filled my senses. Also I had to stay on deck or I'd get seasick. I was thankful for the nice weather.

Our fleet of three frigates and two corvettes left Venice in early April for the islands on the Eastern Adriatic. There were so many and most we found were in good shape. We found lots of survivors that were happy for a semblance of government and normalcy. Venice essentially annexed all the small islands they found and established shipping lanes for our civilian fleet. We couldn't possibly reach every island so we scouted only the largest and let the network spread from there.

Corfu was next. We found the island very well off. The people were alive and zombie-free. They had plenty of food and everything else they needed, except arms. We made an alliance with them where Venice became their "protectors." By "protector" it meant Venice owned Corfu in exchange for security and supplies they couldn't get: a deal we'd made with many islands.

After Corfu our fleet went to Lefkada and then Ithaca.

I was amazed at how much life there was scattered out on the ocean. Islands were pockets of civilization and humanity. It made me a little less depressed about the end of the world. These scattered islands were all that was left. I couldn't help but think about how much we've lost.

We were on our way to Crete, one of the biggest islands in the Mediterranean. If it was alive then that would be great news indeed. It could become the breadbasket for the surviving islands that were quickly coming under the flag of Venice.

"See anything?" Cecilia said in Italian as she walked up behind me.

I looked over as she leaned against the rails beside me. She had on her black sock cap, sunglasses, her long red scarf and a Beretta on her hip.

"I see beauty and life," I said in Italian. Being fluent in Spanish helped me learn Italian rather quickly. Five months and I was speaking and understanding pretty well.

"I'd call this trip a success so far," she said.

"Without doubt. Rome and Assisi can have the mainland. We'll take the islands. Less zombies to clear out."

"More peaceful. More beautiful."

"More beaches."

"I sun burn too easy."

"You spent too much time locked away in a convent."

"No I didn't."

Then Maser came running out of one of the hatches.

"There you are! I've been looking all over for you. We spotted a ship," Maser said, nearly out of breath.

We followed him up to the bridge and I was handed a pair of binos. My good pair George gave me were in my cabin.

Out on the horizon I saw a small speck.

"What is it?" I asked.

"A cargo ship," the captain said. "They're not answering our hails."

"Dead in the water?" I asked.

"Don't use the "D" word," Cecilia said.

"Let's get a closer look. If there are zombies on board, let's clear them out and see if there's anything useful aboard. Do we need a cargo ship?"

"Not really, but we could always use it for parts," the captain said.

He was a retired captain from the Italian navy and was all business. If he smiled he only did it in the privacy of his cabin.

Our small fleet drew closer to the still and silent vessel. It was a large ship covered in rust. It was in poor shape and had clearly been abandoned. Some of the windows were broken and a crane lay toppled on the deck.

"The anchor's up," the captain said.

"And?" I asked.

"That means it's drifting. Strange that it's drifted this long without running into an island or the shore."

"Let's get a team ready to go aboard," I said.

Maser, Cecilia, and me went down to the crew quarters and assembled a team of ten. Then we launched in the small power boats and went over to the enormous cargo ship. I was packing the FS200 for room clearing. Cecilia had her ACR and Maser had a Benelli shotgun. We all wore leather clothing and fully enclosed biker helmets.

We climbed up the ladder to the deck and spread out to cover the whole area. We split into two teams. Maser led one and Cecilia and me took the other. To avoid friendly fire, our teams would leap frog the decks.

I opened a rusty door and the screech it gave off would have alerted anyone on board that we were there. I couldn't see it through her helmet, but I could tell that Cecelia was wincing.

I turned on the flashlight on my FS and led the way down the steep metal stairs, each footstep clanging like a dinner bell. Down below was total darkness. There was garbage and broken glass all over the floor.

All I could see was what the flashlight let me. There was a long hallway with open doors on all sides and every time I moved so did the shadows. My primitive instincts were telling me to run, that there was danger everywhere. I had to silence that part of my mind and focus on what was around me.

I "cut the pie", going around the corners while letting the gun lead the way. If there were zeds around they would have heard us from all the crunching broken glass. So far we hadn't heard a moan.

"Next deck," I whispered to the others.

We went down the ladder two floors. We came into a mess hall where the metal chairs had all been scattered around. There were patches of what could have been dried blood. So far, I wasn't liking the signs I was seeing. It reminded me of the book "Dune" where they'd have "worm sign" only here it was "zombie sign."

I didn't have to say anything to the others. They'd have seen it as clearly as I did.

We went through the galley area and came to a door that said something in what looked like Ukrainian or Bulgarian.

"What's that?" I asked.

"Turkish," one of the men said.

"A Turkish cargo ship then."

We opened the door, I cleared the door way and walked out onto a narrow cat walk. In front of me was a massive sea of blackness. I shined my flashlight in front of me and could barely make out the far wall. This had to be the cargo hold.

I flashed my light down to get a look at the cargo.

All I saw were the unmoving heads of hundreds of standing corpses. I instantly turned my flashlight off. I heard a faint gasp from Cecelia.

Then all at once the moaning began. It was their desperately hungry moan that I now recognized all too well.

"We need to leave now," I said.

Than a voice came from all directions at once.

"Don't leave so soon my friends," the laughing male voice said.

"What's going on here?" I asked, hoping that the red eye's arrogance would make him slip.

"You'll find out soon enough," it said and nothing more.

Crap. That meant he wasn't going to monologue.

"Move!" I shouted and we all took off running back the way we had came. The moans suddenly got louder as they let out their aggressive hunting moans simultaneously. There must have been a few thousand in that cargo hold.

"Team Venture, do you read me?" I called out on the walkie talkie.

"Team Monarch, go for Venture," Maser said.

"Get out of there now! The entire cargo hold is full of zombies controlled by a red eye!"

"Crap!"

We met them up on the deck, but we also met a few zombies coming out of other hatches.

"We need intel. Shoot them and grab their wallets," I said.

"What?" Maser asked.

"Do it!"

Our teams popped the dozen or so zombies that had made it out first. A few went in and grabbed the wallets while the rest covered them.

I was half way down the ladder when the doors burst open and hundreds of undead ran out onto the deck.

A zombie looked down at me and one of my team mates shot it in the head. If fell forward and down, barely missing me and the boat below.

"That would have been a stupid way to die, crushed by dead falling zombie," I said.

I was the last one in and as soon as my butt hit the seat, we took off.

"Captain Andrico, the ship's a transport for a red eye and thousands of zombies. Blow it out of the water!" I called out over our radio.

"Understood."

The turret of the frigate turned and took aim. On land a 155mm was a really big gun. On a navel ship it was a pop gun. Still, it was enough to take out a civilian cargo ship with ease.

The heavy cannon fired and struck the cargo ship just at the water line. It fired again blowing another huge hole in the side. A third round hit the engine and caused a giant plume of black, inky smoke to rise up. Within minutes the enormous ship was sinking with all dead hands aboard.

"What do the wallets tell us?" I asked once we were back aboard our ship.

"This one's from Istanbul," a soldier said.

"So is this one," Cecelia said.

"And this one," Maser said.

"Istanbul, eh? So we got a red eye recruiting in Istanbul?"

"I'd bet more than one. That's a huge city," the captain said.

"They seem to be attracted to populated areas. More zombies to posses I suppose. But what were they doing with a cargo ship? Where were they going?" I asked.

No one said anything for a few moments, but then the captain spoke up.

"They were heading to the islands. They must know just as we do that there are survivors out there."

"That's what I was afraid of."

EIGHTEEN

June 18th

Our fleet was heading to Crete. We looked out for more of the plague ships and warned all islands we had contact with.

I tried to recall what I knew of Crete. I knew it had changed hands from Greeks, Romans, Byzantines, Ottomans, Venetians and pirates. Other than that, I knew very little. I didn't even know what it would look like.

"Where are we going?" Cecilia asked as she sat on the end of my bunk. She was reading and I was too. We had made sure to bring plenty of books. I was trying to read a history book about the city of Genoa in Italian, but some of the words I couldn't make out and had to keep asking Cecilia for help.

"We're going to a city on Crete called Chania. It's a full sized city with an airport so if the infection got to Crete, it would strike there first."

"You think they're alive?"

"Hard to say. Unlike most of these islands, Crete's a pretty big place with lots of tourists coming and going."

There was a knock at the door.

"Come in," I called out

Lorenzo came in and nodded, it was their informal version of a salute.

"What's up?" I asked.

"We just got a message from Venice. They're sending a resupply ship that will meet us at Crete."

"Excellent. Anything else?" I didn't think he'd come down here just to tell me that.

"They say they're bringing something special for you."

"Something special? Like what?"

"I don't know. The Doge wanted to keep it a surprise."

"I had no idea he had a sense of humor."

After Lorenzo left Cecilia turned back toward me.

"A surprise? Curious."

"Very curious. I have no idea what it could possibly be."

"I hope it's a good surprise. I don't like bad surprises."

"I couldn't take another bad surprise."

We read, talked and discussed the future of Venice and the world as we sailed to Crete. There was no communication with Crete so none of us had any idea what to expect. If we had fuel to spare we would have flown a plane over to get a general idea, but Venice to Crete was a long flight. We just had to plan for the worst and hope we were wrong.

The next day we heard them calling out for land. Me and Cecilia hurried up to the deck to get a look. Even through binos the land just looked like a small strip of dark on the horizon. It was another hour before it started to actually resemble land and the closer we got, the larger the land got until it filled our view.

The port city of Chania was there with the white capped mountains behind it. It had old, brightly colored houses that had that rustic charm, sort of like the island of Burano back in Venice.

The city was intact, but when we spotted boats sailing around the harbor, the crew let out a cheer. The people were alive there.

Then I noticed the large, rusty cargo ship with Turkish markings. The people in the boats were obviously humans and were waving at us. I didn't know what to make of it.

Many of the small boats came out to greet us and our large frigate slowed down as it came closer to the civilians.

The crew shouted down to the natives. It was all in Greek so I didn't understand a word of it.

"They're all alive and well here. They say it's the healthiest island in the world," Lorenzo translated for us.

"Ask them about the cargo ship," I said.

Lorenzo turned back to an old man with a white beard, dressed all in black and in a small sailing boat. Lorenzo asked and the old man prattled off a long story of some kind complete with confusing hand gestures.

"What did he say?" I asked.

"He said that yeah, the cargo ship full of zombies came, but when they saw it they didn't trust it and had all their armed men ready. He says they just shot them all, cleaned the place out and hadn't thought about it since. That was four days ago."

"Shot them all? Do they have a military here?"

"A few, sure, but most locals own guns," Lorenzo said.

"What? In Europe?"

"Crete is special. It's against Greek law to own a gun, but they allow Crete to because it's their tradition. They say there's at least one gun in every household."

"I think I like Crete."

Our fleet sailed into the harbor and we took smaller boats over to the shore. The crowds greeted us with cheering and music. Everyone was wearing black and many of the men wore knee high riding boots of some kind. Strange people.

"Why are they all wearing black? I know in Rome they did because it was stylish, but why here?" I asked.

"They wear black as a sign of mourning. I guess everyone has a cause to mourn," Cecilia said.

"Ain't that the truth."

I followed the captain and Lorenzo as we were led to some old government building where a bunch of important looking men and women began talking. I soon became bored because I didn't understand any of it. Neither did Cecilia so we stayed in the back and out of the way.

We were standing in the large lobby of the building and I had my AK slung from its single point sling. Cecilia had her SVD slung over her shoulder as she looked around, appearing to be as bored and confused as I felt.

"Don't say it, Zach," Cecilia said.

"Say what?"

"You know. You say it, no kiss kiss tonight."

I debated for a solid five minutes.

"It's all Greek to me," I said.

She moaned.

"You really had to do it, didn't you?"

"I couldn't help it. It's my nature."

"I hope you like a lonely night."

An hour later Lorenzo came over to explain. They were going to throw us a welcome celebration that night.

"So, it's all good news, yes?" Cecilia asked.

"Not exactly. They lost contact with Rhodes. They were using the internet, but they haven't responded in a week."

"Crap," I said.

"Crap, yes, but I hope its not deep crap," Lorenzo said.

"Either way, we should head there next," I said.

"I think so too," Cecilia said.

"We'll stay here two days to establish our trade agreement and maybe take the place over. Then we're off to Rhodes," Lorenzo said.

"We have enough flags?" I asked.

"If we limit it to one per island," he said.

They threw the party outside in the streets. They set up tables for us and food, loud, obnoxious music and folk dances for us.

Me and Cecilia sat off to the side and were content to watch the festivities. There were plenty of vacant hotels they'd allow us to spend the night in.

We ate to bursting and then me and Cecilia decided to take a little walk around the old city.

It seemed that no matter where we went, the sound of music was as strong as ever. Neither of us spoke. We just walked and held hands as we did.

Eventually, we found ourselves in front of our hotel.

"It was a lovely night," she said. "We don't get many lovely nights."

"Every day we're alive is a lovely night."

"True, but not so festive."

"Or loud. But it's late," I said.

"Not so late. Would you like to come up to my room for a drink?" She said, barely containing a smile.

"I don't drink."

"That's not what I meant."

"I think I would love a drink."

We went up to her room and she sat down on the couch and pulled me down on top of her. We made out to the distant sounds of obnoxious, but happy music. She was usually very "spirited", but this time she seemed somehow more focused and more intense.

I drew her in tight and she pressed herself even tighter against me. It was as if the microscopic space between us was still too much.

She tore off her hat and glasses and slipped off her boots. I unslung my AK and tossed it on the chair beside the couch. Next she undid her pistol belt and tossed it to the floor. We went on for a good long time, enjoying the feel of each other's company.

We still weren't married though and neither of us was willing to go too far.

She fell asleep in my arms.

The next day our leaders and theirs talked on and on about what to do. They liked the idea of a strong government that could bring some order back to the Mediterranean, but they seemed to really enjoy their independence.

An unsaid threat of force wasn't going to work here. Everyone here had a gun. It was like if rural Utah was suddenly transplanted into the ocean. It looked like Crete was going to be an independent ally. Shame. We'll have to try Malta and Sicily eventually. Cyprus would be good to add to Venice's growing domain.

It was good to see that almost the entire island of Crete was alive. They had had a few outbreaks of zombies during the first week, but their firearm bearing populace had dealt with the issue very swiftly.

I wondered what surprises were waiting for us on Rhodes and I also wondered what surprise was coming for me on the resupply ship that would be here tomorrow.

I hated surprises. I'd rather just know and be done with it.

June 20th

I watched the small cargo ship from Venice pull into the harbor. A small corvette escorted it. The corvette would stay with our fleet and the merchant ship would begin the business of trade.

"So, what do you think your surprise is?" Cecilia asked for the hundredth time.

"I don't know. I can't guess. Stop asking."

"Maybe a new car? New tank? Maybe the Doge sent a BMW motorcycle! That would be cool. I hope he sent me one. Maybe I can get the Vatican to send me one. You know, they are still using my picture as propaganda."

"The picture I took? I know."

"I look tough in that picture."

"It's not about being tough," I said as I took a drink from one of the last plastic bottled Coke's on Crete.

"What's it about then?"

"About skill and determination."

She looked up and scrunched her mouth. That was her "concentrating" look.

I had on my best black shirt to match my black tac-vest. I looked down and noticed that the cuffs of my shirt were starting to fray.

The remains of the old world were already fraying at the edges. Eventually, what remained would wear out and we'd be left with nothing, but what we could make ourselves.

Buildings would crumble. Sky scrappers would collapse. Nuclear power plants would burn and records would be lost. Some technology would be lost. Some of it would be small things like mint dental floss. Other things would be more significant. Not everything was going back to how it was. We'd be lucky if we maintained a semblance of what life was like before the Uprising.

Once the cargo ship had docked I went over to meet the captain. He was a Venetian, but many of the men with him were Romanians we had picked up on the way to Cugir.

"Captain Canova, how was your trip?" I asked.

"Calm seas. Couldn't ask for better," the large eyed, thin man said.

"I hear you brought something for me."

"I did."

"Well? What is it?"

He looked around and then pointed toward a group of people. I looked over, but didn't see anything out of the ordinary. I saw Italian and Romanian sailors and some of my people talking and sharing gossip.

Then I saw a small group standing off to the side. I couldn't see their faces, but something looked awfully familiar about them.

I made my way through the crowd of sailors that were eager to get onto dry land and mingle with the local ladies.

Then I saw who they were. Standing there by the railing, looking out over the city were my cousin and her family. Kevin was there with a shouldered AR-10 and Sarah had a light M4. Their three kids were pointing and laughing at something.

"What in the world are you guys doing here?" I asked.

They turned at my voice and quickly gave me large hugs. The kids hugged me around the waist and Lexi shouted "Zachy!" Brian and Christopher began arguing about something and ran around in circles.

"It was too cold in Vernal. We wanted someplace a little warmer in the winter," Kevin said.

"But…how did you even get here?"

"There was a plane going over to England and we hopped on board. Then we took a flight that was going to Venice," Sarah said.

"A flight to Venice?" I asked.

"Yeah, America and Italy are trading stuff now. Where you been bro?" Kevin asked.

"On this boat."

"We didn't get to see much of Venice, but it's beautiful," Sarah said.

"Oh, we brought others with us," Kevin said. He pointed off behind me and I turned to look. Karen and Rebekah were standing by a doorway, each one holding M4's.

"I thought I told you to stay home," I said. I wasn't upset. In fact, my joy at seeing them cancelled out any annoyance. I hurried over and wrapped my arms around them.

"Where's Dan?" I asked.

"He's still downstairs in his cabin," Karen said.

"Probably puking into a bucket. He didn't take to the ocean very well," Rebekah said.

"We came to help out. It's also really boring in Venice without you. I don't speak Italian," Karen said.

"I should be upset that you disobeyed, but I'm glad you're here."

"I'll go get Dan," Rebekah said.

"When do I get a gun?" Seven year old Brian asked.

"When you're older," Kevin said.

"How old?"

"Eighty."

"You piss me off sometimes."

"We can still be friends, right B?" Kevin asked.

"Sure."

I had to keep myself from laughing.

I took my group down to the shore and to a restaurant that was being used to feed the islands guests.

We sat down for some of the local food (which was delicious) and Fish and canned food for free. That alone made the meal worth it. Dan, who was looking rather green, declined to eat anything.

As we sat I asked about how things were in Vernal. Apparently, things were going great. They were establishing control of more scattered towns and finding more survivors. They now had all of Utah, most of Idaho, Nevada, Colorado, Wyoming and had treaties with the Indian Nations in the Dakotas, Kansas and had a few outposts in key locations. Not bad at all.

I noticed that Sarah's belt was covered in medic bags and pouches. A small red cross was sown on her jacket.

"You're a medic now?" I asked.

"They had enough wimps that wanted to remain civilian doctors, so I was volunteered," Sarah said.

"They had me fixing roads. None of those morons knew what to do. I had to show them how to do everything. No wonder so many roads in Vernal were nothing but potholes," Kevin said.

"That sounds about right."

"I did get to wear one of those badass cowboy hard hats though. Got a photo of it."

Kevin took out his cell phone and showed me the picture.

"Why even bother carrying cell phones around?" I asked.

"Take pictures, GPS, Angry Birds," Sarah said.

"Can't survive the apocalypse without angry birds, now can we?"

"I can, they can't," Sarah said, pointing her thumb at her kids who had already grown tired of eating and were playing tag…or some variation of it in the street.

"This place is great," Rebekah said.

She had a fashionable pink jacket with a fur lined hood. Where was Gundoc? He could have painted her M4 pink. I wondered where that Pink Sterling he made was now.

Karen, was wearing a "H.I.M." T-shirt and black PT coat with a hood. Her black hair hung down over her eyes and somehow she had managed to find black lipstick. She would be very sad when the world's supply of black makeup ran out.

Unless she found a way to make more.

"How you doing, Karen?" I asked.

She looked up from her thoughts.

"What? Oh, I'm fine."

"Just thinking?"

"Yeah."

"About what?"

"About all of this. The future. I don't want the new world to be like the old one."

"In what way?"

"The violence for selfish, greedy reasons. The useless wars, the corruption and the poverty."

"That's the dark side of human nature, honey. I don't know if we can eliminate that."

"We can try. Maybe we can lessen it a little? Even a little would be worth trying for."

"Very true. You have a way to do all that?"

She sighed.

"No."

"Keep thinking. Great ideas seldom come easily."

"Or at all."

"If you quit then you'll never find it. Have you been practicing?" I asked, pointing to her M4.

"Yes. We had Torcello all to ourselves. We set out old cans like in the cowboy movies."

"Very good."

"Then we practiced moving as a group of three. I think we got it down pretty good. I'm still faster than Rebekah with the reloads."

"Have you practiced with the irons? Don't get too used to those red dots. Batteries run down and they can be broken."

"I know. Yes, we practiced with irons as well."

"Excellent. For that you get a free island vacation."

She smiled a black smile and leaned her head on my shoulder. Kevin took a picture of it. Cecilia was smiling and Karen quickly sat up, probably feeling embarrassed.

That night we had the hotel all to ourselves. Sarah and Kevin went off to explore the city and Karen and Rebekah babysat their kids. Cecelia loved being with them all. Her and Rebekah got along especially well. Maybe because Rebekah was the more spiritual of them all. Her and Cecilia seemed to have that love of talking about spiritual things that I just lacked. Rebekah had a small military edition of the scriptures in one of her vest pouches. I had done the same thing during my deployments to Iraq. When it was quiet I'd pull out my Book of Mormon or Bible and read. I usually did it only when I was alone. Not because I was ashamed, but because I hated looking like some ostentatious, false piety, kind of pretend Christian.

I didn't really enjoy going to church or talking about my own spirituality. To me those things were much more private and internalized. I kept them inside where I could examine it all in seclusion.

Karen seemed the same way. She was the quietest of them all and I think that she, like me, tended to keep everything bottled up inside her.

In the morning we only had a few hours to show them all the beauties of Crete before we had to board and sail away for Rhodes.

I had little hope that Rhodes would be a vacation. I didn't imagine cheering crowds of people that were glad to see us. Instead I imagined a horde of zombies whose collective moaning created a storm of horrible sound.

Dan stayed in his cabin with Rebekah. She tried to distract him from his sea sickness by reading "The Count of Monte Cristo", but it wasn't working. I kept telling him to come out on deck, but he was afraid of falling into the ocean. Karen mostly sketched horror comics in her sketch pad and I'd offer her advice or show her a few tips on drawing.

In private, me and Cecilia made the best of it. Our little make out sessions usually ended in long conversations about old memories and hopeful futures. It didn't matter what we were talking about because we were together and that was all I required, her love, warmth and kindness.

NINETEEN

June 23rd

Our ship sailed up the coast of Rhodes to the main harbor and city on the northern end. It was a bright sunny day and the island looked like a Mediterranean dream vacation. As we came within sight of the city of Rhodes, I saw towering hotels and white beaches. I saw a lighthouse on an old fortress. The town its self had a castle right in the middle of it. I had done my homework and knew that the castle was the former headquarters of the Knights Hospitallers. It had been the palace of their Grand Master.

Two fortresses. That was comforting because I didn't see any ships sailing in the harbor or anyone waving at us from shore.

When we came close enough we saw a Turkish cargo ship that had run into the docks. Smashed boats and splintered wood were sandwiched between its bow and the land.. It looked abandoned and no one was in sight.

Everyone in our fleet was on guard now and the boats were being readied. We assembled into our teams. Cecilia, Kevin, Sarah, Karen and Elizabeth formed a new team and Maser and Lorenzo led their own teams.

We had trained all winter and I was confident that my men would do what they had to do. I didn't have to worry about them. Karen and Elizabeth needed experience. Training could only go so far. I knew Kevin and Sarah had fought before and I didn't have to worry about them either.

Karen and Elizabeth were young, but people had to grow up fast lately. It was time they earned their stripes. At least we had boats to retreat to and I'd be right there looking out for them.

"Are you ready?" I asked Karen and Elizabeth.

"Yeah," Elizabeth said.

Karen just nodded.

Then a flare shot up into the sky. It was coming from the old fortress at the harbor. All heads looked that way. Through binos we could see someone up on the ancient battlements waving a flag.

"Change of destination," Maser said from somewhere off to my right.

We climbed down into our boats and made our way to the fortress. Some boats were inflatable, others were whatever we had on hand at the time and brought with us from Venice. Some of the teams went to the harbor of the city, but we went to the fortress. There were about a dozen or so zombies at the base of the fortress, but one of them was a red eye. The zombies were standing there, silently and unmoving as we came ashore.

The red eye was standing behind his undead bodyguard. He was a man in a Greek military uniform.

"What brings you Italians here? Expanding your empire? My, how humans are predictable. And we have a few Americans as well. Butting your noses into others business as usual."

"An anti-American demon. I know America has to be good if a bastard like you hates it," I said.

"Now, now Zach. We should be friends! After all…"

I didn't let the possessed corpse finish talking. I hated when they spoke. I didn't like talking to normal people at the best of times.

I snapped up my AK and fired at him. My shots hit a zombie in front of him, but at least two of my bullets struck him. One of them blew his ear off. He roared and suddenly his zombies burst toward us like Olympic sprinters.

Our three teams opened fired. All our bullets riddled the running corpses' heads and dropped them on the spot.

The red eye waved his hand and I was thrown back into the water. It felt like a huge gust of wind that smelt of sulfur.

By the time I crawled back onto shore the red eye's head had been emptied by several bullets.

Cecilia rushed to help me up.

"You okay?" She asked.

"Yeah, just my pride was hurt."

"Hey, you took a hit from a demon like a champ, bro. Nothing to be ashamed about," Kevin said, trying to suppress a laugh.

"Yeah, but still. I wanted to be the one to shoot him. Who did?"

"I did," Elizabeth said, holding up her M4 with the EOTech halo sight.

"Good job."

"I shot it in the nuts," Kevin said.

"Just because you think with them doesn't mean they do," Sarah said.

"Hey, if I just got my nuts blown off, I'd let you finish me off. I think it worked," Kevin said.

We scanned the area for any more signs of threat, but didn't see anything. Then we approached the doors of the fortress. Remains of tourist signs were scattered around and broken, probably from the zombie onslaught.

We knocked with "shave and a haircut" and the doors opened. Inside were about a hundred or so civilians and I only saw four or five guns.

"Anybody speak Italian or English?" I called out in Italian.

"You speak Italian?" Kevin asked.

"I've been here several months," I said.

One of the men stepped forward. He was a short, fat man with a bushy mustache and a balding head.

"I speak English," he said.

"What's the situation here?" I asked.

"That damned boat came ashore and the next thing we knew, we had zombies everywhere. They were running through the streets, killing everyone! There are more survivors in the Grand Master's Palace." He pointed up to the castle in the middle of the city.

"How do you know?" I asked.

"We signal with mirrors every hour."

I looked out to the city and the castle. I was relieved that there were more people left alive, but from the looks of things it had been very bad.

"And the rest of the island?" I asked.

"I don't know," the man said. "Yesterday most of the zombies left. I think they attacking the rest of the towns."

I turned back to my team.

"Zombies don't travel fast. We can catch up and take them out or warn the towns," I said.

"We could take some cars and warn the towns in their path and have those towns warn other towns," Karen said.

"Sounds like a plan," Cecilia said.

"Alright, let's go find some rides."

We hurried into the city and began looking for cars with gas or keys. A rental car place had cars with keys and we found a few remaining tanks of gas.

I rode in one of those small, crappy, European cars with Cecilia, Karen and Elizabeth. Kevin and Sarah rode on a motorcycle they found. We couldn't find enough cars for everyone. Mostly it was a gas issue. There simply wasn't any.

I called up on the radio and told Maser our situation. We had the soldiers without transportation go back to the boats and they'd meet us further down on the island. We had to find the hordes first and then figure out the best place to stop them.

But first we had to warn the towns.

We sped down the small, winding island highway, looking for signs of the undead. We had a tourist map and we split up to cover more towns.

Kevin and Sarah followed our car down the road. My eyes kept looking to the red needle hovering uncomfortably close to empty.

"Up there!" Cecilia said.

Down the road I saw what looked like an enormous crowd of people marching in the road. I slowed down and handed my binos over to Cecilia. She looked through them for a few moments.

"Zeds. A lot of them. Organized. Marching in step," Cecilia said.

I quickly called up the captain and reported our situation.

"We need to get around them and tell the town," Karen said.

"We can't plow through them," I said.

I really wished we had our Centauros right then. It turns out that there are few problems that rolling a tank over it wouldn't fix.

"What do we do?" Elisabeth asked.

Sarah and Kevin pulled up next to us and I told them our situation.

"Too bad we don't have dirt bikes. Then we could just go around them," Kevin said.

"Going on foot wouldn't give us enough time to warm them," Cecilia said.

"I'm not going anywhere on foot unless I have to," I said.

I hate marching and hate is a word I don't use lightly.

"We can't take this car into the dirt?" Elizabeth asked.

"This car would get stuck really fast. The slope to our left is too steep and on our right is a rocky field. One of those rocks would wreck this car in a second," I said.

"We should invest in horses," Kevin said.

"Not an option at the moment," I said.

"We're not far from the shore, right?" Karen asked.

"Correct," I said.

"Why don't we just have our ships blow them up?" Karen asked.

The car fell silent.

"What?" Karen asked.

"That's brilliant. I was in the artillery. Why didn't I think of that? Kevin, you have your GPS, right?"

"Sure do."

"Get the coordinates and I'll send them to the captain."

Once we had a good firing solution I told the captain where to aim that "puny" 155mm cannon of his.

Ten minutes later the first shell struck. The explosion was on the front edge of the zombie formation, but it tore a huge hole in their ranks.

"Too far south. Just a bit to the north," I said over the radio.

The next shell landed a few moments later right in the middle of the zeds. If I thought a 105mm was impressive. The 155mm was shockingly so. I had worked with towed 155mm's, but I never really got to see what happened on the receiving end of one. I recalled the countless hours of going over the crew drills of ramming the shell up into the breech and pulling the lanyard. Sometimes it was fun. If I had gotten to see more of its effectiveness, I might have been more motivated about it.

Three seconds later another shell landed and tore apart even more. The cannon on the ship was fairly rapid fire and as shell after shell landed within seconds of each other the whole road was turned into a lunar landscape. Even the zeds that had tried to run were blown up by the scattered shells.

"Damn me if that isn't a sight to see," Kevin said.

"Boom! Take that suckers!" Sarah yelled out in a victory song.

"That was pretty cool," Karen said.

"Artillery; Queen of Battle," I said, proud to have been a Red Leg at one time. True, it was the Navy that had done it, but I would ignore that.

Now that the road was devastated, we had some difficulty getting through with the crappy, European joke of a car. But somehow we managed to get through and made it to the next small town.

The town only had a few roads going through it with a "main street" that seemed to be ubiquitous for all such rural villages. They had heard the artillery barrage and had three men with shotguns out at a checkpoint.

I let Cecilia talk to the town's people while I got on the radio with the captain. The other squads had found other hordes. However, we didn't find all the hordes. There were more zeds out there and there would be a lot of them. Not only would there be the few thousand from the cargo ship, but there would be the murdered people from Rhodes. We had to take out as many as we could with the naval guns in order to have any kind of chance and a stand up fight would be out of the question.

"What's the plan?" Maser asked over the radio.

What made people think I ever had some kind of plan? I made stuff up as I went along. I never made plans for anything.

"Plans? Our plan is what it always is. We kill them all," I said.

"I like that plan. Simper Fi," Maser said.

"We use the big guns to wipe out the hordes we can find. Evacuate the nearby villages and keep searching for the rest of the zeds," I said.

"Right."

I got out of the car and walked over to where Cecilia was talking to the town leaders. I didn't know what term would be good anymore. Mayor seemed too inadequate now. Chieftain was probably closer to the truth even if most people hadn't realized it yet.

"They want to help," Cecilia said in English.

"How?" I asked.

"They know the roads and paths. They can find the zeds for us."

"Excellent. Tell them we'd be glad to have any assistance."

"Already did."

"Awesome."

Cecilia walked back over to the chieftain and resumed their conversation. I couldn't help but watch her. She was beautiful, but not just in the looks department, but for who she was.

Sarah took out her big, fancy digital camera and began taking pictures of the town and countryside. She was a much better photographer than I ever was.

"Hey, Sarah?"

"What?"

"Want to be Venice's official photographer?"

"Sure."

"Cool. You're on my historian team now."

"Okay."

"So, it's like official now."

"Do I get any perks?"

"You're pictures will be the few documents that tell the story of the end of the world."

"That's all?"

"You get to follow me around and blow stuff up."

"Cool."

Then Kevin walked over with his hands in the air with a "WTF" look on his face.

"What about me?" Kevin asked.

He was wearing his "Heavy Metal Shop" black hoodie.

"You're our combat engineer."

"What does that mean?"

"It means you get to go around with me around and blow stuff up and once in a while build a road or bridge."

"I guess I got nothing better to do."

"Also, we need to find more black hoodies. I want that as our uniform."

"Kick ass," he said with a fist pump.

"Maybe we'll raid Milan for some clothes."

"I could use a new Gucci purse," Sarah said.

"You don't need a new purse, Mom. What are you going to put in it? Credit cards? Cell phone?" Lexi asked. She rolled her eyes as hard as she could.

"Full leather armor and hoods? We need more helmets and a cool symbol," Karen said.

"A phoenix! We're rising from the ashes of a dead world!" Elizabeth said.

"Too girly," Karen said. "We need like a skull with crossed guns and demon horns."

"I like that idea," Kevin said.

"We'll work on that later," I said.

I checked my AK and magazines. All was in its right place. I checked to make sure I had extra batteries for my red dot sight and then checked the water levels in my canteen. I know the camel backs are more stylish, but they always heat up my back too much. I liked canteens better. Did that make me "old school?"

I could really use a Dew right now.

TWENTY

June 24th

I lay prone on top of the hill looking out over the narrow valley that was crawling with the dead. The small town, no more than a few houses, had been evacuated. It was a shame that the people living there had to surrender their homes, but they'd find new ones back in Rhodes.

However, it was necessary. We had looked for a place where the hordes would be bottlenecked the most and it happened to be right here at this town. We used guys on horses to lure the other hordes closer so now instead of several armies of a few thousand, we had a mass that seemed to fill the valley. They were funneling in and filling the place up. The zombies would enter the buildings and search for any sign of life.

The red eye was easy enough to find. He was right in the middle being carried on a make shift palanquin. Arrogant and lazy: just how I liked them.

"When are you going to give the signal?" Cecilia whispered beside me.

"When we got them all inside the valley."

"But what if they start to leave?"

"The locals have that covered."

"How?"

"They're going to set the exit, that narrow canyon over there, on fire."

"Very nice."

"I thought so."

She took my binos and looked around.

"He's a lazy guy," Cecilia said.

Karen crawled up to us from down the hill where the others were gathered.

"Maser wants to know when you're ready," Karen said.

"I'm ready when the zeds are ready. Give them time to assemble."

Karen looked too young to have to be fighting. It didn't seem right, but was it unavoidable? I could have prevented her if I had tried. Why hadn't I?

She needed to learn how to fight because the world was a much more dangerous place. But is she really in more danger now? Before she had been alone and had fallen prey to wicked men. Now she had people to support her and help her. A zombie horde was much less a threat than one evil man.

I watched Karen's cold blue eyes stare out at the zombie horde. What was she thinking? Did she see a threat or an opportunity?

"What are you thinking?" I asked.

"Nothing."

"Karen…"

"Those were all people once," she said almost in a whisper. "Every single one of them was a real person. I wonder if one of them was kind and helped people. I wonder if one of them was going to be the next Einstein."

"Maybe. But their souls are long gone now. They're just empty vessels being controlled by what's left of their infected brain."

"I'm not questioning that they have to be destroyed, I'm just regretting that it's necessary."

"Me too. One death is a tragedy, but a million is a statistic. I don't ever want to think like that. One of those things out there had a life before it and maybe had someone love them like I love you."

Her cold eyes turned back toward me. Her face was unreadable; a mask of calmness.

"Do you mean that?"

"Absolutely. That's not a word I use lightly."

The hint of a smile bent the corner of her lips.

"Thanks, Dad."

It was another ten minutes before the vast horde was fully inside the valley and heading toward the southern exit.

"Fire," I called down to Maser.

Maser then called up on the radio and ordered the bombardment to begin. Less than a minute later the shells began to rain down on the valley. All the ships we had, that could, were firing everything they had. I even heard the shrieking sound of a missile coming in. Missiles would be harder to replace than artillery shells.

The valley erupted into smoke, fire and flying debris. We all stayed down, but couldn't tear our eyes off of the destruction. We weren't cool guys from movies who always turned their backs to explosions. There was something primitive in our desire to watch. Even the local guides came up the hill to stare out over the scene of carnage.

However, artillery couldn't win battles alone and there was a certain point where it became impractical and expensive to continue the bombardment.

Once the horde had been shredded I ordered the bombardment to halt.

"Get ready everyone!" I called out to all our men.

I racked the charging handle of my AK and waited for the explosions to stop.

Once things fell silent I yelled and everyone yelled with me. We rose up and charged into the valley by squads, each with an area of fire to cover. We made sure to stay in a long line to avoid friendly fire and cover as much distance as possible.

Against humans this Civil War style formation wouldn't have flown at all. But against the zeds it worked great.

We walked forward slowly in order to keep our ling together over the uneven terrain of the hill. Going down hill always made you want to go faster, but our men were disciplined and trained enough to know what to do.

The few surviving zeds charged at us in feral, animalistic charges. Apparently, their zombie lord (I still liked that name better) had been blown up because there was no hint of control left. They were just scattered pockets of zombies that we shot to pieces.

I watched Karen and Elizabeth. They kept their carbines up to their shoulders, fingers off the triggers unless they were firing and were careful with their shots.

Elizabeth had a fashionable Italian scarf around her neck and her hair in two long braids. Karen's only adornments were her piercings and makeup. Her hair was cut in a short bob that was partially dyed blue. I had no idea where she had gotten the dye from.

Then I watched as Elizabeth stopped and began to smash in the head of a zombie with her boot heal. I watched the look of anger and rage on her face. No one else seemed to notice or care. Such things were common now.

Zombies had killed Elizabeth's family except for Dan. She hadn't forgiven them and never would.

I was no psychologist, but my guess was that the remaining human population could all use a lot of therapy.

When the valley was cleared we assembled in what used to be the center of town. The buildings were smoking piles of debris now.

"That went well," Cecilia said.

"Not bad at all," Maser said, slinging his M-14 over his shoulder. I don't know what he had traded with the Fiocci guys for it, but he had to have his beloved M-14.

"But there might be more of those dead ships out there," Elizabeth said.

"We need to find them or warn the other islands," Cecilia said.

"They seem to be coming from Istanbul," I said while reloading my magazines.

"What? You want to go there? One of the largest cities around that's covered in undead? Too dangerous," Maser said.

"There are obviously red eyes there and they're not content to just sit there like princes. They're looking to expand and unless we take them out we'll have an undead rival kingdom on our hands," I said.

"Millions of zombies. A few hundred rounds of ammo for each person. Do the math," Maser said.

"True, we need help. We'll have to get Milan, Rome, Assisi and whoever else we can get. Also, we'll need explosives and lots of incendiaries," I said.

"It's still impossible," he said.

"Then we just have to take out the red eyes," I said.

"Can't we get your air force buddies to come and nuke the place?" Cecilia asked.

"They're all the way in Utah and England. I doubt that they'd have the fuel to spare. Also, it wasn't a nuke, it was a MOAB. We don't have any of those either," I said.

"Well, running in with guns blazing isn't the answer either," Maser said.

"Can't we burn the city down? Start a fire and make it spread?" Karen asked.

That wasn't a bad idea, but where would we get napalm? I remembered something from 'Fight Club' about how to make napalm.

"Maybe, but I don't know how to make it spread fast enough. It's not like the city's made completely out of wood."

"Napalm. We can scrounge up enough gas to get some bombers in the air, right?" Maser said.

"I though you were against the idea," I said.

"I am, but if we can get a few napalm bombs or whatever in the right place, we can at least take out a good section of the city."

"The Aviano airbase is near Milan…sort of. I know they've secured it, but they haven't really bothered with the airplanes," Lorenzo said.

"Alright, but remember, an airstrike is going to be a scalpel. When you have a beast as large as Istanbul, there's no way even a dozen airstrikes are going to put a dent in it," Maser said.

"We need more people. Like you said, Maser, simple mathematics," I said.

"I'm sure the Greeks wouldn't mind taking back Constantinople," Cecilia said.

I thought about that. Maybe that could be a motivational thing for the Greek islanders; taking back their homeland. I'd have to work on that later.

We spent the rest of the day searching the hills for anymore zeds, but at nightfall we drove back to the city.

We drove back to the city and to the Grand Master's Palace, the castle that had once been the home of the Knights Hospitallers. From here they had once defended against a massive Turkish invasion though I couldn't recall the story from my head.

We pulled up to the main gate and walked into the imposing courtyard. The captain and a few officials from Venice were already there talking to the civilian leaders. I had no idea what position these people were in. Were they the same leaders that had been in power before the Uprising or did they rise up afterwards? Authority was a fairly vague term at the moment.

While the leaders talked and talked I sat down and began sorting through all my gear and taking inventory. The others sat by me in a semi circle. Some began reloading magazines and others were cleaning their guns.

"Too bad I don't speak Greek. I'd like to hear what they're saying," Cecilia said.

"I think our captain's trying to convince Rhodes that they need to join us," Maser said.

"Even if they don't want to be a part of Venice, we still need their help against Istanbul," I said.

"We haven't convinced the captain of that yet, much less the Doge," Maser said.

"I'm not going to sit around and do nothing," I said.

"Something will be done," Cecilia said.

An hour later the captain came over and stood in front of our group with his hands in his pockets.

"How'd it go?" I asked.

He shook his head.

"They don't want to join us. They'll trade, but they want to do their own thing," the captain said.

"What about Istanbul? That's where these plague ships keep coming from," I said.

"We talked about that as well. They were almost wiped out by one. They do want to help fight them, but they don't know what they can do."

"Manpower. We have guns, we just need more warm bodies that know how to use them," I said.

"That also takes time. Do we have that?" The captain asked.

"We have to make time. What about fighters and bombers? What about getting other naval ships? I know France had a surprisingly good navy. Can we find them?"

The captain thought about it.

"It would take a long time to gather all of that. Are you willing to spend that time?"

"Do we have a choice?"

The palace was unfortunately a museum now so we slept in a less swanky hotel that Rhodes seemed to have plenty of. There was no electricity, but it did have cold running water though. I hated cold. As badly as I needed one I still debated on whether or not to take a shower.

I hated sleeping in strange beds. That was one of the many reasons I didn't like being in the army. I only feel comfortable in a familiar bed and I can only sleep when I'm comfortable.

So I simply laid there for most of the night.

How long was all this going to take? As petty as it was compared to the importance of taking down the zombie lords in Istanbul, I just wanted to go home and live a quiet, peaceful life with my books and my paintings.

The next morning we were greeted with a breakfast of fish.

I was really starting to dislike fish.

July 8th

The Doge had listened to me and everyone else. They were out securing air bases and retrieving ships from Italian and French ports. On Sicily, Crete and Rhodes there were crash courses in basic training going on. All of that was thankfully out of my hands.

I sat on the patio of my house in Torcello and watched the kids play. Cecilia was reclining next to me with a book. Sara, Kevin and their kids had occupied the neighboring house. This was going to be my family's island.

The green canal in front of us was quiet as usual and almost glowed like jade. The two silent churches watched over us and the blue, hot sky above us was reassuring. It was beautiful in Venice during the summer.

Farms had sprung up all over the more wild, and less populated, islands of the lagoon. Raids had collected farm animals so we'd have beef and pork again. As long as we had bacon things would be alright.

One problem persisted though; the shore of the lagoon was still crawling with the dead. We had cleared and secured certain parts of the shore, but Italy and the rest of Europe was still the territory of the undead. There simply wasn't enough bullets to kill them all and we couldn't make enough with our limited resources.

"How do we kill millions of zombies without using up all our ammo?" I asked aloud.

"You chop them up with swords or axes," Cecilia said.

"What? Form a legion of infantry and go in Roman style to kill them? They'd get surrounded really quickly."

"We have to be smart about it, yes? Take them apart small piece at a time. They're numbers aren't growing. What they lose they can't get back," Cecilia said.

"Guerilla war against the undead with hand to hand weapons?"

"Something like that."

"I was hoping for an easier answer."

"I don't give easy answers. I only give true ones."

"Then we need to start making weapons and armor."

"One thing at a time, darling. First, take Constantinople. Then we can take back Terra Firma."

"What about a whole lot of crossbows?"

"Darling? Think about that later, okay?"

"Very well."

Then I heard the sound of a particularly loud chopper. I looked around the clear sky and saw the small form of an approaching helicopter. As it came closer I saw the familiar form that I know I've seen before in Iraq.

The tiger striped Hind attack helicopter came in slowly and touched down in the field behind our house.

"What the heck?" Karen asked.

We hurried over to where the pilot was climbing out.

"Are you Count Hill?" The man asked with a thick Romanian accent.

"I am."

"I'm your new pilot! Your Duke say you like helicopter like this! Isn't she pretty?"

"Yes, she is a very pretty bird," I said.

I walked around the intimidating form of the Romanian Hind attack helicopter and examined it top to bottom. In Iraq I saw our allied Romanians flying these wicked war birds around and was highly jealous. They had the aggressive look of a flying monster. The eyes and mouth painted on the Hind didn't hurt the illusion either.

"Lovely. Hey, Cecilia! We have an attack helicopter!"

"Great!" She said as she walked up behind me.

"This thing is tough as a tank and can carry troops."

"What should we do with it?" She asked.

"Maybe use it for our surgical strike in Istanbul."

"That's a long way away. What else can we do with it?"

"Whatever we want."

The next day I took a boat over to Venice to the Doge's palace so I could thank him. I also wanted to talk to him about Istanbul and retaking the mainland. I didn't want to get involved, but it kept gnawing at my mind.

"That will take many years and much resources," the Doge said.

"Yes, but we need the mainland."

"Not yet. We have more than enough land with the islands. When we gain more people then we worry about more land."

"But what about Milan and Rome?" I asked.

"They can worry about it. Besides, they claim all land in Italy. We'd have to go north of Alps to find land and France and Germany's covered with dead. I hear your brother rules in England. What land are you talking about?"

"The Balkans? Greece maybe?"

"Maybe. But let's talk about this campaign for Istanbul. We are training men, building up arsenals. It takes time. Speaking of which, we have new recruits coming from Crete tomorrow. Train them up."

"I will."

Doge DeCanalli hadn't been joking when he said it would take time. It would take us over a year to prepare for the assault. In the meantime we had been procuring oil wells and refineries, producing arms and ammunition and training and assembling men. We had gathered men and women from all over the Mediterranean and our allied countries. The Greek Islands wanted to remain independent and wanted their new capital to be Istanbul. That was fine because we got the Balkans, Macedonia and Romania and whatever else we could reach from the Black Sea.

Rumors of an undead power in Egypt reached us, but there wasn't much we could do about it yet. Maybe once our air force was powerful enough we could just bomb them back to hell.

There were also reports of England invading France. What the heck was George up to? I hadn't heard from him in a very long time. I hadn't heard from anyone really. Occasionally I'd receive a message on my Blue Force Tracker from Josh and Cappello. I kept asking for them to send me a crate of Mountain Dew.

Then one day, my order arrived.

A week before Thanksgiving a plane touched down at Marco Polo airport, a C-17 loaded with supplies and would return with supplies we traded. There were probably some Americans that wanted to return home as well. I was starting to suspect that Maser was one of them.

Karen and Elizabeth walked on either side of me as I approached the gigantic plane. They were growing much older and already had the eyes of adults. They shouldn't have had to grow up so fast.

Also, they were some of my best soldiers. I kept them out of harm's way as much as possible, but for the times that trouble found them they received more training than anyone else. Others called it training, I called it quality time.

Cecilia was off at the Vatican acting as a go-between for Venice and the Pope. Things weren't going so smoothly between to two emerging powers. I missed her. Strange that I hadn't proposed yet. It had been on my mind, but thinking of rings and weddings felt out of place in this world.

The enormous ramp of the C-17 opened up and an LAV rolled out of the bay.

"I'm sure we can find use for this!" I said.

Some of our pallets of cargo were already waiting to be loaded. One of them was a stash of Romanian PSL's that Utah had requested. There were also hundreds of AK-47's in crates. Fair trade for an LAV. At first they wanted to trade a Stryker, but what good would an under armed high-tech gizmo do me?

The LAV pulled up in front of me, close enough to bug the crap out of me. I saw the turret hatch open and I prepared myself to chew out the idiot commanding it.

The commander emerged from the hatch wearing a helmet and goggles.

"That you Zach?" I heard a familiar voice say. I couldn't place it though.

"Who's that?" I asked.

The man removed his helmet and I recognized him instantly. He had a beard and had let his curly hair grow out, but I knew it was him.

"Cappello!"

"It's me fool! Oh, I brought you something," Cappello said.

He tossed a shiny green object at me. I clumsily caught it and stared down at the beautiful ambrosia in my hand.

"That's one of the last Mountain Dews you'll ever have…until we get the plant up and running again," Cappello laughed.

I quickly unscrewed the top and took a careful, slow sip.

"Beautiful," I said.

"Thought you'd like it."

Then the driver's hatch opened up.

"Is this where we can eat the spaghetti and the spicy meatball?" Hardcore asked in the most exaggerated Italian accent imaginable.

Two of my buddies that I had fought with in Iraq. There were few people I trusted more.

"What in the world are you guys doing here?" I asked.

"We heard you were throwing a party!" Cappello said.

"Indeed we are. You two are welcome to tag along."

"I also thought I'd take the time to vacation in my homeland," Cappello said. Unlike Hardcore who only had a fake accent, Cappello's family really had come from Italy.

"Where you staying? A mud hut?" Hardcore asked.

"I got my own island."

"No way," Cappello said.

"I do. There's spare houses if you want to stay."

"If I like it, maybe I'll bring the wife and kids over," Cappello said.

"I'm sure you will."

I left the unloading and loading to the soldiers and I took my friends back to Torcello. During the entire boat ride back we just swapped old war stories. Karen and Elizabeth seemed enraptured by the stories that seemed too ridiculous to be true. Cappello tried to tell embarrassing stories about me and Hardcore embarrassed me without trying or even meaning too.

This was all very surreal to me. It was as if two separate lives had collided in a dream-like way. They had belonged to a past that no longer seemed my own, but there they were, concrete reminders of what had happened a lifetime ago.

We took our little boat down the small, green canal to our home. I showed them the houses that could be theirs. Military vehicles were parked in the empty fields and a few recruits were milling about between practices.

"You have a lovely little army base here," Hardcore said.

"It's our training grounds," I said.

The girls and I went to the kitchen to prepare supper for our guests. Dan was off training in the youth brigade. Like his sister he seemed to hate the zombies on a personal level and took his training very seriously. They did a lot of target practice with .22 rifles. He said he wanted to become a sniper.

"Tomorrow I'll take you on a tour of Venice," I said from the kitchen.

"I saw it from the boat. It looks like something from a fairy tale," Cappello said.

"It's better up close."

"Isn't it supposed to sink any minute?" Hardcore asked.

"Not yet. She still has some life left in her."

We sat down to dinner and talked all night. Karen asked the most questions, usually about me when I was younger. She was surprised to find that I hadn't changed that much except I was far more foolish and arrogant when I was younger, but wasn't that what defined youth?

I got them caught up on my life here in Italy and they told me all about what was happening in Utah. Sounded like things were really stabilizing out there.

"Shame we'll eventually be at war with Rome in a generation or two," I said.

"Amazing," Hardcore said. "Zombies rise up and kill 99% of the planet and we still don't think that's enough and want to kill the other 1%!"

"I know, but I don't call the shots here," I said.

"Politics like usual. The new world's just like the old one, eh?" Cappello said.

"Afraid so," I said.

"Hey, I hear you're still with the nun!" Hardcore said.

"Yes, yes I am. She's off in Rome right now trying to make the Vatican our BFF's," I said.

"You ain't married her yet?" Cappello asked.

"No, not yet."

"You're living in sin?" Hardcore asked.

"No! Nothing like that."

"Why don't you marry her?" Karen asked.

"Well…I…"

Karen's cold eyes drilled into me.

"I'll think about it," I said.

TWENTY ONE

July 15th

I looked down at the glass counter full of rings. I knew nothing of rings, especially engagement rings.

"Which one?" I asked.

Karen and Elizabeth were both concentrating on the different rings.

"It can't be any old ring. It has to mean something," Karen said.

"It has to speak to who she is as a person," Elizabeth said.

"You two aren't helping."

"Of course we are! We, being women, know what women want!" Elizabeth said.

"Okay then, what does she want?" I asked.

"We can't decide that. That's for you to decide!" Elizabeth said.

"Then what exactly are you helping me with?"

"We'll let you know if your choice is acceptable," Karen said.

That actually sounded somewhat logical.

I grunted and went back to looking at all the rings.

I needed one that was somehow like Cecilia. I needed a ring that was intelligent, elegant, but not stuffy, but also humorous and sharp.

How the hell was a ring supposed to have all of that?

"I give up," I said.

"You can't! You wouldn't give up on Cecilia, would you?"

She had me there.

"Fine."

I kept looking.

Then I saw one in the back. It was a simple gold band with four diamonds spread equally around it and a stylized wave design going from diamond to diamond. Before the Uprising I would never have bought a diamond, but now that the evil that controlled the diamond business was gone, it was safe to buy them again.

I asked to see the ring and turned it around in my hands. I really liked it.

"What about this one?" I asked.

They each looked at it in turn.

"It's not as huge and sparkly as some, but I think Cecilia might prefer it that way. She doesn't seem to like a lot of ornamentation," Elizabeth said.

"I like it," Karen said.

"So, I get your seal of approval?" I asked.

"Yes," Karen said.

"You do," Elizabeth said.

I traded a Beretta for the ring and tucked the black velvet box into one of my tactical pouches on my vest.

"She'll love it," Elizabeth said.

"I'm more worried about if she'll love the words that go with it," I said.

"Of course she will. Don't worry. You'll do fine," Elizabeth said.

"When's she coming back?" Karen asked.

"In a week."

"That long? I can't wait that long to find out what happens," Elizabeth said, throwing her hands in the air.

"Imagine how I feel."

Then three soldiers approached me with Beretta submachine guns slung in front of them. I recognized them from my first group of students.

"Mr. Hill, the Doge would like to see you immediately," the tallest soldier said.

"What about?"

"I don't know, but it is urgent."

"Very well, I'll be right there."

We went over to the Doge's palace, walking through a crowd of pigeons that were pecking around in the square. Officially, this was the only "piazza" in Venice. The rest of the town squares were called "campos" a term meaning "field" from way back when they really were just unpaved open areas.

The three flag poles in front of St. Mark's flew three giant flags of Venice. No more Italian flag and no more E.U. flag. Now it was just Venice and Venice alone.

When we walked into the Doge's palace there were a bunch of suits arguing about currency. Some thought it was too soon to reintroduce currency and some thought doing so would help things greatly. I ignored them and went up the Golden Staircase to the Doge's offices.

Me and the girls talked about romantic ways I could propose while we walked through the endless halls, past the portraits of the ancient Doges. Well, it was more like they came up with romantic ideas and I listened.

When we arrived at the Doge's door I was immediately escorted in while the girls had to wait outside.

In the office were all our officers and most of the senior advisors. The expressions on their faces didn't seem very happy.

"Zach! Didn't expect you so soon," Doge DeCanalli said while waving me over.

"I was in Venice doing some shopping," I said.

I walked over to the table they were surrounding and looked down over a map of Italy.

"What's going on?" I asked.

"We just received word that there is an army of zombies like we've never seen before heading right for Rome. They're coming from the south, most likely Naples and the surrounding areas. They're moving in one massive group," the Doge said.

"How massive?" I asked.

"We have satellite photos," he said. He handed me the print outs.

At first I thought I was looking at images of a forest, but when I saw some of the closer up images I realized that I was looking at a horde of zombies that covered the landscape for miles in every direction. I couldn't imagine how many red eyes were down there to control an army that large.

"And they're headed for Rome?"

"They are. Do you have any suggestions on how to stop them?" The Doge asked. He seemed almost desperate.

"Well, for starters we need to send every fighter, bomber and helicopter at them and send as many sorties as possible. We have to kill as many as we can before they reach our ground forces."

"Right."

The Doge merely nodded to our Air Force general and he left the room immediately.

"We also need to get every troop, tank and APC headed that direction immediately," I said.

I really wish we had some A-10's about now. As it was, our Air Force consisted of five Tornados, seven Euro Fighters and three F-16's. These sorties would use up all the fuel we had stored up for the attack on Istanbul, but we had to do this.

"Have our artillery bring as many white phosphorus shells as we can," I said.

Our artillery brigade were ten 105mm field howitzers that were towed behind trucks, a 203mm self propelled howitzer and a MLRS. The MLRS was our most deadly piece we had, but also the most expensive. We had a limited number of rockets and once those were out we wouldn't be receiving any new ones. I wrote down in my notebook to loot artillery from Romania and the Balkans. I'd have to call the Romanian command that were held up in one of their castles. That was for later though. Whatever they could send now wouldn't reach us in time. We had to get our army moving today or we wouldn't reach Rome in time.

We had three days before the tireless undead army reached the outskirts of

Rome. It would take us a day to prepare, a day to get there and a day to set up. It wasn't great, but at least we had some time.

After the meeting I hurried out of the office and down to St. Mark's Square. The girls were asking what was wrong and I explained to them as I went. The looks on their faces showed that they understood the situation well enough to be afraid.

We took my boat back to Torcello where my recruits, now graduated as auxiliaries, and my amphibious vehicles were. The three AAV's were parked where they always were.

"Load these up and get them to the motor pool in Mestre!"

We'll need every troop carrier and piece of armor we can get. The AAV's would prove a big help. They could carry a whole platoon and had fully automatic grenade launchers. Grenades were also going to be in short supply. The white phosphorus, the rockets and now grenades, valuable weapons that were finite. They'd never be replaced. Artillery shells we could make, but not those American rockets.

I had hoped to use all our special weapons on our assault on Istanbul, but now they were going to be used up in defending Rome. I didn't know if that was the red eye's intention or if it was just coincidental. Either way there wasn't anything we could do about it. Almost five thousand survivors were in Rome and we wouldn't lose the Eternal City for anything.

Cappello and Hardcore came out when they heard the ruckus. I explained to them and Hardcore's pale blue eyes went wide.

"A sea of zombies?" He asked.

"That's what I said."

"Do we have any helicopter blades mounted on the front of tanks?" He asked.

"No."

"Why not?"

"We just don't."

"Wouldn't that come in handy about now?"

"Yeah."

It sounded ridiculous, but I had to admit that I really did wish we had a few of those chopper machines. Maybe I'd have Hardcore think up a bunch of anti-zombie weapons to use in Istanbul to replace the ones we'd be loosing in this upcoming battle.

"Where's that Romanian pilot?" I asked.

"Right here my friend," the pilot said as he swaggered up to me with all the confidence of a Top Gun fighter pilot.

"Are those rocket pods and chain gun fully loaded?" I asked.

"They'd be useless if they weren't," the Romanian said.

"Is that a yes?"

"Yes, it's a yes."

"Good. Get that beast ready for take off. Me and an advance squad are going to Rome today."

"Okay, boss."

I turned back to the others.

"Who's on your advanced squad?" Cappello asked.

"I don't know. I just make this stuff up as I go. That's why I'm not in charge," I said.

"I volunteer," Cappello said.

"Me too," Hardcore said.

"You'll need a medic," Sarah said. I hadn't seen her or Kevin approach.

"I'll be the medic's body guard. I like guarding that body," Kevin said.

"You ain't getting this body any time soon," Sarah said.

"Hey, I said I was sorry about that."

"Not sorry enough."

"I'm going," Karen said.

I was about to argue, but then I saw the look in her eyes. There was no way she'd stay behind.

"Okay," I said.

"Me too," Elizabeth said.

"Alright. We have our advanced squad. Go gear up and bring everything. Bombs, guns, knives, pointy sticks. Bring it all. Especially bring all ammo! Go get ready and meet back here in an hour."

In that hour I was on the radio with Maser and Lorenzo. Those two were more in charge of the regular army than I was. Lorenzo and a few old Italian veterans made the big decisions and I was happy to let them.

But lately I seemed to be doing more. They handled the army stuff alright, but it seemed that I was the only one pushing for the Istanbul campaign. I hated being in charge, but now it felt like I was pulling to be in charge.

"Hey, does this mean our eventual war with Rome is postponed?" Hardcore asked as he came back to the rally point. He was wearing his old digital camo Army uniform with tactical gear in desert colors. He also carried an M4 with a military issue red dot. The chin straps of his helmet were undone.

"Postponed, but not indefinitely."

"Good, I wouldn't want the end of the world to get in the way of our murderous human nature."

Kevin and Sarah showed up next. Kevin had his .308 broadsword made by Gundoc nonchalantly slung over his shoulder and Sarah had large medic packs and two pistols on her hips.

Then came Cappello with his FS2000 and large Kukri on his thigh. Lastly, came the two girls. They both had M4's with red dots, leather clothing and helmets.

"I want a cool helmet," Hardcore said.

"Are we ready? Do we have everything?" I asked. "Now's the time to double check because once that bird takes off, there's no coming back until either the zombie army is dead or we are."

"How do we return if we're dead?" Hardcore asked.

"Because then you'd be part of another zombie army," I said.

"Crap."

"I'm ready…ready to kick some ASS!" Kevin said.

"I'm ready," Sarah said in her calmer voice.

"I'm ready to go fool. You know me. Rock and Roll Cappello."

"Yeah sure, as long as I'm back for dinner," Hardcore said.

I took that as a 'yes' from Hardcore.

"I'm ready," Karen said.

"Me too," Elizabeth said. "Dan's going to be upset that he missed this."

"This is too dangerous for him. There'll be plenty of time for him to fight. He has a whole life ahead of him," I said.

"Can we win?" Cappello asked.

I respected him enough to not lie to him. We've been through too much in Iraq to lie to each other.

"I don't honestly know. There are a lot of cannibal freaks out there. I guess it depends on our allies and how strong they are. We can't do this alone and we can't allow them to do this on their own. Rome needs help and we have to give it to them."

"Alright. Let's go save some Romans," Hardcore said.

"Let's mount up," I said.

Me and my squad climbed into the Hind and we took off. The island of Torcello shrunk away from us and we flew over Venice on our way to Rome. The floating city was now my home and I said a lengthy and silent prayer that I would see it again.

July 15th Rome

The clouds were growing thick and the closer we got to Rome the more it looked like it was going to rain. Just what I needed, to be out in the rain. I hated being wet. However, that was the least of our concerns at the moment.

Our Hind approached Rome and I saw the dark Eternal City with its giant monuments still intact. Even through all this the Coliseum and Pantheon were still standing as they always have. Past them, across the Tiber, was the Vatican where Cecelia would be.

We touched down in the Vatican garden and were met by several Swiss Guards.

"We're glad to see you," one of the Swiss Guards said.

"More of our men are coming," I said.

"We'll need them. We just got more recon photos and it isn't looking good. Follow me."

We followed them into the Vatican Governatorato building where the new Pope was talking to his Swiss guards and what remained of the Italian army. I hadn't heard what happened to the old Pope, but this new one was younger than I was and former military.

As soon as I walked in all eyes turned to me.

"Finally, word from Venice," the Pope said.

"What do you have for us?" One of the officers asked.

"We're bringing everything we have. Our main forces will be here tomorrow night. What planes we have will begin attacks immediately. We are going to set up several defensive positions, strike and then fall back and reform."

"We already have several teams out there right now. We're trying to lessen their numbers, but it's like…picking out grains of sand on a beach," the Swiss Guard commander said.

"Excellent, but this will require much more. We need every big gun, bomb, plane, tank and rock we have to throw at them," I said.

"We have our armor and artillery gathered south of here," an officer said. He had a submachine gun and a beret with a large peacock feather sticking out of it.

"Gentlemen," the Pope said. All eyes turned to him. "We can't fail here. If we fail the world dies. I suggest we do as the Venetians say and start hitting them as hard as we can right now. Otherwise, they'll be too much when they reach Rome.

"If we could kill all the red eyes before they get here that would solve a large portion of the problem, but they'll be blended into the crowd and I imagine that it would take an awful lot to control a horde this size," I said.

The Pope then turned to one of his officers.

"Go get our planes in the air right now. I want non stop sorties until we run out of fuel or bombs," the Pope said.

Then someone entered the room. I looked up from the maps and satellite photos and suddenly all of the conversation around me fell away.

There was Cecilia. She was wearing black BDU's with her body armor and her SCAR slung across her chest. She was wearing her habit again, but that was for PR with the new Papal State.

She didn't see me at first and her eyes behind her glasses were looking to the Pope and his senior officers. Then her eyes came my direction and suddenly we were looking eye to eye. I saw that it took a moment for the realization to dawn on her face, but when it did, I saw that her smile was genuine and all consuming.

She ignored the papal officers and hurried over to me and threw her arms around me. I picked her up and squeezed her hard.

"When did you get here?" She asked, still with that uncontainable smile.

"Just now. How have you been?" I asked.

"Well. And you?"

"I've missed you."

"I've missed you too."

Then the Pope cleared his throat.

Cecilia quickly broke off and straightened her glasses.

"Can we get back to business? Everyone, go get ready. Prepare your men and hit this army of evil hard and with everything we have. Don't hold anything back."

After we left the meeting with the Papal officers Cecilia and I went and found a quiet corner where no one was around. Once I was sure we were alone I drew her in tight and kissed her. She kissed back with a force and passion of a starving woman.

When we finally broke apart she had to take a few moments to catch her breath.

"Is Venice really sending everything?" She asked.

"Yes, we're bringing everything. We're going to use up all the specialty weapons we were saving for Istanbul."

"Good," she nodded.

We walked back to the Hind where the others were waiting.

"What's the plan, boss?" Cappello asked.

"Well, we have to wait for our army to show up. That won't be for several hours. In the meantime we can hit them with our helicopter," I said.

"Right. Let's do it."

We all climbed back in and the Hind took off. We flew an hour south and easily found the undead army. It was indeed massive and covered the entire countryside. It was as if the ground itself was moving. It was night, but the moon was shining and I could see the horde with frightening clarity. I felt their collective moaning more than heard it. It was as if the air was humming from the sound.

"Expend all ammo," I said to the pilot and gunner.

The chin gun opened fire and began blowing holes into the undead ranks. Then the rockets fired and a spread of explosions tore into the horde. It was impressive in its destructive power, but I don't think the horde even noticed.

The Hind ran out of rockets and ammo too quickly and we turned around to head back to Rome.

I kept my eyes on this horde. It had been my first glimpse at this enormous threat. The reality was far worse than the satellite images revealed. I looked over to Cecilia and she had the same look I did; the look in her eyes asked "how are we supposed to stop this?"

I only shrugged.

On the way back to Rome we saw several jets fly by. Mostly there were Tornados, but there were a few Eurofighters.

"Go get them, guys!" Kevin shouted out.

I silently prayed that their bombs would find as many red eyes as possible.

When we got to Rome we found the area where they wanted Venice to set up her army. Rome would be in the center, Milan on the west and Venice on the east.

We laid out all our equipment and I stood there wondering what my weapon of choice would be. Thanks to our Romanian factories, we had more 7.62x39 than anything else. The ammo of the AK was plentiful so most of our forces were switching over to the AK. I would be making several trips so in all likelihood I'd go through everything.

I grabbed my tac-vest that had super large pockets and filled them with 75 round drums for my RPK which was just a stretched out AK-47. Cecilia took her M4 like the girls had.

Once we were ready and the chopper was fueled back up, me and a unit of the Fiocchi guys from Milan flew out and set up defensive position on top of a train station. We blocked off the stairs and waited for the horde to come within range. The Hind was there, ready to take us away if things went wrong or when we ran out of ammo.

We all sat down and rested. There was no telling when we'd be able to rest again. Sarah and Kevin were talking while loading extra magazines and Cappello and Hardcore were in some political argument that was highly irrelevant now. Cecilia sat there with her head rested on my shoulder.

"When do they get in reach of our cannons?" Karen asked.

"Sometime tomorrow," I said.

"They're coming," Karen said.

Already I could hear the collective moans of the horde. I felt it more than heard it. It was a deep, sickly rumbling.

Within minutes they came into view. We were in a small town and they were filling the streets.

"Weapons ready!" I shouted.

We all got to the edge of the roof and took aim. The Milan unit was spread out in other parts of the city. This was about mathematics and not strategy. We didn't have to be together. All we had to do was make every bullet count and take out as many as we could.

"I hope Rome's coming up with a really good secret plan to stop this. Maybe they have a death ray in space," Hardcore said.

"I hope so too," I said. "Remember, only aimed headshots."

I racked the bolt of my RPK and took aim. As soon as I got a clear headshot I fired. Everyone opened up and a rain of bullets began poring down onto the horde. I took aim and fired over and over again.

The horde didn't notice or care about us and just kept going past us. I searched for red eyes, but didn't see any. In the low light of the cloudy morning I should have been able to see them clearly.

Then I saw a zombie wearing goggles. I first noticed because he wasn't moving as sloppily as the others.

"The red eyes have their eyes covered!" I said. Crap. That made things more difficult.

I shot the goggled Red Eye in the head and for a moment the zombies around him paused, but suddenly they went back to marching forward.

My first drum ran dry and I quickly changed. It wasn't a battle, it was a shooting gallery. The only dramatic moment was when Hardcore tossed a grenade into the street. Even then the horde didn't notice.

Eventually, we all simply ran dry. We stood up and watched the river of undead flow toward Rome.

"Too bad we don't have rocks to drop on them," Hardcore said.

"Not a bad idea. Next time we will," I said.

"What's the next town?" Cecilia asked.

"I'm not sure. Why?"

"Maybe the next town we can set on fire. Fill the buildings with gas or something."

"Interesting. That might slow them down."

"I'd prefer a death ray," Hardcore said.

We loaded back in the Hind and went back to Rome. None of us said anything. We had seen and fought our first engagement with the enemy and we all knew was that this was going to possibly the hardest thing we've ever done.

TWENTY TWO

July 17

The tanks and artillery were all lined up ready to roll. I looked at my watch. 2:26am. It was dark from the clouds and I could smell rain. I was tired, tired to the point of my eyes hurting, but I had a lot of work to do.

The Venetian army had just arrived and were assembling for refueling before heading right back out.

My feet hurt and I was sitting down on some crates of ammo. We had been fighting on and off all day. My squad was around me, but they were all I had to think about now. The planning and leadership of the battle was thankfully out of my hands now that the Venetian leadership was here. The Venetian officers were meeting with the leadership of Rome and Milan. Like Hardcore. I was really hoping that they'd come up with a miraculous plan, something that would knock my socks off.

If we couldn't stop them at Rome I don't know what would happen afterwards. I was loading the drums of my RPK for next sortie. Once the horde reached Rome I was planning on switching to my AK with regular mags. Drums were nice for the lack of reloading, but they were awkward to run and gun with.

I'd have to check the batteries of the Red Dot sight before that all went down.

All around me were soldiers running around and getting things prepared for the battle. Civilians were being evacuated north of Rome. The Castel Sant' Angelo wouldn't stop this horde.

"We're heading out in thirty minutes!" A sergeant called out from somewhere.

"A half hour's not a lot of time," Karen said. She was loading up her M4 and eating some Italian MRE.

"Will we run them over with our tanks?" Cecilia asked.

"We'll have to, but probably after we expend most of our ammo," I said.

"Why wait? Just run them all over."

"The problem is the red eyes. They might be able to damage or stop our vehicles and if that happens in the middle of the horde, we'll be helpless."

"So we have to thin the herd before we close in," Karen said.

"How much can we thin the herd?" Cecilia asked.

"I don't know," I said.

When the time came we crawled up on top of an AAV along with several other Venetians and rode out to meet the horde.

We came to a small town where our first large scale stand would be. They had used brush fires to funnel the horde, more or less, into this one area. That would make them more vulnerable to our artillery.

Our cannons were being set up several miles behind us, but our tanks and APC's were here in the town.

I racked the bolt on my RPK and took up position in a line with all the others. By luring them into more narrow streets we hoped to create a meat grinder. The trick would be if we could mount up and bug out in time once we ran out of ammo. For the final retreat I kept a single drum at the small of my back. I'd have to lay down as much fire as I could.

Then I began to hear the distant bass thumping of the artillery firing and moments later of their impacts. It sounded like an epileptic death metal drum solo. Miles away hundreds of zombies were being blown to pieces. Clouds of white phosphorous were falling onto the horde and burning them to ash. It was destruction on an epic level, but still, it wasn't going to be enough.

If there were people on the other side of that bombardment, then I'd feel sorry for them. But as it was, there wasn't and I didn't.

The distant thumping continued for a half hour before I began to hear the faint, penetrating moan of the collective horde.

"They're here, men," an officer said in Italian from on top of a Centauro.

"Alright fellas, time to rock and roll," Kevin said.

"No one get bit, please," Sarah said.

"I'll ask them not to bite me then," Hardcore said.

Elizabeth turned on her red dot sight and stood by my shoulder. Karen was on the other side of her and Cecilia was on my other side.

"Ready?" I asked them.

I got a chorus of nervous murmurs in response.

Then the horde came into view. They poured into the street like a flood. They flowed around cars and dumpsters. They were still too far away for good headshots so we waited. I wondered if this is how the revolutionaries felt when they heard "don't fire until you see the whites of their eyes!" The anticipation was painful. What made it even more painful was the thought of my family and friends being hurt or worse. I didn't want to think about it, but with every passing second the thought permeated my mind. It was fear.

"Fire!" A sergeant called out from somewhere.

My RPK bucked in my hands and I saw the zombie go down. I aimed again and fired. The familiar 'crack' of the rifle felt good and I could smell the gunpowder in the air. All around me was a chorus of gunfire that was like a nonstop stream of firecrackers going off. The pace didn't let up and the zombies were falling in waves.

Many bullets passed through one zombie head and into the one behind it. That was good because it made up a bit for the missed shots. A bullet in the chest meant nothing to a zombie.

We kept the fire hot and intense and didn't let up except to reload. Whenever someone did reload a zombie got that much closer to our line. Still, we were mowing them down like grass.

For a while it looked like we were actually pushing them back as more died than could move forward. I couldn't hear the artillery or the airstrikes, but I knew they were going on.

Smoke was filling the street and the dead zombies were beginning to pile up forming obstacles for the other zombies.

Someone launched a grenade from an M-203 and a hole was blasted in the horde.

"I'm running low!" One of the Venetian soldiers called out.

"Me too!" Another one yelled.

That meant we were approaching our time to bug out while we still had ammo to do it with.

My RPK ran dry and I held up the gun and switched out to my last drum.

Then the officer in charge blew a whistle. That was the signal for platoon 7 and 8 to retreat while 5 and 6 laid down fire.

As the two other units fell back our shooting grew dramatically less and the zombies slowly began to move forward again. Once 7 and 8 were on the trucks and APC's, they opened fire and our two units fell back. As soon as we got behind the APC's our single Centauro opened fire with its cannon and blasted a long trough through the horde.

We managed to retreat without a casualty.

My RPK was smoking and my last drum was bone dry. All I had were my kukri and my pistol.

I was glad to get far from there, but whatever gladness I had was dampened by the knowledge that as soon as we reload and resupply we'd be going right back out there and doing it again.

We made it back to Rome to the Venetian supply point and quickly began refilling our magazines. I had my own little tent where I kept my private arsenal. I put down the RPK and picked up my old trusty AK-47, "Elizabeta." The FS2000 was great for short, close in situations, but a battle like this called for the endurance of a Kalashnikov. I knew I'd need its well earned reputation for reliability. This wasn't a battle where weapon failure was permitted.

We went back out and met the horde on an abandoned highway. The APC's pushed cars to make barricades for us and created a junk fortress. It was ready just in time. The horde came into view and the undead ocean surged toward us.

We didn't wait for orders. We fired as soon as we had clean shots. This time one of our APC's was the AAV and it let loose with a barrage of grenades. Overhead jets streaked by and helicopters launched rockets. Helicopters were in close and that meant the artillery barrage had ended. I hope that didn't mean they were out of ammo. It was far too soon for that.

Other teams were doing the same thing in other locations. Some units had made improvised bombs and were blowing the zombies up. Some had mortars from the Italian army and were providing close range artillery support. It was a symphony of slaughter and destruction with each instrument performing to its best ability in perfect harmony with the others.

And despite all this, it still wasn't enough. The massive horde still covered the landscape. Had we even dented their numbers?

My AK was steaming and hot to the touch by the time we withdrew. I turned off the red dot sight once I was inside the AAC.

"How are we doing?" Cecilia asked.

"It's hard to tell," I said.

"We had to have killed at least five hundred of them," Karen said.

"So, twenty teams, each killing five hundred with every sortie..." Elizabeth said.

"Five hundred is conservative. We killed more than that," I said.

"I know, but I just need a ballpark number. Twenty teams killing five hundred each is ten thousand," Elizabeth said.

"That many?" Cecilia asked.

"If my numbers are correct," she said.

"That's a lot and we've done it twice," I said.

"But to kill five million, we'll have to sortie five hundred times," Elizabeth said.

"I hate math," I said.

"That's impossible!" Cecilia said.

"But we haven't counted the artillery," Karen said.

Five hundred sorties to kill the horde. Cecilia was right. That was impossible. We didn't have the time. They'd be at Rome and we'd have to stop them there. With the red eyes in control I knew that they wouldn't leave Rome standing. We couldn't lose one of the oldest and greatest cities in the world. Most of the art has been evacuated, but the buildings and history were irreplaceable. Maybe it was foolish to worry about such things when survival was in question, but what good would it do to survive if we forgot our past?

July 18

It was raining and I was standing next to my family and friends. I was soaking wet, but that was the least of my concerns. We were on a rooftop in a small town just south of Rome. The city was visible behind us and I could see the sea of undead coming right at us. At least I had a good view of the end of the world.

The generals told us that our rapid attacks had killed many zeds and that it has made a difference. Looking out over the dead filled country side I began to wonder if it was all just feel good lies.

I looked over to Cecilia who stood there, rain poring off of her chin. She was wearing a habit for propaganda. I was taking a few pictures, but I did so only half heartedly. It was hard to care about preserving the present when there might not be a future.

There was so much I wanted to tell Cecilia in case I died. I wanted to give her the ring and make her my wife, but now just wasn't the right time.

"You're amazing," I finally said.

She looked over with her slightly foggy glasses and smiled.

"I love you," she said in a way that made me believe it.

I took her hand and pulled her in for a kiss. We were both cold and wet, but the kiss was warm. I could have kept kissing her for the rest of the day.

"Zach?" She said.

"Huh?"

"You've made me very happy," she said. "I…well…we have work to do. Yes?"

"We do."

"Will we win?"

"I think so. It would be ridiculous for God to preserve us just to end here with the adversary victorious. Besides, if Hardcore's right, then the higher ups have a plan."

"They had better have a damn good one."

"Amen, sister."

"I wonder why they won't tell us."

"In case one of us gets captured and possessed."

The downstairs of the building had a few claymores to protect it. The building had once been a train station and now it was covered in soldiers with guns.

The distant 'thumping' of artillery started and planes began to streak overhead. Geysers of dirt and smoke rose up from the zombie horde where explosions ripped undead bodies apart.

The tanks and APC's formed a wall at the southern border of the town.

"Alright, here they come," I said.

"We'll win, right Dad?" Karen asked.

Her mascara was streaking over her pale cheeks.

"We will. Trust me."

She smiled a genuine smile.

In the meantime I was praying for a miracle.

I carried my AK, but my FS2000 was propped against the waist high wall of the train station roof. When, not if, I ran dry with my AK I would transition to the FS. After that it was my pistols and then my kukri and gunstock club.

"Just like old times," Cappello said.

"Just like it," I said.

"Yeah, except for a dozen insurgents we have a million zombies," Hardcore said.

"A million? That's all?" Kevin asked.

"No, there's a few million out there."

"Too bad we don't have a tac-nuke," Cappello said.

"I'm sure if we did the red eyes wouldn't have tried this," I said.

"How would they know?" Cecilia asked.

"I'm sure they have their sneaky ways," I said.

The artillery and airstrikes kept ripping into the horde with horrible destruction.

Then the wave of zombies came within range of the tanks and APC's and the cannons, grenade launchers and machine guns opened up. A few snipers were picking off zeds one by one. I prayed that they could find some red eyes at least.

"At the battle of Leipzig, during the Napoleonic wars, there were 90,000 casualties in that one battle. If they could do it with muskets, we can do much better with modern weapons," I said.

The barrage of the big guns continued, but the horde surged past the armored vehicles and into the town.

We opened fire.

I began shooting the zombies as they came close to the train station. They knew we were up here and wanted to come get us so we simply had to prevent them from coming up. There were marble stairs leading up to the station's entrance and that was where we shot them down. If they got past we had claymores and if they got past those, the staircase up to the roof was narrow and could only fit maybe two at a time. We could deal with that for a while.

I fired shot, after shot, after shot. Someone had brought a bag of bricks up and was dropping them on the zombies' heads.

The tanks and APC's then began to drive forward into the heart of the horde. It was Grand Theft Auto time. They would crush as many zombies as they could before their fuel ran out.

My AK ran dry and I knocked out the empty magazine with a fresh one and quickly rocked it in. Already there was a pile of mags by my feet.

The horde managed to surge through our deadly fire and entered the station. Hardcore ran over to the detonators and set off the claymores. The explosions shook the building and smoke blasted out into the street.

"Prepare to defend the stairwell!" I called out.

Four men in armor from the museums stood by the stairwell with swords and shields. They stood there, anticipating the knock on the door that would come. The door was locked with a chain, but no one believed that it would last forever.

We kept firing. All I saw of the battle now was the little area in front of the station. The tanks, artillery and jets were in another world. All that was in my world were the people standing beside me and the street full of undead.

Other rooftops had men shooting down into the hordes, each one an island of defiance.

A helicopter flew over head and began to spray rockets into the horde.

Suddenly, a fireball, like from a fantasy movie, shot up from the middle of the horde and engulfed the helicopter. The only comfort was that the helicopter's wreckage crashed down into the horde.

"What was that?" Cappello asked.

"I have no idea. Some weapon of theirs?" I said.

"Do we have some King Koopa jerkwad out there?" Hardcore asked.

A few minutes later a small black, round helicopter approached the train station and landed on the roof. Swiss Guard in their combat uniforms jumped out and ran over to where we were. They ignored us and set up some kind of box while another looked through a fancy set of binoculars.

"What's going on?" I asked in Italian.

"We found him," the Guard said.

"Found who?"

"The Black Eye."

"What's a Black Eye?"

"He's the leader of this army."

Then the Guard with the Binos pointed out into the horde.

"I found him! He's being carried on a throne. Eleven O'clock."

"I see him," the soldier with the large camera looking thing said.

"Paint him," the leader said.

I kept shooting down into the horde, but I kept an eye on what the guards were doing. The officer got on a radio and said some random numbers and letters.

"Watch," the officer said.

Me and Cecilia took a break to reload and watched where they were pointing.

A lone jet streaked high over head. After it passed I spotted the tiny specks of two bombs.

The laser guided bombs streaked downward and found their laser targeted mark. The Black Eye on his thrown was evaporated in a cloud of fire, smoke and debris.

Suddenly all the zombies stopped as if stunned. They paused right where they were and gazed stupidly into nothing. A few moments later they began to move again, but this time they were far less aggressive. I didn't even detect control by lesser red eyes.

"I told you they had a plan," Hardcore said.

"The battle isn't over yet," I said. "Now it's winnable though."

My AK ran dry and I put it down and snatched up the FS. I turned on the Red Dot and began firing.

The four men in armor opened the door and let the zombies come through only to be hacked to pieces like they were in a Tyson's Chicken factory. It was a mechanical process. A bloody, but simple one.

The vehicles, now that the red eyes were gone, were able to tear through the undead ranks with reckless ferocity.

The Swiss Guard pulled out P-90's and began firing down into the street as well.

Then I saw the artillery. A self propelled 203mm rumbled into the street and leveled the cannon. When it fired it broke all the windows around it and the enormous shell cut a swath through the horde a half mile long before it detonated and created a giant hole. In other parts of the battle the artillery were now being deployed as direct fire instruments of mass carnage. The 203mm would wait for the street to fill in again and fire another round. It was a leisurely and devastatingly effective way to whittle down the undead army.

I slung my FS and took out my camera. I had to document this battle. It wasn't over, but it was already won. Somehow I knew it was over. There were hours of fighting left, but they had teams divert the zombies in the rear away from Rome. They'd be dealt with later.

By sunset there were only scattered pockets of zombies and they were being destroyed by crossbows and halberds.

Every bone in my body ached from exhaustion.

We stumbled our way back to the Venetian rally point. I put down my weapons and collapsed to the ground. Cecilia lay down next to me.

"What a day," she said.

"We're alive though."

"We are."

She sat up and looked down at me. Her shirt and habit were soaked and I could see the weariness in her eyes. Her hand rested on my chest and she bent down and kissed me.

"I want to go home," she said. "With you."

"Then let's go. As soon as our Hind is refueled."

Already I could hear people playing on guitars, singing laughing. The celebrations were starting already. Venetian officials were on radios telling the people back in Venice that the battle was won.

I sat up and took a few pictures of it all. The victory needed to be documented as well as the battle.

The pilot came over and told us when the Hind was ready to leave. My friends, family and me boarded the helicopter and flew back to Venice. We all slept the entire trip home.

It was the middle of the night, but I could see lights on in Venice and fireworks shooting up into the air. They were still celebrating.

We flew on to Torcello and touched down on our quiet island.

Karen and Elizabeth stumbled, half asleep to their rooms. I carried my things to my room and dumped them all in a pile. I'd worry about it all tomorrow.

Then I thought of Cecilia. Perhaps we should celebrate in some small way. If she wasn't too tired I'd make her something to eat.

I went to her room and saw that her door was still open. I peeked in. She was sitting on her bed and drying her hair with a towel.

"You hungry?" I asked.

She looked up and smiled.

"Sure," she said.

"I'll make you an omelet to celebrate."

"We're alive. That's all the celebration I need."

I walked over and sat down beside her.

"Want to sit up on the roof and watch the fireworks and fall asleep in each other's arms?" I asked.

"Hard to say no to that."

I took her by the hand and led her up to the roof. We laid down some blankets and sat down.

We watched the distant fireworks illuminate the low, foggy clouds over Venice.

"It's beautiful," she said.

Then I remembered the ring.

"Hold on, I have something for you."

"Something for me?"

"Stay right there."

I ran back to my room where my tac-vest was and grabbed the ring from the pouch. I hurried back up to the roof.

She was leaned back on her elbows and she had a huge, nerdy smile on her face. I sat down and looked into her dark brown eyes. I had to control my breathing and act as calm as I could possibly be.

"Cecilia, I love you. That's no secret. I want to be with you and I want you to always be there with me no matter what happens. I want you to be with me until the end."

Then I pulled out the ring and her eyes went wide and her mouth opened. She quickly covered her mouth with her hands and I saw the glistening of tears pool up in her eyes.

"Cecilia, will you marry me?"

I waited there a few moments while she cried. I had hoped for a quick answer, but it seemed that she was too busy crying.

"Cecilia?"

She managed a quick nod and then threw her arms around me.

"Yes!" She finally managed to get out.

A wave of relief swept over me and I took her in my arms and kissed her.

TWENTY THREE

Two Years Later

March 3rd

I watched as a new class of recruits repeated weapons drills again and again. Most had freshly made AK-47's from the factory in Romania. Some had Beretta rifles that we traded Milan for, but our trade with Milan was growing less and less by the month. The more independent they grew, the less they cared to share.

It was a good thing that we didn't rely on them for our arms and ammunition anymore. It did limit what we had though. But then again, if you had one gun for the end of the world, why not an AK? We also could make RPK's, PSL's, PKM's and a few other variations. My FS2000 will eventually become something of an oddity and little more. Something for a museum.

Some of the recruits were Greeks and they were growing more eager to take back Istanbul. They were already calling it Constantinople.

I only taught a few of the advance classes. One benefit of being "Duke of Torcello" was that I didn't have to do much real work. I delegated and watched over the proceedings. Cecilia sat beside me reading a history book and I sat there on my laptop writing my own history book about the Uprising.

It had been a relatively peaceful two years. We secured more islands, mines, factories and farms. We were slowly building a sustainable nation. Married life was very good. Karen, Elizabeth and Dan were older and were becoming dedicated soldiers.

Lexi and my girls had started their own band. They added more solar panels so they could play electric. Lexi was lead guitarist, Elizabeth was bassist and Karen was drummer. They didn't have a singer yet. Mostly they played covers which was fine by me. The old rock songs needed to be preserved.

Sarah was sitting under a tree teaching a combat first aid class and Kevin was teaching hand to hand. When he wasn't teaching he was helping the Venetian government make bridges and repair roads. He was far more important in that regard than I ever was.

Perhaps my ownership of Torcello was undeserved, but I didn't really care. It was mine and me and my family would own it for generations.

Cappello had moved to Venice and taught convoy tactics and Hardcore found a Romanian woman and was one of the Doge's personal bodyguards.

Karen and Elizabeth were watching over their group of female students. They taught a beginner class as well.

"How's your book coming?" Cecilia asked.

"Slow. I'm trying to put in every picture I can, but I have to choose and I hate not putting something in."

"Why do you have to choose?"

"Space. Paper and Ink are going to be expensive and I can't make the book as huge as I want to."

"You have some good pictures of me, yes?"

"Of course. You were inspiring during the battle of Rome."

"Is that what you're calling it?"

"Well, the siege and then the raising of the siege I lump under one battle."

"Makes it easier, I suppose."

"Well, I'm not a fantastic historian."

"Yes you are. Don't try to tell me anything different."

"You're a little biased."

"Only a little. I'm still ninety percent right. When will we be ready for the war?"

"This summer."

"I know that. I was asking if you had heard anything more specific."

"Sometime in June."

"Will we be ready?"

"I think so."

"I was hoping for a more definite answer."

"So was I. How are things going with Rome?"

"Not good. They're still accusing us of stealing Ravenna."

"That's not good."

"Nope."

We sat there silently in the shade for an hour.

"Have you heard from George?" She asked after a while.

"I've heard about him, but not from him. Apparently he's running off to Russia or something like that. No one would give me the details."

"That's odd."

"It is. Josh is in Washington D.C. cleaning the place up. I don't know why he didn't just stay in Vernal."

"Why didn't you stay?"

"I felt out of place there."

"Like a third wheel?"

"Fifth wheel and yes, I didn't feel that I belonged."

"But here you could be someone."

"Here I could at least be myself."

"And so you could marry me in St. Mark's!"

"Not many could say that they were married there. I did want to get married here at Santa Asunta, but when the Doge invites you to be married in St. Mark's you don't exactly turn that down."

"As soon as we can make it down to Rome we'll be married in the temple, right?"

"Yes! It'll have been a year since you were baptized. The Pope wasn't too happy about that."

"Well, they don't like us Venetians anyways."

"Not at the moment."

Then I saw Karen running up the path that ran alongside the canal. She came up to us without a hint of being out of breath. She had been working on her cardio.

"The Doge's coming. He just landed at our pier. Elizabeth is leading him," Karen said.

"Did he say the reason for the visit?" I asked.

"No, I ran here as soon as I saw who it was."

I looked over to Cecilia who merely shrugged.

"Alright, let's go meet him," I said.

I got up and then helped Cecilia up. The three of us then walked back toward the dock and met the Doge and a few other officials halfway.

"Zach! Good to see you," Doge DeCanalli said, as soon as I got close.

"Doge. What brings you to my quiet little island?" I said as the sound of live fire exercises went off in the distance.

"Just doing an informal inspection. I want to see how our recruits are doing and if they'll be ready by late June," the Doge said.

"They'll be ready by then. We have a lot of veterans that are helping out."

"I'm afraid we have too many veterans. I wish we lived in more peaceful times."

"True. We're all veterans now."

"Even the children."

We walked down the path toward the two churches and the old piazza.

"I do love this island here," the Doge said.

"Me too. My family is very happy here."

"I'm glad to see that it's being put to use again. It has such an old history. Fitting for Venice's official historian."

"Oh? It's official now?"

"It is. You and your team."

"Thank you."

"Our satellite images confirm that Istanbul is the center of activity. They're bringing in ghouls and sending them out to other towns and cities. I think they're hunting out pockets of survivors."

"Any word from England?"

"They say that they have no one to spare. Milan and Rome have already agreed to it, but I wouldn't be surprised if they try to back out just to get more concessions from us. We can't let Ravenna go."

"Why?"

"If we do that, they'll ask us for more land and expect us to give in. If we stand firm now, they won't try to take anything else. Also, Ravenna is a traditional Venetian city."

"I suppose we couldn't trade Ravenna for another city?"

"I tried that already."

"Will they really go to war over this?"

"As it is now? No. They wouldn't. But I don't think the next generation of leaders will remember the horrors of war as clearly as we do."

"It's an eventuality then."

"Indeed."

We stopped in front of the cathedral of Santa Maria Assunta.

"I always liked this church. Your petition to turn this into a Mormon church has been denied, but you can convert the Byzantine church of Santa Fosca right here."

I looked at the round, Greek Cross shaped church. It was smaller and far simpler, but it would do nicely. It would be nice to not have to have services in my living room.

"On behalf of the ten Mormons left here in Venice, I thank you."

"It was the council's decision. I would have given you Assunta."

"Rule by Majority, right?"

"That's how it should be."

"So, we're planning on starting the campaign in late June?"

"Yes and we'll be attacking Istanbul on July 1st, but do not tell anyone. That is very classified information."

"My recruits will be ready, but will Venice? Do we have enough ammunition?"

"Ammo for small arms, yes, but I can't guarantee how much of the bigger stuff we'll have. Our navy is low and our artillery stockpiles still haven't recovered from two years ago."

"We'll make do. What are Rome and Milan saying?"

"They say it can and should be done. They're as eager to stop this threat as we are. We don't want all of Eastern Europe heading at us like southern Italy did."

"At least they're confident about it. I hope it's a deserved confidence."

"Oh, Cecilia, the Pope asked about you," the Doge said.

"He did? What did you say?"

"He said that he's willing to pretend that you didn't switch religions and that you'd be reinstated without question."

"That's very kind of him, but I've made my decision."

"That's what I told him you'd say. Also, Zach, have you heard from your brother George? The Ogre King as he's being called now?"

"I haven't. Last I heard he was heading to Russia."

"I see. He's an unknown factor in all of this. He's still on the other side of the Alps, but I don't think those mountains would prove much of a barrier against him."

"You don't think he'd come all the way down here and attack us, do you?"

"I don't know anymore. Right now I'm thinking of a war with cities that used to be in the same country with us. I don't know what's normal right now."

"Normal doesn't exist."

We went inside the ancient church of Santa Maria Assunta that had stood since the sixth century and sat down on one of the pews. Karen sat behind us, leaning back with her legs crossed in an unlady-like fashion. Cecilia sat beside me with her hand in mine.

We looked up at the giant mosaic of the solitary figure of Maria, dressed in a long black robe and looking directly at us as if she knew all the answers.

"That is a remarkable image," the Doge said.

"One of the finest outside of St. Mark's and Constantinople," Cecilia said.

"She's seen Venice go through hard times before. Do you think she believes we'll be alright?" The Doge asked.

"I think so. She knows the plan, but isn't telling us," I said.

"I've never been a religious man and even less so lately, but sometimes I get this idea of a grand plan and that we're all playing our parts in it," the Doge said.

"You may be right about that," I said.

We sat there for a while, looking at the majestic Mary that stared down at us.

"Doge?" Karen asked.

"Yes?"

"I was looking through a history book and it talked about the Doge wearing a special hat and robes. Why don't you get something fancier than a suit?" Karen asked.

"Fancier? Like a tuxedo? I wouldn't want to go around in a tux for the rest of my life."

"No, but you can throw on a sash, a robe or something like that."

"I'll see what I can do."

Maybe it wasn't such a bad idea. Looking the part of Doge could help the moral of the people and help with the negotiations with Rome and Milan.

June 14th

I stood in St. Mark's Square in formation with five hundred other soldiers. My friends and family stood next to me in our line as a distinct unit. We were the 101 Training platoon.

However, we weren't there for training. We were gathered there with the rest of Venice's armed forces preparing to leave on what they were already calling a Crusade. Our navy was ready and all our equipment was already loaded up in the ships.

All that was left was to satisfy the Venetians love of pageantry. So, we were all here lined up in neat little rows as if any of it even mattered. What good were pretty formations and marching when the enemy was utterly unaffected by any of it? Except to make officers feel good, formations and marching were useless even before the Uprising.

The Doge was giving a cute little speech about bravery and honor. Why? We all knew what was at stake and what was expected of us. No one here had escaped the apocalypse without loosing someone.

Next up to give a speech was Lorenzo who was now the official general of the land forces. I didn't listen and let my mind wander off to what my next chapter of my history book would be.

Surrounding our little army were the civilians that were staying behind. Among them were Dan and Sarah and Kevin's kids as well as Cappello's wife and kids. It was a fairly large crowd of a few thousand people, but considering that we all fit comfortably in the city's square was a reminder of how many people the world had lost.

As the officials and officers gave mercifully brief speeches the crowd was silent and all I could hear were their useless words and the flapping of the oversized, maroon, Venetian flags. These flags normally showed a winged lion holding a book in his paws. The book was the Book of St. Mark, but today the flags showed the lion holding a sword, a symbol that Venice was no longer at peace, but now at war.

After the pony show they gave us an hour before we had to report to our boats. We spent that hour in our apartment listening to music and eating a good meal. Dan kept saying that he should be going and that he was old enough.

I didn't want to let Karen and Elizabeth come either, but they were very good and had been trained too well to leave them behind. Like it or not, they were an essential part of my team.

Eventually, we had to say our goodbyes and I promised to bring him back a souvenir of Constantinople. He didn't seem impressed. I made Maser promise to take care of him while we were gone.

Maser had officially retired from combat services. I couldn't blame him. I was still relatively young and I felt too old for this crap.

We took gondolas out to the gray Naval ships and climbed aboard. We found our cabins and settled in for the voyage. It was me, Cecilia, Karen and Elizabeth in one cabin and Cappello, Hardcore, Sarah and Kevin in the other. The space was tight and the beds were tiny bunk beds.

If there was one thing I hated, besides being cold…and hungry…and tired, it was sleeping in an unfamiliar bed. There wasn't much, or any, privacy aboard the ship so "fun time" with Cecilia was out of the question. Most of our troops slept in the cargo holds of civilian cargo ships. They were all crammed in there like sardines.

Somewhere out there were the make-shift navies of Rome and Milan. We would meet at Crete and together sail to Constantinople.

We spent the time simply talking and making up stupid stories. Occasionally I'd tell them a story of my time in Iraq. Whenever they wouldn't believe me I'd call in Cappello so he could verify. For some reason me and Cappello could tell the same story, but they'd believe him and never believe me.

"Yes, I'm serious. It's all true," I said one evening as we were settling in for bed.

"I don't believe it," Elizabeth said.

"It's true. I swear," I said.

"There's no way a First Sergeant would tell soldiers to go back and change into a proper uniform during a surprise attack. He would have to be deaf, blind and stupid," Karen said.

"I promise. At Abu Garhaib, April 2nd, 2005 we were attacked by a large insurgent force and it was a pretty big surprise. I ran out without my over shirt and some were still in their gym clothes with their body armor and guns. It was quiet one minute and then suddenly all hell broke loose. Mortars and machine guns were going off everywhere and no one knew what was going on. It was like WWIII. And during all this, our First Sergeant was trying to get people to go back to their barracks to change into "proper" uniforms."

"I don't get it," Cecilia said. "Didn't he see the danger?"

"Of course, but he was so rigid in his love of regulations that he forgot the real reason of the army: to fight," I said.

"Is that why you always show such disdain for uniforms, formations and ceremony?" Karen asked.

"That's part of the reason. I've seen how it gets in the way of actual important things. Am I going to have to get Cappello in here to confirm this?"

"Did he get fired?" Elizabeth asked.

"He got reassigned," I said. "Also, that wasn't the end of his stupidity."

"How can there be more? He's already the world's biggest idiot," Cecilia said.

"No argument there, but yes, there are more tales to tell of his deeds and adventures."

" Our towers had machine guns that were defending the base. Well, they were running out of ammo and so some of our guys decided to go resupply them. They couldn't find our arms room guy and so they broke into the arms room and went to grab a Humvee. The Humvees were also locked so they cut the chain and loaded up. Well, our hero saw them and demanded that they go back and properly sign out for everything. Keep in mind that the battle was going crazy all around them. Our guys politely gave him the bird in a manner of speaking. The First Sergeant demanded to know who they were so he could right them up and one of them told him his full name, rank and unit and dared him to try to stop them."

Karen shook her head and Elizabeth groaned.

"How could someone be so stupid?" Karen asked.

"He was caught up in the bureaucracy and forgot what was important. Remember, never let the small details blind you of the bigger picture," I said.

"I would have court-martialed him," Elizabeth said.

"I would have put him in front of a firing squad," Karen said.

"It's true," Cecilia said. "Back in Vernal, I heard him and Cappello talking about it.

"Can you imagine someone worrying about proper uniform during the Uprising?" Karen asked.

"I can," Elizabeth said quietly.

"What do you mean?" Karen asked.

"When everything was going crazy and we didn't know what to believe about dead bodies coming back to life, me, Dan and my dad were packing up our RV. Dad kept telling us to make sure to pack warm and cold weather clothing, just in case."

The room fell silently. None of us liked to talk about those times.

I thought about the people I had lost. I thought about my college professors who were most likely dead. I thought about my college friends, my friends and extended family. I thought about my sister and her children. I thought about my grandmother and aunts and uncles. They were all gone. I wondered if some of them were finally destroyed when Ogre nuked Salt Lake or if they were shot in a raid or perhaps they were still roaming around an empty Salt Lake.

Then one morning the captain called me up to the bridge. The sailor who woke me seemed agitated so I hurried up to follow him. Up on the bridge the captain was looking out with a long telescope.

"What's wrong? I asked.

"We're approaching the Dardanelles," he said.

The Dardanelles were the straights that led to Constantinople.

"Awesome," I said. "So, why bring me up?"

"Because we fear an ambush," he said.

"Why?"

"Because if I were defending Istanbul, that's where I'd try to block any enemy fleet."

"I see."

I could see the rolling, hilly shores on either side. The coast undulated in and out and up and down giving the enemy plenty of places to hide. We sailed slowly and with all hands on alert.

Then from out of a small alcove, hidden by a large hill, two rusty cargo ships plied into view heading directly toward our fleet. They were close, almost on top of us.

"What do they plan to do?" An officer asked.

"I think they plan to ram us," I said.

"All ships open fire!"

Our lead ship was already sailing past, but the two death ships were coming right at the center of our fleet. They weren't changing course and one of our troop ships was right in their path.

"Don't let them hit that troop ship!" The captain yelled.

Too slowly the cannons on the warships began to turn towards the large, fast moving hulks.

The cannons fired and shook the ship beneath my feet. Explosions erupted all over the lead death ship, shredding it to pieces. However, it was large and it kept going, though it was now barely visible with all the smoke and fire coming from it.

The two ships were almost there. Our ships were trying to move out of the way, but the slow troop transports could only move so fast. One of those ships carried a hundred men with all their equipment. One ship lost would be devastating.

"Fire!" The captain shouted again.

Another barrage blasted the first death ship and this time it stopped and began to go into the water nose first.

The second ship slipped past the smoking wreckage of the first and sped right for a troop ship.

I thought of the hundred soldiers aboard that ship, watching that death ship heading right for them. There weren't enough people left in the world to lose a hundred.

A few ships were able to fire safely at the remaining ship, but it wasn't enough. The smaller barrage blew several holes in the ramming ship, but it kept coming.

"We're not going to get it," the captain muttered.

"Sir, look! The Princepessa is moving in to intercept!" An officer called out.

One of the light Roman frigates was speeding to move between the cargo ship and the death ship. All our warships kept firing and smoke and fire was pouring out of the enemy ship, but it wasn't stopping.

Then the Princepessa rammed into the side of the enemy ship with a twisting metal sound that filled the air. The force knocked the enemy ship off course and stopped it in its advance. The front of the frigate crumpled and the enemy ship began to capsize onto its side. Like footage of a building falling down, we watched the death ship capsize and splash into the water.

"Good job Princepessa!" Our captain called over the radio. "What is our damage? Will you be able to continue?"

"We're currently assessing the damage."

Our fleet halted while the Princepessa looked over their crumpled bow. A few hours later we were able to continue. The damaged ship trailed in the back.

I would have to thank the captain. He had saved hundreds of lives.

"Commander Hill, we're coming into view of Istanbul," the captain said.

I put the binos up to my eyes and looked where the captain indicated with his outstretched arm.

Up ahead, in the bright sunlight I saw the sprawling view of Istanbul with its gleaming domes and tall minarets.

Finally, we had come to our goal. The battle to retake Constantinople was about to begin.

TWENTY FOUR

June 21

Our ship surrounded the horn shaped peninsula of Istanbul. From the safety of the ship I could see the dome of Hagia Sophia. It was a magnificent ancient church built by the emperor Justinian. It had to survive. All the gunners knew not to target landmarks such as that. When we went into the city I was going to have to go inside the great church. It had been a life goal to see the great Hagia Sophia.

I met with my squad out on the deck of the ship.

"What's the plan?" Cappello asked.

"First, our planes will fire bomb the edges of the city, clearing out as many as we can while leaving the historic center intact. Our separate units will attack the city from different directions and lure their hordes out into six distinct groups. Then we will call fire support to weaken each horde."

"Sounds iffy," Hardcore said.

I had to agree with Hardcore. The plan sounded less than perfect, but it was all we had.

The airstrikes began and napalm and white phosphorous were being dropped on the outskirts of the enormous city. It had long overflowed the ancient walls of Constantinople and sprawled out in all directions. We'd set fire to the outskirts and let it burn. That would hopefully take care of a good percentage of the zombies, but the survivors would either go out or retreat back inward.

From the water we watched the planes streak over head and the distant thumping and flashes of the bombings went on for hours. By the time night fell an orange glow filled the sky on the far side of what we could see of the city.

We put on our night vision goggles and were dropped off at the northern shore where there were was less urban areas. Most of our armored vehicles were already waiting for us and piles of destroyed zombies showed the effectiveness of our advanced parties.

We loaded up in our AAV and once everyone was ready we rolled forward. Our armored group drove forward toward the burning city until we began to encounter scattered groups of zeds. These groups weren't controlled and weren't much of a fight.

It wasn't until the flames were in view did we encounter something like a main force. There were thousands of them, but our armor opened up with .50 cals, Mk-19's and 105mm's.

I stood in the turret of the AAV that I had found on my first trip to Italy. It was an old friend now and I knew every nut and bolt.

I also knew the sound and smell of gunfire. The air filled with the smell of gunpowder and smoke. There was also the smell of rot underneath everything else.

Our bullets and grenades tore into the zed horde. This wasn't a battle: it was simple mathematics. It was a chore. Something to do before the real battle started.

Before we finished with that horde, another came in from our right. We shifted our formation to an "L" shape to defend from both sides.

"Everyone, move forward! Run them over!" I called out over the radio.

At that signal, everyone moved forward and plowed into the hordes.

Our men didn't fire their small arms. They were saving their ammo for once they went inside the city.

There were suburbs filled with undead and we continued fighting well into the morning. We'd enter the streets and run over and shoot any zed we found.

"Commander Hill, we're running low on fuel," the driver said.

"We had enough fun for now," I said.

I called up the rest of my team and we turned back to the rally point for resupply and chow. Vehicles and men were still being unloaded and without logistics officers telling everyone where to go it would have been a complete mess.

Similar battles were going on all over the outskirts of Istanbul. After we ate and refueled, we went back out. No one really said anything. We all felt it. This battle was important. If we lost here our children would be fighting them for years to come.

It was more than that though. We felt the evil that hung over the city. It was thick in the air like someone had covered us in a freezing, wet blanket.

It took three days of nonstop fighting to clear the suburbs. By that point we were already low on ammo and fuel. We had all our small arms, but the big guns were running low. We'd have to save what was left for the assault on the historic city center where they believed the "Black Eye" was living.

By the feeling of the city I felt that there was something worse than a "black eye" lingering here.

On the night of the third day I lay in the back of the AAV next to Cecilia. We shared a sleeping bag.

"We're making progress," she said.

"But not enough of it."

"We'll make it."

"We're almost out of supplies. How many rounds you have left?"

"Not many."

"How much gas you think is left?"

"If we don't win quickly we won't win at all."

"Then we'll win."

"Not unless we do something."

The high command was content to slog it out in a meat grinder until they were out of gas and bullets, but I was not. I couldn't sit by and read my books and enjoy peace and quiet when an undead ruler was trying to destroy my home.

I had to take action.

All my life I had avoided positions of leadership and importance. I couldn't do that now: not when the goal was so close.

The suburbs were far from clear, but they were clear enough to keep our backs safe while we went into the city the following morning.

On the fourth day we found a path through an already burned out section of the city and all six units gathered.

Once everything was under way we rolled into the heart of the city. Once we reached the ancient land walls of Constantinople, thousands of zombies began poring out. These were definitely controlled by red eyes or worse. They ran strait for us and began trying to climb up onto our vehicles.

Our big guns opened fire, ripping into the hordes that poured out of the ancient gates. It wasn't just the gates that they came out of, it was every opening there was and there were a lot of them. They came out and began to surround our small army. We kept the fire poring down on them, but no matter how many we killed, they kept coming.

"Pull back before we're surrounded!" Lorenzo called over the radio.

Our vehicles began pulling back while sustaining our rate of fire.

Artillery was called in and what remained rained down on the hordes, blowing them to pieces. The ships off shore were firing the last of their shells and the cannons on the beach fired what little they had left.

The explosions made the hordes disappear in clouds of smoke and dust, but when it all settled, the zombies kept coming.

There were no clear open areas nearby so we pulled them into what streets were unblocked. Once they were bottle necked in dozens of streets we pulled another Grand Theft Auto move and ran them over.

We were behind a Centauro when suddenly a giant blast knocked the vehicle over. The path of the blast came from a burned out house and our Mk-19 opened up, killing the red eye that caused it.

However, zombies were charging toward the downed vehicle. We opened up with our machine gun and Mk-19, but too soon our ammo ran out.

"I guess we do this on foot," Cappello said.

"I was hoping to stay clean for just one battle," Hardcore said.

We jumped out, got in a line and began to open fire with our rifles. My AK barked out over and over again. With the zombies as tightly packed as they were, our bullets tore through several of them. That was fortunate because we didn't exactly have infinite ammo.

We were holding them off, but that would last only as long as our ammo did. I dumped magazine after magazine, knocking the empties out with a fresh mag. Heat waves were coming off of my barrel and the muzzle flash was growing as more and more powder was burnt up with every shot.

"I'm almost out!" Cecilia called out.

"Me too!" Hardcore said.

When I was down to my last mag there were only about a dozen of the undead left in our street. I fired all but one magazine of my pistol. The last mag I always saved in case I had to off myself or anyone else.

We were all out and the zombies were coming closer.

"This will get messy," I said.

I pulled out my gunstock club. Cappello pulled out his baseball bat and everyone else pulled out whatever they were carrying.

I really hated this. I hated being scared and I hated having to fight for my life. Most of all, I hated that my family was in danger.

We maintained our line and let the zombies come at us.

As the first one entered within striking distance I smashed his head with my synthetic, modern club. I felt the blow in my arm travel up to my shoulder. One of them grabbed my arm and I kicked him off, but another quickly grabbed my other arm. It's teeth tried to bite through my leather sleeve, but I pushed it away.

That came way too close.

Cecilia hit the last zombie in the head with a hammer and we regrouped to check for injuries.

"Everyone okay?" I asked.

They were, but another horde was coming, a smaller one of only about twenty or so.

Shots rang out and dropped the small horde. I looked back and saw the crew of the toppled Centauro.

"Thanks for the help," I called out.

"No, thank you."

Now, completely out of ammo we fell back all the way to the resupply point. Ammo was already running dangerously low and fighting was still going on all over the city.

"Grab what you can. We're heading back in," I said.

They had more 5.56mm ammo than anything else so I put back my AK in the AAV and took out my FS2000. This was perhaps the last hurrah of the FS. I doubted more ammo would be forthcoming if we went to war with Milan.

I turned on my red dot sight and we climbed back into the AAV. Our armored group came up to a battle in progress and we rolled in, crushing the zeds beneath our tracks.

Now came the hard part: I had to tell the others about my plan.

"Guys, I have an idea," I said. We were inside the AAV and I was looking at a map of the city.

"What's that?" Cecilia asked.

"The zeds and red eyes are distracted right now. Why don't we roll in to the old town, find this Black Eye and take him out?"

"Hey, I was just thinking that suicide might be a great plan. Glad to see we're on the same wavelength," Hardcore said.

"Yeah, that's kind of reckless," Cappello said.

"Shouldn't we try to take this guy out while we still have ammo?" I asked.

"We still have a few rounds with the Mk-19. Might as well," Cecilia said.

"I like the plan," Karen said.

"Let's do it," Elizabeth said.

"Hell, if it means killing this zombie lord sooner, I say we do it," Kevin said.

"I'd prefer to do it without getting killed though," Sarah said.

We drove passed the ancient land walls and into the historic part of the city. The fire had caught in some parts, but most of the city was a modernized jungle anyway.

"Where are we going?" Kevin asked.

"The satellite photos showed a lot of activity near Hagia Sophia," I said.

"Wait, I thought we weren't supposed to touch the church," Cappello said.

"We can't destroy it, but that doesn't mean we can't shoot the crap out of whatever's inside."

None of them seemed to like the idea, but they agreed.

We and the few armored vehicles that followed us tore down the main street of Istanbul heading toward the giant, domed church.

June 24th. Istanbul

We drove through the strangely quiet streets of Istanbul. In the distance we could hear the muffled shots and explosions of battles raging all over the suburbs. However, the streets were clear of zombies. All of them had to be out fighting our army.

We were inside the AAV and I let my people focus on getting to the church. I tuned out the squeaks and noises of the engines and treads and focused on trying to calm my mind. This was possibly insane. I didn't know much about these Black Eyes and didn't know if we could take them, but we had to try. I saw what happened when we killed the Black Eye outside of Rome. It had severed all the links with the red eyes and with the regular zeds as well. There were too many zombies for our forces to destroy. If we didn't kill this zombie lord, we'd lose this battle.

I looked down to the FS2000 on my lap. I only had five mags for it and three for my pistol. Were we really prepared for this?

Then I looked over to Cecilia who sat across from me. She had her M4 between her legs, barrel pointing down. I could tell she was nervous because she was fidgeting and kept adjusting her glasses.

"We'll be alright," I said to her.

She just nodded and managed a faint smile.

I wished I had a bigger gun.

As I looked around the AAV I realized that I couldn't risk any of these people. I didn't want to lose a single one. But if this Black Eye wasn't killed then many more would die.

The AAV pulled to a stop and the escorting Centauros pulled up in a circle around us. I got up in the turret and scanned the open area. The sky was overcast with a slight drizzle, but with the sun going down it was growing dark earlier than it should.

"Any sign of movement?" Cecilia asked.

"No, nothing yet," I said.

Then I saw something move at the door of the giant church.

Twenty figures were walking out of the giant doors. In the dim light I could see the glow of their red eyes.

"Open fire!" I shouted.

I quickly grabbed the handles of the Mk-19 and pulled the trigger. The grenade launcher barked and three grenades arched out and exploded on the steps sending red eyes flying in every direction.

But several of them survived and ran towards us. One of them unleashed with a bolt of force that rocked the AAV and almost made me fall out of my chair.

The next second the red eyes were pounding on the doors.

"Hey, Hill, we're going to try to get them off of your APC," a voice said on the radio. "Can your armor stop 7.62?"

"I think so," I said.

Then I heard loud metallic plinking like the worst hail ever.

"You're good," said the radio.

We opened the door of the AAV and stepped out.

"I'm sure there's more inside," Cappello said.

"Maybe a whole army. I mean, that is a pretty big church," Hardcore said.

"It's a very big church," Cappello said.

There were about thirty of us and we got out of our vehicles and walked up the stairs. The doors were wide open and there was light inside. As we walked in we saw that every candle and then some was lit. The golden mosaics of the church glittered in the flickering lights and shadows danced all over the place. Also, as Hardcore so eloquently put it, it was a pretty big church.

Then three figures emerged near the alter. Two were wearing long black robes with hoods and the third was wearing a white cloak with a hood. I couldn't see the others' faces, but the one in white had her hood down. She was simultaneously the most beautiful and hideous thing I've ever seen. She was tall and thin with an almost impossible delicacy about her. She had long white hair that hung to the floor and an almost innocent, elven face. Her eyes were black, but it was more than that, it was as if they sucked in the light around her. I could see the aura of darkness that surrounded her. One moment her face would look peaceful and almost angelic, the next it would look as if it were full of rage and venom. Her hands were long, boney and ended in sharp claws.

"I think we should cross the streams," Hardcore said.

"Screw that, blast her," Kevin said.

"Who are you supposed to be?" Karen called out.

The black, hollow eyes looked at us from the raised alter. Instead of crucifixes there were stone pyramids with wings carved on the front. It didn't quite look Egyptian, but it felt far more ancient. The white haired woman's clawed hand brushed the unholy image as she stepped forward.

"I won't tell you my name. You haven't earned that privilege yet," the white haired woman said in the sweetest, purest voice I had ever heard.

"I'm guessing you already know who I am," I said.

"Of course. We've been following your family for some time. Your brother George has embraced his fate as leader. Why haven't you?" She asked.

"Because I don't want it? You're supposed to be some super demon and you can't figure that out?"

The woman smiled with her blue lips and took a step forward.

"Is it because you'd rather spend time with your new family? You'd rather make love to your wife and play with your adopted children than waste time dealing with other people's problems. What if I were to take away those obstacles?"

"Zach," Cecilia whispered.

"I'm kinda busy," I said.

She looked like she had more to say, but I had a devil in front of me that demanded my attention.

Then the woman reached up with her hand and suddenly my head began to hurt like I had never felt. I fell to my knees and felt myself screaming though I didn't hear anything.

"You're in my power. What did you expect? You come in here into my center of energy and expect to have power over me? I think not. You know nothing of me, not even my name."

"I know your name," Cecilia said.

"Oh? Do you?"

"Lilith," Cecilia said.

As soon as she said her name, the pain left. I quickly stood up and aimed my FS right at Lilith's head.

"Oh, so you do know a little," Lilith said. "Well, it won't help. I can kill you right now. But instead I'll spare you because I think that you could be useful. You can lead my armies from the capitol of my new empire and take this world. You can be king of Europe! You can rule it as you please, create a safe haven for humans. I won't interfere. Think of how many lives you can save."

"Hey, skank, if you're trying to make a deal, then you're not as strong as you say you are," Sarah said.

"Right, honey," Kevin said. "I hate long conversations. I'd rather be doing something. I say we do something."

"I must agree with my good fellows here. I say we kill them and break that stupid little alter of theirs," Hardcore said.

"Waste 'em," Cappello said.

Then Karen suddenly fired, hitting Lilith in the neck. Black blood spurted out of the hole before it closed a second later.

With that we all opened fire. Bullets tore into Lilith and her two black cloaked companions.

One of the men in black raised his hands and a blast of fire tore through the church hitting some of the men from one of the Centauros.

I placed the red dot of my sight right between Lilith's eyes and fired several times, almost emptying the magazine. Black holes appeared where I hit, but she didn't even seem to notice.

Lilith dashed forward quicker than I could see, grabbed another man and ripped him to pieces. Blood sprayed all over her white cloak. I fired again and one of my shots hit her in the eye. She staggered back, clutching her face.

"Go for her eyes!" I shouted.

Kevin fired is .308 Broadsword and hit one of the black robed men in the eye. The back of the demon's head blew out and it dropped like a rock.

"Woohoo!" You see that, honey?" Kevin shouted.

A blast of energy struck in front of us, knocking Karen, Elizabeth and myself onto our backs. A second later one of our men shot that robed demon in the eye and it fell dead.

I looked over as I stood up and froze in place.

Lilith was standing in the middle of us with her hand around Cecilia's neck.

"One move and I'll decapitate her," Lilith cooed.

The radio in my ear piece chimed in.

"Commander Hill? What are you doing in the church?" Said the unfamiliar male voice. I didn't have time to deal with that. My wife was in the hands of a very powerful and very evil demon.

"What do you want, Lilith?" I asked.

"I want you to surrender to me and join me. You'll have your own kingdom where people can live in peace. You can write all the books you want."

"Commander Hill, I'm glad you're here. It makes our job easier," said the voice on the radio. I wanted to tell him to piss off.

"Zach, don't worry about me, just kill her," Cecilia said.

"Don't be noble. Heroes don't have happy endings," Lilith said. "Zach, why settle for this little woman when you can have me? I can be and do everything you've ever wanted."

"No," I said. "You're nothing but a shallow, useless thing that's destined to lose in the end. You should know that you can't win against God. You know this and you ignore it."

"Yes, but think of how much pain we can cause him with every one of you that we drag down with us. It's not about winning, it's about revenge."

"Cecilia has everything you'll never have. She's also much prettier and funnier and smarter."

"What do you mean? I have everything! I have her life in my hands. I have your happiness in my hands. I have an empire in my hands!" Lilith said with a hint of anger.

"No she doesn't," the radio voice said.

Then I heard an ear shattering crack and Lilith's head exploded. Her body fell limp and Cecilia scrambled away.

I looked up to where the sound came from and saw two men dressed all in black with a .50 cal sniper rifle. They were up in one of the small windows lining the base of the dome.

"Commander Hill, hurry and cut out her heart!" The radio voice said.

I yanked out my bayonet and drove it into her chest. As I worked to open the rib cage I saw her head start to reform again.

Sarah knelt down beside me and took out a pair of pliers.

"Let me do it," Sarah said. She was a nurse and had seen lots of battlefield wounds in the past three years. "Don't be a pussy. You have to put some force into it."

As she pulled the ribs apart Lilith's head was starting to come back together. One of her arms began to twitch and her long fingers curled.

"I would suggest picking up the pace, gentlemen," Hardcore said.

I grabbed the heart with one hand and sliced it free with my bayonet. Lilith stopped moving.

The two men in black ski masks and NVG's moved up beside me and grabbed the heart from my hands. They wore subdued patches of the Swiss Guard. One of them set down a small metal box filled with yellow powder and took out a flare. They placed the heart in the box and set fire to it with the flare. The flames came out blue and green and crackled like a wet log.

"Excellent work, commander Hill," one of the special ops guys said.

"Yeah, without your unplanned distraction, I don't know how we would have done it," the other operator said.

"Wait, who are you guys?" Cappello asked.

"We're part of a quick strike team. While our main force drew out the zombie hordes, we were to move in and take out the brain of the operation," the first operator said.

"Just the two of you?" I asked.

"There were more. There were more Black Eyes than we had anticipated. We were glad to see you, Hill."

I looked around the church. All my people were still alive. I checked on each one of them and then took Cecilia into my arms and kissed her.

"You'd take me over her?" Cecilia asked.

"Well, she's a little too demanding."

"She was kind of a bitch," Cecilia said.

"Kind of."

Karen and Elizabeth hugged us and Hardcore began laughing.

"We did it!" Hardcore said. "We killed the queen demon and saved the world! You can't say that every day. If there was still Facebook I'd have to post this. I'd even post pictures because if it isn't on Facebook, it didn't happen."

That did remind me. I took out my camera and began taking pictures. We all posed over the body of Lilith and one of the operators took the picture.

I think we were allowed to gloat.

TWENTY FIVE

Five Years Later

December 11th

My feet hurt so I sat down on the "Giants' Stair's" of the Doge's palace. It was the traditional staircase where the Doge's would be inaugurated. The courtyard of the palace was full of officials and military officers.

Although I was retired from active duty I was still their head trainer and had my place reserved. I tended to keep to my own small island and paid little attention to the local politics. Even at the end of the world there was still politics to annoy me.

"What's this all about again?" I asked.

"The Roman and Milanese ambassador are coming with some special intermediary," Cecilia said.

She sat down beside me and rested her hand on the butt of her pistol that was strapped to her thigh.

"Will any of this do any good?" I asked.

"Seems like it. They're all stubborn people that want to be the alpha dog."

"You'd think they'd seen enough killing. .99% of the world wasn't enough for them?"

"Maybe this mediator will help."

"Is this guy Gandhi?"

"I have no idea. They're keeping it all hush, hush."

Then I heard the sound of the approaching helicopters. Down in the courtyard I watched as the Doge and top men of the Senate readied themselves.

Reluctantly I stood up and watched the helicopters come into view and then descend back out of view as the walls of the palace came between us and the city square where the three helicopters were landing. One was from Rome and bore the Papal symbol of crossed keys. The second was from Milan and had the red cross as its symbol. The third helicopter was an American Black Hawk. That surprised me. I didn't expect the mediator to be American. English, perhaps, but not American. We hadn't heard from them in a while, at least nothing officially. Now that everyone was becoming more self sufficient, trade across the Atlantic was dying out.

A few minutes later the two ambassadorial teams entered the palace courtyard. The band started playing and I waited for the American delegation to come in.

I saw a group of armored men and women enter. By the way they moved I could tell that they were professionals and knew what they were doing. They had a very modern and tactical air about them.

Then I saw the mediator come in.

It had been almost a decade since I last saw him, but I recognized my brother instantly.

"It's George!" I said.

"Is it? When did he get an eye patch?" Cecilia asked as she squinted.

I unceremoniously made my way forward, but was stopped by one of George's body guards.

"Don't get too close, jack off. I'd hate to shoot you and have an international incident," the bodyguard said in English that sounded strange to my ears.

"I'm the Ogre King's brother, moron. Let me through or I'll have you reassigned to northern Alaska."

The guard hesitated and looked back over his shoulder.

Then a tall, young man with a long beard and long hair approached. He had two men beside him that looked identical. They seemed familiar.

"It's alright," the tall man said. "This is Zach Hill, George's brother."

"Yes, Sir Kilo," the guard said.

"Kilo? That you?"

"Who else? I also have the twin terrors with me," Kilo said, nodding his head to the two men beside him.

"Wow. You guys are grown men now."

"And you sound like an Italian," Kilo said.

"The king wants to see you," one of the twins said.

They led me and Cecilia past the groups of delegates and officials to where George was talking to the three Italian princes. When he saw me approach he motioned for the leaders to be quiet and he turned to face me.

"Zach, it's been a while," George said.

"Too long, I'd say. You shoulda called or…pony express."

"You're still with the nun I see," George said with a slight smirk.

"I'm not a nun anymore," Cecilia said.

"Clearly. So, this is where you've been chilling during the apocalypse, huh?" George said.

"It's as good a place as any, especially if you like seafood."

"I thought you hated seafood."

"Most of the time. At least I got my own island."

"I got my own island too. It's called England."

"Go ahead and brag. I have everything I need and want."

"Glad to hear it. You all are doing good here, better than most places."

"We're doing well enough to start a war. That's the milestone of civilization I suppose."

"There won't be a war," George said.

"You sound pretty confident. You just got here."

"I have a fleet of warships heading this way. If they don't give up this idea of fighting for useless reasons, I'll annex all of Italy. Hell, I might just do that anyway."

"Take Italy? I guess that would be better than letting us blow each other up. I don't think they'll be very keen about the idea."

"Tough. I'll have to explain it to them in terms that they'll understand. Trust me, I can be persuasive."

Honestly, I didn't like the idea of Venice being subject to anyone. I guess I had gone native.

"Well, when you're done bullying the leaders of Italy, you should come to my house for dinner. I have a house here in Venice and my island's just north of here."

"I'd like that very much."

I let him get back to the important duty of intimidation. I didn't stick around for the negotiations, but later I heard that it took the threat of three aircraft carriers and twenty other warships to get the three Italian leaders to agree to a peace treaty and accept the 'protection' of the Ogre King.

That night George and his three eldest sons came to my small island and me and Cecilia made them dinner. Karen kept asking for stories and Elizabeth and Dan kept asking for training advice. They took their role as senior trainers seriously. Sarah and Kevin's daughter kept asking about zombie killing tips and if he'd seen any ghosts or vampires.

Cappello, Hardcore, Sarah and Kevin were all there. It was strange in a surreal, dream-like way. After so long I had my brother there in this new world that was separate from any old one. It was strange, but it was also very nice. It felt comfortable and it felt good.

I sat beside Cecilia who held my hand as we talked. George offered me lands in Poland and I accepted, but I had no intention of leaving Venice. It was my home and it's where my children had found homes.

George let me use the satellite phone to talk to my twin and parents. That felt even stranger. He was in charge of the eastern United States. It seemed I held the least amount of land than any of my siblings. It didn't bother me. My ambitions were in another direction.

After I said goodbye to my twin I presented George with a finished copy of my history book. I watched him as he flipped through the pages. I had used some of the last printer paper and printer ink that Italy had to make the ten copies.

"Very nice, bro," George said.

"It took me a while to finish. I only finished two months ago."

"You're slow, but you did it. I don't know of any other real attempt to document everything that happened....hey....you have a picture of the MOAB going off in Sandy Utah! Finally, I have proof that I didn't nuke Salt Lake!"

"I'll make sure the next printing has that photo grainy and blurry and I'll reword it to be vague and confusing."

George spent three days with us and then he left to go back to America. I was tempted to go back with him and see my old home again.

As he left on a boat to take him back to Venice I stood there and watched. The sun was setting and the lagoon was sparkling in whites, yellows and oranges. Beside me was Cecilia who took my hand and rested her head on my shoulder. Karen, Elizabeth and Dan were laughing about something from somewhere behind me.

Maybe others wanted power and fame. Not me. This was all I wanted for it was all that was really important. I had done my part in history and now I'll spend the rest of my life enjoying my family.

I had every intention of growing old and dying there on that island. My children would live there and their children would live there. The zombies were all but extinct in the civilized parts of the world and soon history would be back on its normal track again. It would go on as it always had and soon this would all pass into legend and other stuffy history books.

Centuries from now they'd probably doubt the existence of the Ogre King or his brother that went off to Italy and fought Lilith in the rechristened Constantinople. It was a strange life and it would be hard to believe, but this time the legends had the help of photographic evidence and numerous interviews with eye witnesses. No, the things I saw and did weren't going to be brushed aside as fantasy.

"History shall be kind to me for I intend to write it." - Winston Churchill.

About the Author

Zachary Hill has written stories as long as he can remember. In high school he filled up notebooks full of stories. In army basic training, after lights out, he wrote using his flashlight and notebook. During his two deployments to Iraq he wrote stories in his down time.

Zachary Hill graduated from Southern Virginia University with degrees in History and Art. He taught English in Italy and fell in love with Rome and Venice. He has done illustration for Larry Correia's *Grimnoir Chronicles.* He loves pizza and Mountain Dew.

You can find him at his blogs at *Broken World* and *Minimum Wage Historian.*

www.ingramcontent.com/pod-product-compliance
Lightning Source LLC
Chambersburg PA
CBHW050526260626
47157CB00004B/1491

9781618080578